CLINICAL ERROR

JOHN EGERTON

By the same author

The View from Serndipty Hill

Clinical Judgment

Clinical Trial

Clinical Deception

Clinical Option

CLINICAL ERROR

ONE

Cancer.

A word always spoken in a voice that contained a tone of warning. A condition that applied to other people, something that came as a punishment for doing certain unhealthy things, or as a catastrophe which struck the very unlucky. It was something that had not affected Diana directly, although her grandfather had died of – hushed voice – the big C. She had been too young to remember much about him, there was a vague recollection of a thin and trembly old person who had left them before she had really gotten to know him. Cancer, she considered, was something that attacked older people, she was, as yet, immune to the disease. At the age of twenty-five she was immune to most of life's fatal events. There was though the little girl, a neighbor she knew only vaguely, who had become sick and died very quickly of what they had called cancer. Diana had been young at the time but had been affected deeply by the reaction of her parents to what was horribly sad and frightening news. But this monster of a disease was something to anticipate and hopefully avoid in the distant future. How had this happened to her?

The blurring of vision in her left eye, the black spots, had been a nuisance but only that. She had not felt ill. In fact she had been enjoying life as never before. A new job with a start up magazine, a handsome and manly boyfriend, a life in the country with the city of Austin only a short distance away.

Then the vision in her eye had become dramatically worse. By the time she had the appointment for her exam she could see very little with her left eye.

"I want you to see a specialist," said her optometrist.

"What's wrong?"

"I'm not sure."

An hour's stay in an uncomfortable waiting room, another hour being shuttled between machines that required her to lean into eyepieces and stare at bright lights that hurt and blinded her. Then another wait in a tiny exam room.

Dr. Wright was very pleasant although he did seem to be overwhelmed by the amount of work he was trying to cram into a short time.

"It's a tumor," he said.

The word hit a blockade of denial as her brain refused to recognize its significance. "A tumor?"

"It's a growth at the back of your eye. It's already invaded your retina which is why your vision has gone from that eye."

Diana was listening but the words were not sticking, they were like drops of water falling onto waterproof material running away without leaving an impression.

"Can you take it out?"

The look on Dr. Wright's face scared her.

And the word came to her.

"Cancer, is it cancer?" It was a silly question she knew but it just came out.

Dr. Wright nodded. "I'm afraid so."

"In my eye?" This was not what Diana had expected. At worst she thought she would need to wear glasses, a rather futile form of denial she realized, as the vision in that eye had become virtually non-existent. Cancer? Thoughts raced around her brain, alarm bells, denial, her dead grandfather, the young neighbor. She swallowed and cleared her throat; she was not sure she could control her voice. "So, what do we do now?"

Diana listened while Dr. Wright explained the options, none of which sounded at all pleasant. One option, to do nothing and let the cancer spread and devour her whole body, she considered briefly and rejected. She left Dr. Wright's office knowing that in the very near future she would have her diseased eye cut out and later would have a prosthetic eye to replace it. She did not sleep that night. Her eyes had always been her pride.

"What beautiful blues eyes you have," had been said to her many times. Would the artificial eye be a match for her remaining beautiful blue? They showed her what her replacement eye would look like. It wasn't too bad, considering that her diseased eye was now losing its color. She tried to convince herself that everything was going to be okay. When she thought otherwise she pictured the cancer spreading and eating up her body. But she still woke at night, her body soaked in sweat, dreading what was going to happen to her. Why? What had she done to deserve this? She prayed that she could wake up in the morning and find this was just a bad dream.

And now she was in the hospital feeling drowsy from something they had given her before wheeling her into the operating room. There was a clattering atmosphere of activity. Diana wanted to let sleep take her into more comfortable surroundings but her mind was racing with images of what they were about to do to her. The sharp scalpel slicing through the muscles that held her eye, cutting the optic nerve, and the freed globe of her beautiful blue eye being lifted from its socket. She tried to force the gruesome pictures from her mind.

Somebody spoke to her, asked questions. Diana mumbled answers but her concentration was elsewhere. A young woman introduced herself as her anesthesiologist. She looked no older than she was and Diana felt a pang of alarm that this young woman was going to be responsible for making sure she would survive the anesthetic. She was aware of the rapid thumping of her heart, she wanted to stop all this, to wait another day. She didn't want to lose her eye, even though she couldn't see with it. She began to feel a sense of panic. She opened her mouth to tell them to stop but before she had formed the words her brain seemed to do a somersault and she lost all contact with the world.

She was having a nightmare, dreaming of the surgery she would be having tomorrow. She drifted back into the sound sleep she had been in. Then she heard her name being spoken. Like a swimmer rising to the surface after a deep dive she slowly became aware of her surroundings. She could feel hands touching her wrist, adjusting something there. The soft voice echoed her name. She was suddenly awake.

They had told her there would be pain. The muscles that had been attached to her eye would still contract as they tried to move the eyeball now removed. She winced as she felt the pain, it was a very unpleasant sensation.

She was dreaming of course, just like the dreams she had had since her diagnosis, every night dreading what was to come.

The pain came back, and with it a closer contact with consciousness, she was waking from anesthesia. It was over. She forced herself to feel relief that her surgery was done and that she had survived the experience. Her blurred mind told her think positive.

The pain from her empty eye socket hit her again and she moaned. Well, they had warned her.

Then the world seemed to stop. Her mind, addled by the anesthetic, was clearing rapidly. She winced again with the stab of pain and realized something was very wrong. She had to be mistaken, her brain was confused by the anesthetic. She took a deep breath and concentrated, forcing her mind to focus. A wave of panic seemed to flow through her, she wanted to press a pause button and reverse time. The message she was getting was now certain. The pain she was feeling was coming from her right eye, or rather from the socket where her right eye had been. Her right eye, her good eye.

She felt a scream build in her chest, a scream of agony and regret, a scream of anger.

But all that came from her mouth was a whimper of sorrow.

TWO

Kate Westbrook drove into the doctors' parking lot and searched for a space, hurrying along lines of vehicles already secure in their places. She turned into another line, her heart thumping with frustration and the prospect of having to find a space in the general parking area of the hospital. That would entail a long walk back to the building and she was already running late. She braked hard, the tires making a brief screech of frictional protest as her car jerked to a stop. The reversing lights she had spotted a few cars ahead indicated that her search was at an end. The red brake lights stayed on though. What was keeping him? She checked her wristwatch and whispered a curse. The exiting car slowly reversed out of its slot, hesitated for a long moment, and crawled away. Kate nipped into the empty space, cut the motor, and scrambled from her car. She checked her watch again. The meeting would have started. Another whispered curse. Then her phone sounded.

She checked the caller ID and recognized the name of one of David's patients. In their shared practice they each had their own patients and, unless one of them was away, it was unusual for a patient to call the other doctor. Kate let the call go to voicemail as she hurried toward the hospital building. She checked the message as she strode along the corridor toward the annex of the main dining room in which the meeting was taking place. It was not urgent; the call back would wait. But why had she received the call?

The monthly meeting of the Family Practice department had already begun as she pushed through the door of the room. Alongside one wall there was laid a buffet meal. Around the room were tables mostly occupied by now with people eating. Kate decided against helping herself to food and found an empty seat. As Chief of Staff of the Hill Country Healthcare hospital she tried to attend the meetings of all the specialty departments. It was only last year when she had been Chief of Family Practice and would have been chairing this meeting herself. She wished she was conducting tonight's meeting as she listened to the present chair wax long and repetitively in an extended monologue. Her thoughts drifted. David Mansfield, her partner in the medical practice they shared, had been withdrawn and quiet the last few times they had spoken. She recalled the energetic enthusiasm of the man when they first met over a year ago. He was forty-five years old, ten years her senior, she was working in the Hill Country Clinic as a salaried doctor. David was running a concierge practice, a family practice in which for a monthly fee the patients had full access to the doctor via telephone or e-mail. It had been so successful that David had asked her to join him. She was enjoying the experience of being able to spend more time with individual patients than she had in the busy clinic when she had to cram as many patient appointments into the day as she could. She now included house calls in her daily schedule, which was one of the reasons she had arrived late to this meeting.

She looked around the room. A large proportion of those present looked as though they would rather be somewhere else. She recognized a few faces that held expressions she knew promised speeches as soon as the opportunity arrived. Her concentration again wandered.

She had things to do this evening, she checked the list in her mind. She felt her phone vibrate and did not recognize the caller ID when she glanced at the screen. By the time she had left the room to answer the call it had gone to voicemail. She listened to the message and found it was from another of David's patients. She called the number back.

"I've called Dr. David and he hasn't called me back," said the worried voice. "It's about my little boy."

Kate listened as the mother described her son's symptoms and then gave instructions as to what to do. "You might want to bring him in to see Dr. Mansfield in the morning," she said before ending the conversation. She then forwarded the patient's details to the practice record-keeping number with a dictated note on the advice she had given. There would also be a reminder for David's nurse to follow up with the patient tomorrow morning. Kate slipped the phone into her purse with thanks for modern technology.

She started to head back into the meeting, hesitated, and gave way to the easy temptation that told her she had made her presence known, would be of no more use there, and did not want to suffer through any more of the verbal diarrhea that would be oozing from the few who loved to hear their own voices. She strode down the corridor and out to the parking lot.

The drive to the office was maybe a hundred yards although not in a straight line, it seemed a lot further. She drove anyway for she did not relish the thought of walking there and back in the increasing dusk. Kate was looking forward to finishing her day and driving back to her home and her lover with whom she shared a house.

She parked in her usual spot at the rear of the office block. David's car was in his spot too. Strange. Why was he not responding to his calls? Was his phone not working?

Kate punched in the code for the lock and opened the door. She stepped inside and stopped abruptly. Something, she was not sure what, set off a warning in her mind. There was a scent, metallic and acid, faint but definite. There was a silence, an inaudible buzzing of absent sound. Her footsteps in the tiled corridor felt foreign and obtrusive.

She walked past the door to her own office and further down the corridor. David's office door was closed. She knocked on it gently. Silence. She pushed it open, slowly. The smell was strong here, she felt her skin tingle, she knew she was about to discover something she did not want, she wished for a pause control, a cancellation of the inevitable but she knew that was impossible.

The smell brought back a distant memory, not a recall that required any effort rather a stab of recollection that forced itself into her brain like a painful wound. She was a teenager. The house had been empty, or so she thought. As she let herself in through the front door she smelt that smell, the smell that was strong and metal in her nostrils right now. She had walked slowly into the den of her house and stopped as if hitting a solid wall. As she remembered the sight and the shock it had given her which lasted for years to come and was probably engraved in her brain forever she felt a spasm of nausea that threatened a violent vomiting attack. She closed her eyes and took deep breath. Her father had been slumped on the den carpet, unconscious or dead. But it was not the sight of the body on the floor that struck her most it was the voluminous spattering of blood all around the room. The walls seemed to be covered in the dark red staining, there were pools on the carpet, the furniture was soaking in it. This was the smell, the scent of spilled blood. She remembered too the half empty bottle of whiskey toppled over on the table. That and the many before had been the cause of her father's liver cirrhosis and the swollen esophageal veins that had ruptured and caused him to vomit the volumes of blood that now covered the room.

But David had not vomited the blood that was spilled in his office. This was blood that had flowed from his brain when he pulled the trigger on the gun he held in his mouth. It flowed in a clotted stream across his desk. Spatters of flesh and brain were sprayed against the wall behind him, his shattered head lay crookedly on the desk.

Kate closed her eyes in a gesture of disbelief but immediately opened them again. What had happened? And why?

THREE

Kate poured her second cup of tea and took a large gulp. She felt as if she had sand under her eyelids. She rubbed at them and yawned deeply.

"You okay?"

Jack sat across the table from her nibbling a piece of toast. They had both spent an almost sleepless night. By the time the police had done their work and David's body had been taken away it was already late. They talked until the early hours and then they both lay in the dark while their brains digested what had happened and worked on what the future held.

It seemed obvious that David had committed suicide although they could not think of a reason why and he had shown no sign of stress or depression that might have been a warning. The police detective who had questioned them had given the impression that suicide was not the only possibility. At one stage in his interrogation Kate had vaguely suspected that he was considering her responsible for David's death. It was ridiculous of course but how was she to know how a policeman's mind worked.

She looked across at Jack. He was already showered and shaved, his fair hair was cut short, he was dressed in a sport shirt and slacks. This morning's meeting was important to him, to them both. She was grateful for his support last night, she knew he had other things on his mind. He would be back by this evening, perhaps the problems he was dealing with might be in the process of being solved. Her own day would be a challenge too. She looked forward to a joint celebration of things improving. Then an image of David's bullet-splattered brain flashed into her mind and celebration was not a word she should have imagined.

"I have to go," said Jack. He stood from the table, his tall body seeming to unwind as he rose. He hugged her and she felt his firm muscles embrace her. Their lips touched and there was a hint of passion. Then he was gone. Kate finished her tea and prepared to face the day.

She drove along the quiet street of houses perched on the hillside and looking down onto the river valley below. The narrow road wound in a steep descent to join the main highway. Jack had a commute of almost an hour to his office in Austin, the journey to her own office took less than half that time. Today she was a little faster. She realized she was driving more quickly than was usual, too much caffeine, anxiety, lack of sleep. Who knew? And her mind was plowing through the puzzle of what had caused David's death and what she was going to do to keep the practice going. Thoughts bounced around her head, she needed to make decisions but as soon as a solution came to her another possibility popped into her perception.

The road ran through countryside with the occasional homestead along the way. They had decided to settle in the small community of Mill because it represented peace and

13

tranquility within a reasonable distance from the growing metropolitan area of Austin. In the three years they had lived there they had seen the village grow, housing developments had sprouted on its periphery, traffic had become noticeably more busy. But Kate still enjoyed the separation from the hectic urban pace of Austin life.

The town of Deep Wells was a buffer between Mill and Austin, a settlement originally separate from but now becoming a suburb of the city. It valued its independence though, as was demonstrated by the impressive complex of the Hill Country Healthcare Medical Center. Newly built and still expanding, its pale limestone-walled buildings contained medical offices of many specialties as well as the hospital. Kate drove through the landscaped grounds and parked in her space behind the office building. Maureen's car was already there. She had spoken to their office manager last night, she was not surprised to see that she was taking charge this morning. As she opened the door and entered the building Kate smelled the faint odor of stale blood. She fought back the nausea it seemed to induce.

Maureen was in her office, talking animatedly on the phone. She ended the conversation and put down the phone as Kate arrived at the doorway.

"They want to keep Dr. David's room closed for at least today." Maureen's frown was more pronounced than usual. She was a serious person. In her mid-forties she was no slave to fashion or style. Today she was dressed in a plain white blouse and black slacks. Her hair was a mousy color with hints of gray, cut short and combed straight. She peered at Kate

14

through heavy rimmed spectacles. To Maureen, problems were meant to be solved, if there was no obvious problem then she would search for one and very often find it. She was an excellent manager.

"They?"

"The police. They have to do some more work in there they say."

Kate felt a spasm of anxiety squeeze her chest. She remembered the detective questioning her last night. Was it possible that David had not taken his own life? And if his death was suspicious would she be investigated as a possible suspect? Kate pushed the thoughts aside, she was being paranoid, feeling the lack of sleep affecting her and the extra cups of tea that made her anxiety worse.

"Angela says she can't come in today. I've just spoken to her."

Angela was David's nurse. In Kate's mental planning for the next few days she had banked on her being around to answer calls from David's patients and to see routine cases in the office. Kate was fully expecting to be overwhelmed with work dealing with David's patients as well as her own, Terri, her nurse, was busy enough as it was but with Angela missing Kate worried about her workload.

"Why?"

"She's very upset about Dr. David and she doesn't think she could face things here."

Kate felt a wave of anger well up inside her. Of course Angela was upset, weren't we all?

She resisted the urge to say something bitchy and let her choice of words fade below the surface of her thoughts. The look on Maureen's face told her that they shared the same opinion of spoiled little Angela.

Her cell phone sounded and she checked the caller ID before answering it. It was a call from a patient she recognized, a minor medical problem easily dealt with over the phone. When the office was staffed she would rout her cell phone calls to the office line so that she could deal with the patients who came to the clinic without interruption. There would be the added load of David's patients and Kate anticipated a busy day. She still felt a protective mental shell of denial that he was dead. The shock of last night had left her with a numb feeling of disbelief. Like a nightmare that lives in vivid memory but you know you are now awake and that was in a different world.

"Do you want me to contact the locum agency?" asked Maureen. They had used this agency to hire a temporary doctor to help out when either of them had taken time off. They had had mixed luck with the doctors provided, one was quite outstanding, a young woman who dressed as if she was on vacation but practiced medicine with a mature and professional touch. A middle aged male locum had proved to be a pompous and lazy doctor.

"Yes, see if you can get, oh I can't remember her name."

"Dr. Archer, she's good."

"That's right, Shirley Archer. Okay."

A door opened at the rear of the building. Kate's nurse, Terri, and their receptionist, Ruth, appeared. They looked as though they could be sisters, tall, blond, in their mid-twenties. They had been informed of the happenings of last night and had expressions of numbed grief. They took up their duties in silence. Kate switched her cell phone to the clinic system and went to her private office. Sitting at her desk she turned on her computer. The list of office appointments was full, Ruth would be busy juggling the patients who had appointments with David and trying to fit them into her own full schedule. She clicked the mouse and checked her house call list. Not too bad for a normal day, but this wasn't a normal day. She leaned back in her chair and closed her eyes. A wave of fatigue flowed over her like an uncomfortable blanket. She shook her head trying to rid herself of the webby tendrils of sleep that threatened to envelope her. She rubbed her sandy eyelids and wondered if coffee was a good idea. She decided that it was and by the time she saw her first patient she was aware of the caffeine induced tremor in her fingers.

The patient, Grant Lewis, was a man in his forties. He was waiting for her in the exam room. He had an expression suggesting he was frightened, his eyes seemed to pop out of their sockets and he kept glancing from side to side. Kate noticed that his hands were shaking too. Her computer showed that David had seen the man just a few days before and had diagnosed a sinus infection. A prescription for amoxicillin, a penicillin antibiotic, had been called in to a local pharmacy.

"I feel worse now than when I saw Dr. Mansfield," said Grant. He had a nervous twitch and his speech was slightly slurred. "I can't sleep, I keep having these horrible nightmares."

Kate asked more questions and examined him. There was nothing obvious to find that would explain his symptoms. She checked his record again. Apart from a note to say he was allergic to fluoroquinolones there was no significant medical history. A flutter of remembered facts stirred in her tired brain.

"What happened when you took the antibiotic you are allergic to?"

"I felt really weird and my heart was thumping. I had nightmares then too. Do you think I'm allergic to this antibiotic too, I've taken it before with no problem."

"I think we need to run a few tests." Kate began to enter a request into the computer.

"These pills don't look like the last prescription, they were capsules not tablets like these." He was holding a bottle. Kate reached out and took it from his shaking hand. She stared at him for a few seconds, he was looking really sick. She glanced at the medication he had handed her. She held the bottle closer and read the name on it. Levaquin, one of the fluoroquinalone family of antibiotics, the medication that Grant Lewis was allergic to. She looked back at him, the frightened look was now wildly panicky, she could hear the wheezy sound of labored breathing. She grabbed his wrist, the pulse was irregular. She needed only seconds of listening to his lungs with her stethoscope to determine that he was developing bronchospasm, an asthma-like constriction of his airways. Grant Lewis was going into anaphylactic shock, an extreme allergic reaction that would rapidly have fatal consequences if not treated aggressively. She moved quickly.

Rapidly she asked Terri to get her life saving medications. Maureen was instructed to call for an ambulance. Kate rummaged in the refrigerator in the treatment room and found the injectable epinephrine. Grant had collapsed onto the floor of the examination room by the time she returned. She carefully inserted the needle under the skin of his arm and slowly pushed the clear liquid into his body. Epinephrine helped to block the allergic response but it also was a powerful stimulant and could affect the heart's rhythm, a potentially lethal complication.

Grant's breathing was becoming increasingly labored, Kate was tempted to inject the epinephrine more rapidly but remained patient. Terri arrived with another syringe. "SoluMedrol," she said. A corticosteroid that would act as a powerful anti-inflammatory antidote to the allergic response.

"Find a vein."

Terri wrapped a rubber band around Grant's arm and fingered the blood vessels on the back of his hand. She rubbed the area with an alcohol swab, touched the needle of the syringe against the skin and was about to ease it into the vein bulging beneath. Grant gave a wheezy cough and his arm jerked violently. The syringe in Terri's hand was knocked away and clattered to the floor. A stunned moment of silence. They both knew that their patient was in shock and that every second counted. Terri looked up, the expression in her eyes was one of apology.

"Get another," said Kate, regretting the gruff tone of her barked command. She pushed the last of her dose of epinephrine and pulled out the needle.

Grant's eyes were rolling in their sockets, he was sucking in air and trying to force it through the narrowing air tubes in order to breathe in more life-sustaining oxygen. Kate had seen this before, the fight for life, the blue-tinged skin as the blood became deprived of oxygen, the fading of the battle, the closing of the eyes, the breathing slowing, and then stopping. She was helpless to do any more than she had.

Terri raced back into the room, a fresh syringe in her hand. She found a vein in his wrist, held the syringe firmly and pushed against the skin. She knew that she had to thread the needle into the lumen of the vein and get the steroid injection into his bloodstream. She drew back on the syringe and blood appeared. Success. She pushed the needle into the vein hoping not to puncture the blood vessel and exit the other side. She pulled at the syringe again and more blood appeared. Then she pushed and emptied the contents of the syringe into the open vein.

Grant was unconscious, his breathing was shallow. The blue tinge was starting to show on his earlobes.

"Oxygen," snapped Kate. The mask was at hand. She held it against his mouth and waited. It would take so little time for the steroids to work but they had very little time. They could hear the sound of the ambulance siren in the distant outside. In the confines of the room they waited. Would he continue to breathe on his own? Would his heart maintain its regular rhythm?

The room was suddenly invaded by two medics. Large men dressed in dark blue uniforms. Kate explained what had happened as they quickly assessed the situation. With very little comment they took charge. An IV was started, a gurney appeared and Grant was moved onto it. He seemed to be breathing more easily now, the steroids were probably kicking in. As they wheeled him from the room Grant opened his eyes and stared vacantly at Kate. She reached for his hand, walking beside the hurrying gurney as they made their way to the waiting ambulance.

FOUR

Jack Stone parked his truck in the multi-storey lot belonging to the marbled high rise that was home to the law firm that represented him. He entered the spacious foyer and rode the elevator to the fourth floor. As he walked out into the corridor he reflected again that the luxurious surroundings enjoyed by his lawyers were paid for partly by himself.

He wondered how Kate was feeling. The evening had been hell, the night too. He so admired her. The black haired pale-skinned beauty he had first met at that conference only a few years ago. He was pushing the software his company produced for the medical profession, out of his context for he was not in sales but relevant as he was the brain behind the development of most of it. She had been curious but skeptical, he had been captivated by those deep brown eyes, the look that bored into him, an invitation, perhaps. Was it this that had encouraged him to hang onto her attention? She seemed to be interested in what he had to sell and stood close to him as he demonstrated what his computer could do.

"Could I send you more details, do you have an e-mail address?" It was such a corny approach and he still cringed when he remembered it. But e-mail contact led to a short and passionate courtship.

Kate had been offered a job in Austin and he had been unable to let her go and followed her there. Her career had blossomed, she built up a busy practice while employed through the hospital and now was independently successful. His own career had followed a similar path. The company that had brought him to Texas from his London home had treated him well. His decision to move with Kate and become an independent enterprise should have led to positive results, and it had - until now.

There was a single desk in the huge foyer. Behind it sat a young woman with blonde hair arranged in an incredibly elaborate style. She was dressed immaculately in a pale blue suit. She smiled politely and greeted him with clichéd properness. Jack could not help comparing her to one of his robots, prepared and programmed to behave impeccably.

After a few minutes wait he was invited into Roger Fado's office. His lawyer was a man a little older than he was, in his late forties Jack guessed. He was tall and walked with a stoop, as if trying to avoid hitting his head on some invisible overhead object. He had a Dickensian seriousness but was always friendly and spent a great deal of time considering minor points of any problem they discussed, expensive time that Jack sometimes, no, often thought might be unnecessary. Today, after formal greetings and enquiries as to health and circumstances, Roger launched into the main business.

"Mr. Windle has become quite aggressive," he said, regarding Jack beneath raised eyebrows. A pause. "His attorney claims that you have fraudulently acquired designs that he developed and which he should be paid for."

Jack felt a rage build up and fought to keep his emotions under control. Tom Windle was his partner in their startup company, 'Clinotics'. It had been his idea originally, Tom had been a colleague working for the computer giant that had brought him to America. They had talked about the robot scheme over a beer or two and eventually had set up Clinotics. They had raised a considerable amount of cash from investors and both had money of their own at risk. The business seemed to be developing well, they had their prototypes, the machines were functioning as expected, there had even been some promising innovations.

Then Tom had begun acting strangely, becoming withdrawn and secretive. His claim that Jack had stolen his ideas and the lawsuit he had initiated to obtain damages had come as a complete surprise. Jack had almost convinced himself that this was the American system, that it did not mean what he thought it did, that lawyers here had different rules. But, unbelievably, the situation had progressed to what it was. His mind wandered as to how he had arrived in this predicament, and deviated to the problems Kate was facing. He found he was not really concentrating on what Roger was saying, the legalese, the lack of sleep, the distractions overwhelmed his focus.

"So it could cost millions."

Suddenly he was paying attention.

"Millions?"

He listened while Roger explained the process of what could happen if Tom continued on the path he had started. There were the legal fees of course, then there was the chance, more than a chance, the possibility that judgment could be in Tom's favor.

"Is that likely?"

Roger paused, rubbed his chin for an awkward moment. "In this sort of case there is no certainty."

A silence filled the room. Jack felt the need to say something definitive. Roger had said his piece. There was a decision to be made but there was not a good choice available. Jack was lost for words, his mind was fatigued, tired and full of unsolved problems. He wanted to quit, to take a time out, to rest. But the world kept on turning, he could feel Roger's eyes on him. He was wasting expensive time.

As he walked from the impressive office suite and toward the elevators Jack hardly noticed his surroundings. He thought over what had just transpired. From the brink of a hard-earned success he had been sucker-punched by who he thought was a trusted colleague. Looking back now, though he realized he had ignored early warning signs, intent on moving forward, only seeing the positive, denying the possibility of what was now happening. Tom was a crook, Roger had made that quite clear, but being an immoral cheat did not necessarily mean he had broken any laws. Jack had a double anger, that he felt toward Tom and that he had toward himself for walking into this situation. What should he do? Roger had given alternatives, each choice was one that had some major risks. He had a short time to make a decision.

The parking garage was full, his footsteps echoed against the concrete and metal, there was an odor of rubber and exhaust. His head was spinning with a painful mixture of thoughts. He slipped into the driver's seat and pressed the start button. As the motor kicked into life he closed his eyes for a moment allowing his mind to settle. A picture of Kate flashed and caught his attention. How was her day going? She would have to organize the practice to cope with the death of David. There would be a big load of patient needs to take care of, there would be the grief and the stress involved in the circumstances of how David died. Jack had not known Kate's partner very well although they had met socially several times. He had not seemed the suicidal sort, although what is the suicidal type? He seemed self confident, perhaps a little too confident, and always exuded an energetic personality. Why would he want to blow his brains out? Did he have some secret stress that he had kept hidden? Jack thought of his own situation, the churning tension going on in his mind, and the outward impression he must be giving to the world. Who knows the inner secrets of one's fellow beings?

As he exited the garage he was greeted by the glaring brightness of the midday sun. He reached for his sunglasses and slipped them on. Easing into the Austin traffic he joined the crawling stop-and-go stream and headed south. The traffic eased and speeded up as he left the main city area, time to reflect as he settled into the journey home.

Where would Kate be? At the office, or the hospital, or making house calls? She had been busy enough when there had been two of them and now she was on her own.

It was half an hour later when he was approaching Deep Wells that he reached for his phone. It was possible that Kate was at the hospital although more likely that she was at her office. He glanced at the phone, the screen showed a list of his favorite contacts, he found Kate's name. As he looked up from the screen he heard a loud blaring of a car horn. He saw the pick-up truck speeding toward him and tugged at the steering wheel. It was over in a split second, he had no time to think of a reaction, not even the regret in breaking one of his own rules about using a phone while driving. He managed to get the truck into his lane and felt the rush of air as the pick-up swerved and almost touched him as it sped past. Jack slowed and let his rapid heart rate calm. A close call, very close. Sleep deprivation, stress. Perhaps, but he had made a serious error. He put down the phone and found a place to park off the main highway.

She answered the call on the third ring. She sounded tired. He was conscious of the tremor in his own voice as he spoke, he concentrated on keeping his tone steady.

"How's it going?"

"Okay," she said without conviction.

"Can I do anything?"

"Not really. I'm at the office trying to keep up with a whole bunch of patients. How did your meeting go?"

"Oh, okay." He felt he was echoing the tone of the word she had just used. "Lunch?"

"Haven't got time."

"I'll bring you a sandwich."

He stopped at a Subway and bought a Veggie Delight with extra jalapenos. The smell of it as he set it down on the passenger seat set his mouth watering.

The parking lot of the clinic was almost full; Kate was having a busy day. He found a space and turned off the motor. A flashback to the previous evening came to him as he looked toward the building: the smell, the sight of the blood, the unreal feeling as they had tried to take in what had happened. Was Kate going to manage all of this? And then his own problems. He felt the pain squeeze his chest. He sensed the closing of his lungs. He fought the feeling of losing consciousness. For a moment he thought he was going to succumb to the dark cloud that was descending over him.

FIVE

Kate came out of an exam room and was preparing to go into the next when she spotted Jack in the corridor. There was something wrong. Nothing obvious but she could tell that he did not look himself.

"You okay?"

Jack smiled. "Sure. Got you a Veggie Delight." He handed her the wrapped sandwich.

She stared at him for a moment. "You look different, strained."

"Probably just tired. How are you doing, you had as little sleep as I did."

"Well, I guess we both should get an early night."

They shared the sandwich in Kate's office. They ate in silence, each surprised by the hunger they felt.

"That's better," said Kate mopping her lips with a paper napkin. She looked at him, those brown eyes searching. He met her gaze and had the familiar melting feeling inside as they made silent contact. She was suspicious that something was wrong with him, he had to concentrate on not allowing anything to show. He smiled.

"Yeah, I was hungry too."

Terri tapped on the open door. "You've three exam rooms full," she said with an apologetic half smile.

"Okay, I'll be right there," said Kate. "Sorry honey. Busy."

"See you this evening." Jack kissed her lightly on the lips and watched her as she grabbed a medical chart and opened the door to the first exam room. He left the building, blinking in the bright sunlight. The memory of his previous attack was still vividly etched in his mind. It had taken him by surprise, which was worrying. He could usually detect warning symptoms before anyone might notice. Kate had never seen him experience one of his episodes.

Kate worked through the afternoon without a break, conscious that she was spending less time with each patient than she would like. It reminded her of working in the clinic where the main object was to see a high volume of patients in as short a time as possible. It was late when the last patient left. She and Terri went through messages and Kate left her nurse to deal with return phone calls. She had two house calls to make, some other requests had been handled over the phone or the patient had been persuaded to come into the office.

The late afternoon traffic was beginning to clog the main highways, Austin was spreading its transportation problems far afield. Kate was familiar with alternate routes and managed to complete her house calls in a reasonable amount of time. She had a couple of things to do in the hospital and then she would be on her way home. As she walked from her car and into the air conditioning of the building she felt the fatigue of the day weigh on her like a heavy blanket.

She checked a patient on the surgical floor, a social call really as the surgeon was strictly the attending physician but the rules of their concierge practice required more than the minimum attention. Then she headed for the medical floor on a more personal mission.

Grant Lewis was in the intensive care unit lying under a white sheet and attached to tubes and wires. A machine was breathing for him, rhythmically pumping air through the connection intubating his trachea. His eyes were closed, his face was pale and ghostlike. Kate checked the medical chart and then the computer. Grant was lucky to be alive, although by the look of him she could not be certain he was lucky. His blood pressure had been almost non-existent when he had arrived at the emergency room. He had had a cardiac arrest which took quite some effort on the part of the medical staff to correct. He seemed now in stable condition, but what sort of condition, she wondered. She stood at the side of his bed and touched his hand. The skin felt cool and dry. Instinctively she felt for the pulse in his wrist. It was full and regular, the screen on the wall would have told her the same thing but somehow the old fashioned physical contact was more satisfying. She released her hold and was about to turn away when Grant's eyelids flickered. She grasped his hand. His lids opened and the blank uncomprehending eyes tried vaguely to focus on her, then gave up the effort and disappeared again behind closed lids. Kate stayed for a minute but Grant showed no more signs of interaction.

As she left the hospital her phone sounded. A patient had expected a prescription to be called in earlier and the pharmacy did not have it. Kate called the office computer and accessed the patient's records. She checked what the prescription was and called the pharmacy to authorize it. Had Terri been distracted or just overworked? Today had been a challenge. Kate dreaded the days to come.

Dusk was fast approaching as she left the hospital parking lot. The roads were quiet though and she felt the first moments of relaxation of the day as she headed toward Mill and home. Questions buzzed through her mind. Why had David Mansfield prescribed such a potentially toxic antibiotic for a simple upper respiratory infection? His usual habit was to treat with a penicillin class drug or a cephalosporin unless the patient was allergic to these medications. And how did he miss that Grant Lewis was allergic to fluroquinolones? That one prescription mistake had almost cost Grant his life and he was still at great risk.

She stopped at a red light and turned on the radio, selecting a station playing soft country and western music. She would be home in ten minutes. She looked forward to a quiet evening and an early bedtime.

Her phone sounded. She answered the call remotely, glancing at the screen of her phone and recognizing the caller ID as one of her patients. Flora Robbins was a middle-aged woman who Kate had seen in the office quite recently. She listened to the woman's complaints, her mind trying to recall what her recent visit had been about. Warning signals waved flags as she listened. She asked a few questions and made a decision.

"I want you to go to the Emergency Room."

"But can't you call in a prescription?"

"No. I'm not sure what is going on with you but you need to be examined and have some tests done."

"Can I wait for the morning?"

"I think this needs to be dealt with tonight."

There was a short silence as Flora Robbins considered her options."

"Really Flora, this could be serious."

"Well. Okay."

"I'll call the ER and let them know you'll be coming." Kate disconnected the call.

The lights were on when she arrived at the house. Jack greeted her with a hug. "Busy day?"

Kate nodded and hugged him back. "Got to make a call." She waited for the switchboard to connect her to the Emergency Department, accepting Jack's offer of a cup of hot tea. The ED clerk came on the line.

"Hi Dr. Westbrook, can I help you."

Kate gave her patient's details and a brief summary of their phone call and of her suspicions.

"I'll let Dr. Butler know."

"Dr. Butler?" Kate knew all the ER doctors, she had regular communications with them but she had never heard of a Dr. Butler.

"Oh, he's new. Very nice really."

"Well good. Thanks a lot." She ended the call and took the teacup that Jack held out for her. She had never believed that she could have fallen into the British habit of drinking tea at any time of the day, and actually enjoying it. She sipped and the warm slightly milk-flavored liquid flowed soothingly over her tongue and down her throat. Was it the taste or the texture, she wasn't sure, but it was a very pleasant sensation.

They chatted about their individual days and the problems they had encountered. It was later than they had planned when they headed for the bedroom. Sleep came quickly.

Kate had no idea what time it was when the sound of her phone roused her very slowly from a deep slumber.

"Hello." She was aware that her voice sounded dry and slurred. She forced herself to concentrate, to drag her mind from its pleasant somnolence into the real world of the dark night and its demands. It was Mark Butler, the new ER doctor. He was talking about Flora Robbins. Kate was awake now and was acutely aware of what he was saying, which seemed puzzling and disturbing. He described his initial examination of Flora and what the tests had shown. He had sent her home as he did not consider her symptoms warranted admission to hospital but she had now returned and was in serious condition. He was preparing to admit her to the surgical floor and wanted to know which surgeon Kate would like called in to consult.

The conversation was brief. Kate put down her phone and settled her head on the pillow. Sleep was very near but her brain was busy. Why had Butler sent her patient home? Had he missed something in his exam, were the test results accurate?

And what of Flora, would she survive the night?

SIX

Jack watched Kate drive away early the next morning. She had been uncharacteristically quiet as they ate a scrambled egg breakfast together. He had been vaguely aware of the conversation she had in the middle of the night, another problem on top of what was already a heavy burden. He had allowed her the privacy of her own thoughts, he had his personal decisions to make. She had kissed him goodbye, there was no animosity, they each had to deal with their own troubles, although in the end they would share them.

He sat at the table and scribbled notes. He sent out e-mails and then picked up his phone. Jack had developed some persuasive marketing skills which he would have to use to the best of his ability if he could salvage what he had invested in Clinotics.

"Carl Maxwell," said a gravelly voice after three rings.

"Hi, Jack Stone, how are you?"

The "I'm fine" reply did not sound as friendly as Jack would have hoped. He took a deep breath and began his spiel. Carl was one of his major investors, a canny businessman who was in this company for nobody else but himself. Jack thought he should emphasize the advantage to Carl in keeping him, Jack, at the helm of the company. As the conversation ended he was not convinced that he had succeeded.

Several more phone calls and a succession of email exchanges sent Jack's mood sliding into a morbid trough. He poured himself a cup of tea and drew arrows and words on the paper before him. Roger Fado had been right, unless he could persuade a majority of the board that his way was the best for the company then he would have to fight a possible losing battle for control.

Jack was in an unfamiliar conflict zone. He had always found the mysteries of high tech easy to maneuver. He had risen high in the ranks of the company that rewarded him with his posting to Houston. There he had met Kate and they had fallen in love. Her move to Austin had persuaded him to quit the job and form his own company developing robotic machines. He had been biased by Kate's career into concentrating on robots that could take over certain medical tasks. Investors had liked his ideas, Tom Windle, an expert in marketing from the firm, had joined him and things were looking extremely promising. Until Tom came out of left field – that was an American expression that flew into his mind although he had no idea of its origin – and was trying to take over the whole enterprise. Why did he assume that people all over the world played by the rules? They did of course but not everybody's game was cricket, they played their own game.

Jack leaned back in his chair, took a long swallow of tea, and closed his eyes. Should he fight this and face the battle and the risk of bankruptcy or should he just give in, admit that he had been out maneuvered?

He did not think so.

He stood up and mentally slammed his fist down on the table. An image of Tom Windle and his face with the pseudo sincere smile and his firm handshake flashed into his mind. No, this was a fight he would win.

With luck.

The drive to his office in Austin was usually a time of peaceful thought, an opportunity to catch up with his ideas without the intrusion of external stimuli. Jack often wondered about this rationale, he was manipulating a vehicle among similar moving vehicles, a task that required a certain amount of concentration, and yet he found he could do so completely automatically and focus his thoughts on other things. Just like his robots, programmed to behave, to react to circumstances, to play by the rule. The rule he had invented for them. He was now faced with a game – some game – that was played under rules that were unfamiliar to him, dirty rules he thought. They called it business. In the quiet uninterrupted peace of his truck ideas blossomed in his head, rules were made by man, man could change them.

He drove by the Medical Center in Deep Wells and imagined Kate in her neat white coat with her efficient and empathetic tone and her gentle touch and the adoring patients she cared for so much. Things had been going so well with the practice, Kate was busy but happy in her work. She had seemed to get on well with David although they were colleagues rather than friends. Why did he do what he did? It must have been suicide, what else could it be? But the police were pursuing their enquiries.

He left Deep Wells, the Medical Center receding and disappearing in his rear view mirror. Ahead was the road to Austin and thickening traffic.

His office was on the second story of a modern building. There were two desks although almost always he worked here on his own. He could have done his work mostly from home but he preferred to keep the business separate from his personal life and he found it easier to concentrate in the neutral environment here. He checked his computer and noted the few replies to his e-mails. They did not reflect the positive response he had hoped for and his heart sank a little further. He entered his password and opened the program that was his own personal workshop, the site at which he had developed the technology that made his robots not exactly unique but different enough to be commercially special. He found it hard to believe that Tom could so blatantly claim credit for the work he, Jack, had done and was cleverly spinning it so that the investors saw only extra profit for them in Jack's ousting.

Jack worked for over an hour. He stared at the screen, the idea was there and the outline of how it could be done. It would take a while to figure out exactly how to finish this but it could be done. Unfortunately his plans would involve Kate. Would she have the time and energy to do what he was planning to ask of her? Either way life was going to be difficult for them in the near future.

SEVEN

The office was buzzing with activity when Kate arrived. She had received a patient call on her phone during the journey from her home, she gave the message to Terri and switched her calls through to the office phone. From her office she checked with the hospital on the status of the two patients admitted last night. Grant Lewis was doing much better, it was anticipated that he would be discharged home today. Kate had to wait to speak to the charge nurse when she called the surgical floor.

"Sorry to keep you waiting Dr. Westbrook."

"No problem." Although Kate was aware of her waiting room beginning to fill up. "How is Flora Robbins doing?"

A few seconds silence. Bad news or just the nurse checking the chart?

"Well, she's in the ICU, shall I transfer you?"

Another minute or so, Kate could almost hear the ticking of a clock as she sensed the precious moments of her day being wasted in waiting.

"ICU, Taylor speaking."

Kate repeated her question as to Flora's condition and listened to the nurse's response. As she put down the phone at the end of the conversation she had a looming feeling that something nasty was going to happen. Again questions as to why she had been misdiagnosed in the ER came into her mind. She pushed them away for the moment and prepared for what promised to be a hectic morning of trying to see more patients than she had time for. She knocked on the first exam room door and pushed it open. Let the day begin.

At the end of the morning Kate felt exhausted and over stimulated, a lot like the feeling she had when she worked in the clinic. She was forced to devote less time to each patient than she felt was needed because she had the added load of David's patients to treat. It was well into what should have been a lunch hour when the last patient of the morning left. It was while she was going over the telephone messages with Terri that Maureen appeared.

"I've managed to get a locum, she can be here for this afternoon."

Kate felt a sigh of relief deflate her into a state of semi-relaxation. A busy office schedule and some house calls and who knew how many phone messages had promised a continuation of the morning's cruel pace. But now there was help on its way.

"Shirley Archer?" She remembered the doctor who had stood in when David took a vacation. She had been efficient and pleasant and the patients had loved her.

Maureen shook her head. "She's not available. They're sending a Dr. Snooks, Sally Snooks. They say she's very good."

"They said that about that man, whatever his name was."

Maureen nodded. The experience with the male locum had not been good, he had been a pompous retired GP who thought he knew it all and was not liked by their patients.

"Fingers crossed," said Kate.

40

Maureen pulled a face. "Crossed."

Maureen had been out for some food and Kate took a few minutes to feed herself. She was sitting at her desk and had just taken a mouthful when Maureen knocked on the open door. Standing behind her was another woman who Kate had not seen before. She was probably a little older than Kate but it was difficult to tell.

"This is Dr. Snooks," said Maureen. "Dr. Snooks this is Dr. Westbrook."

Kate got up from her chair, busily chewing and hurrying to swallow what was in her mouth. She caught an expression on Maureen's face. Dr. Snooks stepped forward to shake hands and Kate realized what the look on Maureen's face meant. The locum doctor was of medium height, she had long hair that hung straight to below her shoulder blades. She was dressed in a strange looking robe-like garment that reached her ankles. On her feet were rope sandals. She looked like the pictures Kate remembered seeing of hippies.

"Hi, I'm Sally," she said stretching out a hand. Her voice was pleasant and musical, her handshake warm and gentle.

"I'm Kate. Thank you for coming."

"I'm afraid you and Dr. Snooks will have to share your office," said Maureen. "The other office is still – er – closed."

A minor consideration that had not occurred to either of them. Maureen quickly organized an arrangement of chairs that would allow the two doctors to share the desk.

The afternoon began. Kate felt a noticeable reduction in her workload. She caught an occasional glimpse of Sally as she slid from exam room to exam room. Terri did well to keep up with two doctors.

Later Kate went over telephone messages with Terri and was comfortable leaving Sally to see the rest of the office patients as she set out to do the three house calls that had been requested.

The first visit was to a patient who had seen David in the office the week before. Kate checked the record. Jane Sommers was a woman in her forties who had complained of shortness of breath. David had done a thorough exam and had ordered lab tests and a chest X-ray. The lab tests were all within normal limits but Kate could not find a result of the X-ray. Had the patient actually gone for the X-ray yet? Kate left a message for Terri to check with hospital to find out if the test had been done and, if so, what was the result. She spoke into her phone asking for directions to Jane Sommers' address and followed the automated voice instructions onto the highway.

She had left the clinic with only the locum to see patients. Kate had reservations about Sally Snooks. How would the patients in this concierge practice react to her? She did not project the image of someone who might offer the pampering special treatment the practice specialized in. But what was the choice? The locum service had only Sally who was available and she, Kate, could not keep up on her own.

"Turn second right and your destination is on your left." Her phone's GPS had guided her accurately. She parked in the quiet street in front of one of a row of houses.

The door was answered by a worried looking man wearing blue jeans and a scruffy Tee shirt.

"Hi, I'm Dr. Westbrook."

He introduced himself as Len and led the way through to a bedroom at the back of the house. Jane Sommers was lying in bed propped up on several pillows. As she entered the room Kate could see that her breathing was labored. She asked some questions, pulled out her stethoscope, and listened to Jane's chest. The faint heart sounds were not encouraging, the moist crackles she could hear as she put the stethoscope on the back of her chest were warning signs. She pulled the stethoscope from her ears and was about to speak when her phone sounded. She glanced at the screen, it was the office. Some instinct told her she should answer this.

"Excuse me." Kate touched the screen and was listening to Terri. She ended the call and turned back to her patient. "That was my nurse, she has the result of your chest X-ray. The reason you are short of breath is that your heart is not functioning properly." Kate was reluctant to use the term heart failure, it had such a negative sound, that would come later.

Jane looked puzzled. "Why is that?"

"The cold you had a few weeks ago, I'm guessing that the virus may have affected the muscles of your heart. It's called cardiomyopathy, it means the heart muscle is weak and is finding a problem pumping blood through your body."

"But they said everything was okay."

"Who did?"

"The lady from your office."

Jane was obviously confused, a possible result of her failing heart or perhaps something else. She needed treatment urgently now though, and Kate explained that she would arrange for her admission to the hospital. She called the admitting office and then contacted Dan Rule, one of the cardiologists she usually referred patients to.

As she drove to her next call Kate wondered how the miscommunication over Jane's case had happened. There was no record of the abnormal chest X-ray in her chart, she had checked on that, and there was no note made of any call to tell her of her test results. The delay in diagnosis and treatment could prove harmful to her recovery, or result in a condition from which she would not recover. If Kate was correct and Jane was suffering from a viral-induced cardiomyopathy then there was a very real risk of serious and permanent damage to her heart.

She was still worried about her patient when she returned to the clinic after the other two calls had been made. There was also a niggling doubt as to whether their locum doctor was suitable for the practice. Kate parked her car and saw that Maureen's car was still there. She would get a progress report.

"Nobody complained," was the office manager's reply to her question. And then Maureen raised an eyebrow in a way she had when an unspoken question lingered in the air.

"She does dress – er- strangely," said Kate. Maureen nodded in silence, she was not going to be dragged into any gossip. Kate respected her not making a judgment without evidence to back it up. She determined though that she would sneak a look at the charts of patients Sally Snooks had seen this afternoon to check up on the locum's performance.

She spent the next thirty minutes at the computer in her office.

There was one more visit to make before she headed home.

The ICU was bustling with activity, there was a hum and hissing of machinery, bleeping and pulsing of monitors, nurses and technicians staring at screens, doctors striding around.

Kate found Flora Robbins' bed. Flora had her eyes closed but opened them as she felt Kate's touch on her wrist. Her response was dulled, she was not able to communicate well.

Kate had noticed the machine at her bedside and had already guessed Flora's prognosis before talking to the charge nurse. She left the unit and the hospital feeling as if a heavy cloud was weighing her down. As she started the engine of her car her phone rang.

EIGHT

Jack sat on the wooden decking at the back of their house. It was almost dark now and he could see the village lights twinkling in the valley below. He sipped from his teacup and checked his wristwatch. Kate would be home soon, she had called to let him know she was on her way, it was time to light the barbeque. He would put the burgers on the grill as soon as she arrived. He turned on the gas and the lighter clicked several times until the flame whooshed into existence. He sat down again and breathed in the fragrant evening air. It was peaceful here, a faint hum of distant traffic was the only sound made by humans, the buzzing of night insects and the call of a whippoorwill took precedence. But, peaceful as his surroundings were, Jack felt far from calm. His mind was full of unanswered questions regarding his own problems; he was also concerned that Kate would be overwhelmed by what she was having to face.

He heard her car draw into the driveway and got up to greet her. She looked tired but as beautiful as ever. He wondered if he would ever not experience the flipping of his heart at the sight of her. They kissed.

"Hungry?"

"I guess so, I've not had a lot to eat today."

Jack fetched the hamburgers and took them out to the grill. Kate followed him onto the decking. She took a deep breath and let the silence soothe her racing mind. The day had been busy, and worrying. She had dealt with the call she had before she left the parking lot. Her phone had sounded again when she was halfway home, she was able to use Bluetooth to talk to the patient. She thought of the days, and nights, stretching ahead when she could expect her phone to demand her attention. What the long-term future held she did not know.

The aroma of the cooking meat set her mouth watering. Jack tossed the buns on the grill for a few seconds, let the burgers sit for some minutes and then served them up with tomatoes, lettuce, and onions. They ate at the outside table. An owl swooped silently by, there was a high-pitched chirping from some invisible creature.

"How did your day go?" Jack broke the silence.

Kate had so many things rush through her mind she didn't know quite where to start.

"The good news is that we've found a locum who seems to be okay. I had my doubts about her, she is sort of eccentric but I checked her patient records this afternoon and she seems very competent."

"And the bad news?"

Kate paused and took a deep breath. She had been mulling over the questions that were bothering her all day. She tried to condense them into a short recitation that would not turn out to be a rambling list of complaints. Grant Lewis and the prescription mistake. Flora Robbins and the misdiagnosis. Jane Sommers and the miscommunication over her X-ray result.

"You've had a bad day."

"Some of my patients have, I can't believe that we make such awful mistakes."

"We?"

"Well, I'm talking about the medical profession as a whole."

Jack reached out and took her hand. "I read somewhere that medical errors are the third commonest cause of death in this country."

"What?" Kate knew that mistakes occurred, but number three cause of death?

"There is some controversy about the figures but some people estimate that around four hundred thousand people die every year because of a medical mistake, that's about the same as people who die because of cigarette smoking."

"Hmm. Should we put a warning notice on the entrance to hospitals like we do on cigarette packs?" Kate smiled at the analogy although the implication was not at all amusing.

"I'm sorry," she said. "I'm going on about my problems. How was your day?"

Jack smiled. "Not too bad. I think I can see a solution in the near future." It was not entirely true, he was still a long way from resolving his situation but Kate had enough to worry about right now and he wasn't going to burden her further. They sat and watched the lights of the village. A crescent half moon rose in the sky sending a faint silver glow over the trees and shrubs that covered the land leading down to the valley. Kate felt the tenseness of the day begin to fade away, there was still a bothersome anxiety that lingered in the background of her thoughts but she managed to ignore it. They shared a fatigue and each sensed the other's needs. Together they went inside and locked the door.

They left the bedroom curtains drawn back. They could see the blanket of stars from where they lay in the bed. He touched her and she moved into his arms, their lips meeting gently and then hungrily as passion ignited. Jack caressed her flesh as if it were an act of worship. She moaned softly as her skin tingled and warmed. He felt her response and was aware of his own uncontrollable arousal. For minutes they floated on a cloud of ecstasy. Then, overwhelmed by desire, they joined in a mutual physical need and together surged into an explosion of delight.

Spent and relaxed they rested in each other's arms and let sleep take them.

It was still dark when Kate surfaced from her slumber. A movement had disturbed her and she was conscious that Jack was turning over in bed again. She tried to ignore him but he was muttering softly. He was usually a sound sleeper, was something bothering him, something he had not told her about? She remembered what he had said about the deaths from medical errors and her problems from the day before came marching into her thoughts. She must have dropped off to sleep again for the sun was just about to rise when she next opened her eyes.

"Jack," she asked over breakfast, "are you sure everything is okay. You were quite restless last night."

He smiled. "Of course, don't worry about me." There was something reassuring about his clipped British accent, he always sounded so calm. It was something that had attracted her when she first met him. She met his gaze. And wondered.

Sally Snooks was already working when Kate arrived at the office. That was good, Kate was beginning to think that her original impression of the locum was not a correct one. She met Maureen in the corridor, she had an expression that sent alarm bells ringing in Kate's head. Silently Maureen nodded toward Kate's office and followed her into it. Maureen closed the door behind her.

"What's the matter?"

"There's a man in the waiting room, says he needs to see you."

"A patient?"

Maureen shook her head. The alarm bells rang louder, Kate felt her mouth go dry. Were the police following up on David's death, did they think she might be involved? Even though she knew she was innocent she had heard of cases where police suspicion had led to a person being brought to trial.

"I'll send him in." Maureen left and returned in a minute with a middle-aged man. He was of medium height, had thinning gray hair, was dressed in a plain shirt and slacks. He was not a person one would notice in a crowd. His attitude did not seem friendly or even polite.

"Dr. Kate Westbrook?"

"Yes."

"I have to serve you with this." He handed an envelope to Kate. She felt her heart skip a beat and seem to sink in her chest. For a moment she contemplated not accepting the envelope but realized that it would not help her. She reached out and took it. The man turned and walked away.

Kate tore open the envelope and pulled out its contents. Her hands were shaking as she read the subpoena. She thought of other colleagues who had described how they felt when this had happened to them and now she was experiencing exactly the same emotions. It was a document all doctors dread receiving. As she read the dry and formal legal descriptions informing her that she was to be sued for malpractice her head began to spin. She staggered to her desk chair and slumped into it. Maureen stepped forward.

"Are you okay?"

Kate raised a hand and nodded. Words were stuck in her throat.

"Bad news?"

"Lawsuit." Kate could not believe it. What had she done, or not done, to warrant this? The name of the patient she was accused of harming – such a cruel word to use – was familiar, she needed to review the chart and see what this was all about. A curse word found its way to her lips.

NINE

Kate spent twenty minutes on the computer studying the medical records of Donald Templer, the patient she had 'harmed'. She really could not see where she had made any mistakes, a denial she guessed that was common in people in her position. She was late in starting to see her patients and felt the stress as she tried to catch up on time. There was covert feedback from a patient who had been kept waiting too, not a spoken complaint but a subtle perception of attitude. She was also distracted by the lawsuit and her thoughts kept drifting to the details of Donald Templer's records. She told herself to forget it and concentrate on the patients she was seeing this morning. Medical errors occur when other things interfere with the doctor's judgment.

David's office was now able to be used, the police had finished whatever they had to do there and the room had been cleaned up. Sally Snooks took up residence there leaving Kate sole use of her own office. Halfway through the morning Maureen informed her that Angela had called to say that she would not be coming back to work, she was too upset. Kate had never liked David's nurse, she acted like a spoiled child and Kate had the impression that she was intrinsically lazy. She had been her nurse for two weeks when David was away and Terri was on vacation, Kate remembered the relief when Terri returned to work. But now they needed a nurse to help Terri.

They probably also needed another doctor to take David's place, Kate could not continue running the practice on her own and to hire a full time locum would be cost prohibitive. That little problem would have to be dealt with later.

At the end of the morning Kate was reminded that today was the date for her weekly meeting with the hospital CEO. As Chief of Medical Staff she was the liaison between administration and the doctors working in the hospital. As usual the meeting was held in a small conference room in the hospital. A collection of snacks had been laid out and Kate helped herself to what she considered the least unhealthy items. She sat at the table which was also occupied by Heather Roth, the hospital secretary, a woman in her late twenties, blonde, well dressed, and overtly ambitious. Tim Lake was assistant to the CEO, in his thirties and a little obsequious but polite and non-threatening. Michael Maloney was in his forties, slightly overweight with a sandy bush of hair and a ready smile. He was known as a shrewd and ruthless man dedicated to his job of running an efficient and profitable hospital. Today his smile was not quite so ready. He greeted Kate with commiserations on David Mansfield's death. "Terrible thing to have happened," he said as he shook her hand. There was obviously something else on his mind for he munched on his food as if it was an enemy he was trying to destroy.

"Well, might as well get started," he said, mopping his lips with a paper tissue. "Tim, anything to report?"

Tim Lake recited some new rules that would be applied to Medicare patients, there was a gloom around the table, an acceptance of the increased regulation of medicine by the government.

Michael Maloney spoke next. "You may have heard rumors about an unfortunate case in the OR last week." He looked around the table noting any reaction. Kate wondered what he was talking about. She listened as he described the removal of a young woman's healthy eye leaving her sightless. This was a nightmare situation for any surgeon, not to mention the tragic situation facing the patient. Maloney was clearly angry at what had taken place. "I've looked into this and there is no explanation as to why it happened or who is to blame." There has to be someone to blame, medical errors did not occur on their own. She thought of the misfortunes in the office that puzzled her. Nothing as bad as what had happened to Diana Bond but who was to blame?

Michael Maloney continued by stating that there would be a thorough investigation of the surgical mishap and that steps would be taken to ensure such a thing did not happen again. He made reference to some structural improvements planned for the hospital building, thanked them all for coming, and declared the meeting closed.

There was not the flippant social chitchat that usually followed these meetings, the atmosphere had a certain tenseness. Kate was relieved to walk out into the hospital corridor having said a hurried goodbye. She caught the elevator to the ICU and checked with the charge nurse. Then she walked through the Unit to where Flora Robbins lay. The portable dialysis machine was no longer at the bedside, the charge nurse had told her that Flora was receiving treatment in the main dialysis center. Her kidneys had shut down as a result of the dehydration she had suffered. An eventual recovery was expected but not guaranteed. She did look less ill than she had the previous day. They talked briefly before Kate left to check on Jane Sommers. At the entrance to the ward she almost bumped into Dan Rule. "Ha," said the cardiologist, "I was going to get in touch with you. Jane Sommers, congestive cardiac failure. I think you're right it looks as if that recent viral infection is to blame. I've started her on an ACE inhibitor and diuretics and we should see some improvement in the next few days. I'll keep you informed."

Kate thanked him, she wondered if he had any idea of the miscommunication that had delayed treatment of her condition. Checking the time she walked briskly back to the office, she had a few minutes to spare before her first patient of the afternoon. She was anxious to study the records of Donald Templer again, what had she done to harm this particular patient?

She sat at her desk and tapped the mouse, staring at the computer screen. Templer's chart came up just as Terri knocked on her door. "Sorry to interrupt but I have this problem." By the time Kate and Terri had sorted out the problem with a patient they had seen that morning it was time to start seeing the afternoon patients. Kate was very tempted, almost compelled, to go back to her computer and Donald Templer and had to tear herself away from the screen. It was much later when she found time to search the records.

Donald Templer was a man in his early fifties. He had mild hypertension controlled with medication but had otherwise been in good health. She had seen him once for a routine check in the year she had been with the practice. She had seen him again several weeks ago. She remembered that consultation. He had complained of a dull headache and a rapid pulse She had found nothing abnormal on examination and had advised him to go home and rest and to call her if anything changed. He had told her that was impossible for he had to drive to Houston on some important business. She had secretly wondered if his symptoms were the result of a stressful situation. He had not called her again and this was the last entry in his medical record. She read through her notes again, checked on the vital signs and her exam findings. What had she done wrong? It should have been easy to dismiss the legal challenge as a mistake, an enquiry into what might have been a clinical error but was not. It should have been but Kate found it impossible to ignore the anxiety that was burning her brain. She dealt with the details that would complete her day and left the office, locking the door behind her.

She could lock up and leave the office, she thought wryly. But her worries she would have to take with her.

TEN

Jack drove into Austin and to his office, not because he needed to work there today but for a more specific reason. His night had been disturbed by dreams, not so much random dreams that float into sleep and take you on unplanned journeys. These dreams were extensions of what was weighing on his mind during his waking hours. He had come far in the development of his robots, he had given up a successful career with an established company and risked his future on his own initiative. The surprise and the hurt he had felt when Tom had done what he did were now turning to a slow burning anger. He would not allow defeat, he would come out on top of this situation. His ideas were still vague although he knew in which direction he should go. His mind worked as it would in a chess game, anticipating his opponent's next moves and working to prevent or neutralize them. Possibilities of what might happen in the very near future had popped into his mind yesterday and had translated into disturbing dreams during the night.

He left the house late enough to avoid the usual rush hour traffic in Austin and was parking his car less than an hour later. He unlocked the door to his office and pulled it open. Officially he kept the key but he knew there were other keys around so several people could have access to the building. This had not worried him particularly before but last night's dreams had suggested things that raised a few alarms. As he stood at the open door now he paused and listened. The room was silent. Then a sudden sound made him jump in that split second before he realized it was the air conditioning switching on. His imagination was playing tricks. He told himself it was only a dream that worried him but his logic realized it was more than that.

Jack spent an hour in front of his computer screen. He had his own password but who knows who could have hacked into his system. What he had planned would require absolute secrecy and he was not going to use this computer for his work on those plans. He changed his passwords anyway as if that would make any difference. Then he backed up relevant information on flashcards and deleted files on the computer. He would be using his home computer from now on.

He checked his e-mails and felt the hairs at the nape of his neck rise as he saw one from Tom. As he read it he was aware of his teeth grinding. He resisted an angry reply and turned off the computer. The familiar clutching in his chest sent a wave of alarm shoot through him. He concentrated on his breathing as he found himself short of breath. The tingling in his fingers was not a good sign. Jack forced himself to his feet and walked to the door of the office. Perhaps some fresh air would help. He stopped at the door and fought for his breath. Gradually it came under control. He waited for the dizziness to lessen and then left his office, locking the door behind him.

The sun was bright, the air warm and humid. Jack needed to walk, to burn off some of what was bothering him. He strode along the sidewalk. His office was off the main streets of downtown and traffic was light here. The sidewalk was shaded by trees. He crossed the road at a four way stop and wandered into a small park-like area. There were several benches and he sat down on one. A man ambled by on the sidewalk he had just left. There was nobody else around. In the middle of this busy city Jack felt alone, and a little lonely. A car slowed at the stop sign and rolled through it without hurry. And then silence apart from a dull roar of traffic from surrounding streets and the song of a bird high in a tree above him.

Jack sat for some time letting thoughts run around in his head. The dream returned and he felt a sense of alarm that he was here all alone and unobserved. It seemed that he was far more vulnerable here in the city than he was in the cozy country – well almost country – street where they lived. He shivered in spite of the warmth and got to his feet.

A few cars passed him as he walked back to his parked truck. He glanced behind as he entered the parking lot, there was one other person on the street. It was while he was unlocking the vehicle that it occurred to him who the person was. He drove from the lot and headed for the main roads that would lead him out of the city. A car was following him. He knew he was being paranoid but he took a turn before he needed to. The car behind kept following, he noticed it was a black Toyota. Another turn that would take him back to where he had started out and the other car stayed with him. Jack felt a knot tighten in his abdomen. Why was he being followed, for he was certain he was? He stared at his rear view mirror, there were two people in the car, he could not make out details but they both appeared to be men. What to do? Stop and confront them? Two against one, he could probably handle that, he had received a thorough education in the martial arts, but he had no idea if they were armed or what their intention was. Drive to a police station? He hadn't a clue where that would be. Instead Jack drove out of downtown and onto the familiar route to Deep Springs, and beyond, to Mill. He vaguely hoped he would see a police vehicle along the way. What he would do when he arrived home he did not know.

The traffic lightened and the Toyota made no pretence at keeping hidden, staying close behind him. Jack was feeling increasingly desperate, he would be arriving at his empty house soon, on a quiet street where probably no one else was around. He would stop and get out of his car. And then what?

The idea came suddenly. He reached the outskirts of Deep Springs, the buildings spread from the roadway to his right. He accelerated slightly and then swerved into the entrance to the hospital. He heard the screech of tires as the driver behind jammed on his brakes. Jack checked his rear view mirror, the Toyota had driven on. He drove within the grounds' speed limit and found the entrance to the Emergency Room. He parked as near the door as possible keeping an eye on the entrance from the road. He was prepared to dash into the relative safety of the hospital if his followers returned, but there was no sign of the Toyota.

After five minutes Jack drove out onto the road again. The traffic was moving smoothly, he saw no sign of the Toyota. As he left Deep Springs and headed toward Mill he wondered what it had been all about. There was no question that the car had been following him, had last night's dreaming made him over suspicious? Had the men in the Toyota mistaken him for someone else? Was there some unexplained reason for them following him? His mind began to accept the fact that perhaps he was wrong to assume that the situation had been threatening. And then a soft voice interrupted the reassuring calm of his logic. What if they knew where he lived and perhaps had gone on ahead to wait for him? Why would they do that? He thought of his dreams and the ideas that had disturbed him. Why should he have a strong feeling that he might be in danger? There were too many whys.

In Mill he drove through the small town center with its shops and galleries. There were a few people strolling around, visitors mostly, Mill was a popular tourist attraction. Jack turned from the main highway and drove up the hill to Middle Way Road. Their house was halfway along it, an unimpressive structure from the road but commanding a stunning view from the decking at the back. The street was empty, no parked cars, no people. Jack pressed the remote and waited for the garage door to open fully before driving in. As he pressed the remote again and the door slid closed a thought occurred to him. A car could easily be parked within walking distance but out of sight from the house. Was it possible that someone could be waiting somewhere in or at the back of the house? His senses were sharp as he let himself in.

It was warm in the house; there was the faint aroma of the omelet he had cooked for his breakfast. There was a silence as if the place was sleeping. Jack walked through the rooms, hesitating at each entrance, prepared for action if that was required. It was not. He turned on the air conditioning and slid open the doors leading onto the wooden decking. The air outside was warm but felt fresher than inside. He took a deep breath and stretched his muscle tensioned body. The village glimmered in the sunlight, flashes of light reflected off distant windshields. He could relax again.

Then the dream returned.

ELEVEN

Kate drove through early afternoon traffic to the only house call she had scheduled for the day. Her morning had been hectic and many of her problems were still unresolved. Sally Snooks was only available for two weeks so another locum would have to be found then. Kate was faced with the decision as to whether she could continue to run the practice on her own or needed to find another physician to join her. That would decide if she needed to employ a nurse to replace Angela, Terri was coping well but Kate knew that she was under enormous pressure in keeping up with two doctors.

A voice from her smartphone told her to take the next turning right. She flicked her indicator and drove onto a narrow road that became a quiet country track.

"You have reached your destination," said her phone.

Kate parked on the verge near a small cottage-like house. She had checked her computer for details of the patient she was about to see. Olga Bebb was a sixty-one year old woman who had seen David in the office almost four weeks previously. She had complained of pain and aching in the muscles in her shoulders and back, worse in the mornings. David had taken a good history and had performed a thorough exam. He had listed his differential diagnosis and ordered lab tests. A high sed rate had confirmed the diagnosis of polymyalgia rheumatica, David had prescribed a course of corticosteroids.

Two weeks later there was a note that a telephone call had confirmed that Olga's symptoms had improved dramatically. A follow up appointment had been arranged. Today Olga's husband had called to say that she was complaining of troublesome headaches and her muscles were really hurting her.

Kate pressed the doorbell button and heard the faint sounds of a complicated chime of bells from inside the house. A few seconds later the door was opened by a skinny man with a wrinkled face and strands of gray hair spreading across his balding scalp. He looked surprised to see her.

"Hi. I'm Dr. Westbrook."

"Oh yes. They said that Dr. Mansfield was – er – deceased."

"Yes."

There was an awkward silence and then Mr. Bebb – as Kate assumed he was – invited her in.

Olga was in their bedroom, the drapes were drawn and the room was in semi darkness. Kate introduced herself again and asked Olga about her symptoms. Then she examined her. Olga winced as Kate pressed gently over her temples.

"Does that hurt?"

"Yes it's really tender there."

Kate stood back from the bed. "I think you have a condition called temporal arteritis. It's an inflammation of some of your blood vessels and it's associated with polymyalgia. We need to increase your dose of steroids and get a biopsy of your temporal artery to confirm the diagnosis." Kate hesitated, should she mention that loss of vision was a complication of temporal arteritis? She decided that this information would come later, she would be initiating treatment immediately.

"So your muscle pains improved quickly when you started the medication Dr. Mansfield gave you?"

"Dr. Mansfield never gave me no medication."

"The steroids, you said they made you feel better."

"Never did feel better. Feel a lot worse now."

"But you've been taking prednisone, the steroid?"

Olga had a beagle-like expression, a sad look that did not change much. Now her eyebrows arched slightly and her eyes seemed to question Kate's intelligence.

"I've been taking Advil and that didn't help at all. I don't know anything about predsone."

"But you said you felt better."

"Never did feel better. Keeps me awake at night, the pain."

Her husband was nodding in agreement. "Me too," he muttered.

Something was wrong here. Kate wondered if Olga might have some sort of cognitive disorder, an early dementia. Had she really forgotten her prescription of prednisone and that it had improved her symptoms? She reached for her phone.

"I'm going to send a prescription for more prednisone to your pharmacy. A much higher dose than what you've been taking." Olga frowned but Kate continued. "It's really important that you take this medication." She held Olga's gaze and then turned to her husband. "You understand?" He nodded. Olga shrugged. Kate wondered if she should emphasize the risk of her losing her vision if she did not comply. "There could be complications," she said compromisingly.

Kate promised to arrange an artery biopsy and let them know the details, emphasized again the importance of filling her prescription and left the house.

Her appointment book at the clinic was full. She finished seeing patients, dealt with the afternoon's telephone messages and checked in at the hospital. Her day was over, apart from the calls she was likely to get before the office opened again in the morning.

The drive home was like an oasis of peace in the desert of her busy day. She turned on the car radio and listened to a news program but her thoughts kept interrupting what was being broadcast. Olga Bebb's story did not make sense. She was either suffering from something more than polymyalgia rheumatica or somebody at the clinic had screwed up mightily. Had David not called in the prescription for prednisone? Had he been distracted by something, maybe the something that had led to his suicide?

Was this another medical error? The number three killer.

She emptied her mind and changed channels. Country music filled the car. She turned up the volume.

TWELVE

Michael Maloney stared at the document on his desk. The envelope it had come in bore the name of a law firm. It was a request, no a demand, for copies of the medical records of Diana Bond. Maloney was expecting the inevitable suit but not as soon as this. The removal of the wrong eye was indefensible malpractice and the result, total blindness, was a highly significant damage to the patient. He could think of no argument that would lessen the hospital's liability. What had happened? Nobody in the operating room could explain why the young woman's good eye had been removed, everything had checked out, the records showed that. He thought of the poor woman, the sight of her in the hospital bed when he had visited her as soon as he had been told of the incident. There was a patch over her right eye, or rather where her eye had been. There were tears running from her cancerous left eye. He had offered condolences that felt as useless as they undoubtedly were. He remembered his emotions as he left the ward, a deep sympathy for the patient and a frustrated anger that such a thing could have happened and the effect it would have on the hospital. Michael Maloney was something of a perfectionist and as CEO he was responsible for what happened in the hospital.

"Damn," he muttered as he pushed the letter away.

He turned to his computer screen and clicked with his mouse. He selected a file, "Incident Reports". This was a daily report he dreaded and yet welcomed. Any event in the hospital that did not fit into a completely satisfactory category necessitated a report form to be completed. He dreaded it because he did not want to see something like the surgery he had just been reading about and he welcomed it because it showed that mistakes were being monitored and hopefully prevented from being repeated.

The first item today was a complaint by a nurse on the surgical floor that a doctor had been rude to her. Maloney forwarded the item to the Chief of Staff and the Chief of Surgery asking them to investigate and deal with the complaint.

An internal medicine physician had reported that one of his patients had been improperly treated in the Emergency Room. Maloney remembered a recent incident when a patient had been sent home from the ER and had returned later needing to be admitted to the hospital. He checked to see who the Emergency physician had been this time. Mark Butler. He clicked on the screen and brought up the previous report. Mark Butler had been the doctor on duty that night too. Maloney could not remember ever meeting this doctor but two complaints in such a short time spelled trouble, he would contact the Emergency group who contracted with the hospital and ask them to look into it.

A mistaken dose of medication given to a patient. A readmission to hospital within twenty-four hours of being discharged. A doctor's telephone orders not being recorded correctly. The list was short but too long for just one day.

Michael Maloney exited the program. He checked the time, he had a meeting in half an hour. He made sure he had all the information he would need. Then he picked up the lawyer's letter again. This was going to be nasty.

Jack was sitting in his study when Kate arrived home. The door was open, she walked in and touched him on the shoulder. "Hi," she said.

"Hi." He looked tired, his smile a heavy expression.

"Tea?" said Kate as she headed for the kitchen. She had picked up Jack's British habit of drinking hot tea, a dash of milk in the cup first, the tea made in a pot with boiling water and allowed to brew for a few minutes. In the daytime she reverted to coffee but now a cup of tea would be quite welcome.

She took the cups back into Jack's study. As she handed him his tea she noticed something in a corner of the room. It was a skeletal mass of metal with four spindly legs and several horizontal propellers. "What is that?"

"My latest invention," said Jack grinning proudly.

Kate frowned a silent question.

"It's a robotic drone. You know the robots I've told you about, they can communicate with patients then diagnose and treat. Well those are office based but this," he made a 'Ta Da' sound as he threw an arm out toward the strange looking object, "makes house calls."

"House Calls?"

"It uses GPS to find the house then it can communicate with the patient, transmit information back to the office and prescribe whatever is needed."

"Sounds futuristic."

Jack smiled. "Well that's the whole object."

Kate knew that Jack's project had to do with computers and robots and that he was working on the use of machines in diagnosing and treating patients. More reliable than people and much less expensive, he had explained. She could use a computer and was adept at handling her smartphone but when Jack tried to explain the details of what he was doing she found her mind wallowing out of its depth. Now she stared at the drone in the corner and marveled that such a thing could find its way around by itself.

"How does it communicate?"

"Voice recognition. You tell it something and it responds. It can have a perfectly logical conversation with a patient and ask the appropriate questions. There's a dock that the patient can put a hand and wrist in and the machine will measure vital signs. A camera can scan the patient and match up what it sees with what the patient has said about symptoms. This information is fed into the computer and a diagnosis is made. Less chance of a mistake being made than if a human is doing the same thing."

The mistakes that Kate had seen recently came to her mind, she could agree with Jack.

"Have you finished for the day?"

"Just about. Another cuppa?" Jack went to the kitchen and refilled their cups. They took them onto the decking and sat looking down to the village where evening lights were just coming on.

"How was your day, have they decided anything about David?"

"Suicide, although there apparently wasn't a note."

"Any family?"

"Only his ex wife and they've been divorced for years."

"And the practice?"

Kate hesitated, where should she start, her mind had been stuffed with problems while she had to focus on the many patients she had seen all day. What was still bothering her most was the case of Donald Templer, not the most serious of clinical problems – although she still did not know what his present condition was – but one that affected her personally. To be accused of malpractice, of causing harm, of causing pain and suffering, was something that hurt most doctors to the quick. It was how things were she knew. The Lotto mentality of some people who hoped to make money because of sometimes an unavoidable complication of nature. She was in a profession that was particularly vulnerable to the legal hawks eager to plunge and snap up the money that could be claimed and willing to share it with the poor victims of whatever misfortune medical mismanagement could be blamed for.

"So what is this man, Templer, complaining of, what did you do to harm him?"

71

"I don't know. We couldn't get hold of him today. We'll try again tomorrow."

She wondered if Jack would be interested in the Emergency Room mishap with Flora Robbins or in Jane Sommers' heart failure but she did not mention them.

"Mistakes happen I suppose. Scary to think how we all trust our doctors."

Kate laughed. "Not always, you should have seen the high tech nerd, not a term of abuse, I admire nerds, who came in today with a stack of printouts of his research into the medications I had prescribed for him last week."

"Complaints?"

"Not really, just questions. And I like that. Anyway we managed to agree that I had made the right choice."

Jack smiled and took her hand. She felt comforted. The memory of Grant Lewis and his anaphylaxis flashed but she told herself that Jack had had enough of her problems for tonight. It was something that bothered her though, a mistake that had harmed a patient, had almost killed him.

They ate a sandwich and drank more tea. They kissed and touched and felt the night air caressing with the night sky glimmering above and night sounds hovering around them. Then, lying naked in bed, they whispered words of love and lust, felt the passion unite them and relaxed into a dreamless sleep.

Tomorrow was another day.

THIRTEEN

Flora Robbins was not in her room and her chart was missing from the nurses' station. For a moment Kate had a premonition that something bad had happened. The nurses were all busy so she used the computer at the station to access Flora's records. Kate scrolled through the chart until she found the latest progress report. The surgeon's note indicated that he was satisfied with her recovery as far as the surgery was concerned but was still worried about her kidney failure. The nephrologist was cautiously optimistic that she would recover renal function in time. She was suffering from acute tubular necrosis, damage to a part of the kidney caused, in her case, by dehydration. Kate wondered if Flora would be in this condition now if she had been admitted earlier. She and her chart were now in the renal unit where she was undergoing dialysis. She had seen this condition before and usually the outcome was good, but not always.

Kate scrolled back to the Emergency Room records. It was obvious to her that Flora had been suffering from what is called an acute abdomen when she presented that night. Kate herself had suspected that she might have had some sort of obstruction to the bowel from the conversation they had over the phone. Her diagnosis had been proved correct during the subsequent surgery. She re-read the notes, this was more than a simple error, what had Mark Butler been thinking of?

On the medical floor she asked the charge nurse how Jane Sommers was doing.

"Doctor Rule is worried about her. She's not responding to treatment as well as he hoped." She brought up the chart on the computer screen. Several of the lab test results were out of the normal range. The latest chest x-ray showed "possible minor improvement."

Kate went to Jane's room. The patient was propped up on several pillows, a nasal cannula fed oxygen into her airways. Kate spent a few minutes in what was essentially a social visit. As she left she again wondered if earlier treatment might have made a difference.

Sally Snooks was coming out of an exam room when Kate arrived at the office. She smiled politely and said "Hello." Kate wondered at the first impression she had when meeting Sally. She looked just the same now, an oddly dressed hippy-like person, but she somehow was fitting in to the practice very well. She was proving to be extremely proficient and had a bedside manner that patients really appreciated. Kate was sorry that she could not stay on as a locum for longer. Sally knocked on the next exam room door and disappeared inside. A willing worker too.

Maureen was smiling.

"You look happy."

"I think I've found a nurse."

"Tell me about her."

"Well –er."

"Something wrong?" Why should Maureen be smiling if something was wrong?

"It's not a she, it's a he."

"Okay, tell me about him."

"His name is Nick White, he's been working in a hospital in Austin but is moving to live in Deep Wells and would like to work near his home."

"Does he have any experience in Family Practice?"

"He said he worked in a clinic for about a year. He sounded very nice on the phone. I asked him to come and meet you this afternoon, is that okay?"

As the day progressed Kate watched Terri dash from exam room to exam room, pick up the phone to deal with messages, dial prescriptions into pharmacies. She needed help, Kate hoped Nick White might be suitable.

There were two house calls scheduled for the day, Kate could fit them in at the end of the morning if she didn't break for lunch. As she drove away from the office she wondered about Jack's robot drone. Would she feel comfortable allowing a machine to take over her work? It made sense, robots were used in surgery although the surgeon was usually near at hand. Voice recognition was everywhere, she could talk to her phone and get solutions to complicated questions in seconds, so she could believe that a computerized robot might be a brilliant diagnostician. What was causing that seed of doubt in her mind? She had felt a similar doubt before joining David in his practice. The idea of a concierge practice was relatively new and was not entirely accepted by the medical profession, or the general public for that matter. That people could pay for privilege was a political controversy. Since working in the practice Kate was persuaded that the efficiency and cost saving benefits of not having to deal with insurance companies allowed her to have fewer patients and to spend more time with each individual. Patients paid a monthly fee and had unlimited access to their own doctor, no office call payments, no extra payment for necessary lab tests. She was committed to being on call all the time but modern technology made some of that burden easier. Back to technology and robots. Would that make life even more simple? Kate arrived at her first house call before she could think about an answer.

For some reason Kate had expected a young man but Nick White was in his mid fifties. A tall slim man with graying hair and a kind friendly face. She liked him immediately.

"I worked as an engineer for NASA in Houston," he said when she asked about his experience. "I always wanted to be a nurse so when I retired I went to nursing school." He smiled and small lines wrinkled the skin at the corner of his eyes. "It's been five years now."

He told her about the jobs he had had and gave her copies of references. Kate explained how the practice worked and what his duties would be. She explained the circumstances of David Mansfield's death. Nick White seemed visibly moved.

"Are you okay?"

"Yes, of course, I'm sorry. My wife passed away in the same way. Almost ten years ago now."

"I'm so sorry."

He smiled and held up a hand. "Please, that's history now, I didn't realize your partner had committed suicide, it came as a shock."

Maureen spent some time with Nick and it was arranged that he could start work the next day.

Kate's cell phone sounded as she drove home that evening. She listened to the voice-mail message and decided that she could return the call when she got home. She thought of how easy it was to be in contact with her patients. Would a drone work the same way as the house calls she had done today? Then she thought of Nick White. He seemed to be a good example of the advantage of human contact. How do you train a drone to smile in the reassuring way he did?

FOURTEEN

Jack had not left the house for over forty-eight hours. His brain felt fried from staring at the computer screen and working out complicated machinery. He was under the pressure of time, he had to produce results before the board of directors of the company met and voted on his fate. He stretched his desk-chair-stiffened frame and walked out onto the decking. The air smelled fresh and clean, birds were singing. He moved back into the house and put on a pair of sandals. A walk, quick and brisk, was what he needed. He closed the door behind him and walked out onto the road. He stopped and went back to the door. It was not the habit of people in this street to lock their doors when they left the house and he had not done so. But something told him that maybe he should. He had left a lot of information and equipment out in the open for any intruder to examine or take. He slipped the key in his pocket and set out to walk.

The sun burned down and he enjoyed the welcome patches of shade as he passed under the live oaks lining the road. He turned a corner and headed along a narrow road that would lead him in a circle back to Middle Way Road. In an empty lot were two white tailed deer. They looked up from their grazing and he could sense that they were tensed to leap away if they detected him as a threat. He quickened his pace and felt his muscles respond. A memory of his training in the military made him smile. The minor discomfort he now felt was nothing compared to the torture he was put through to toughen up his body. It was later that he thanked his trainers and was able to endure combat situations that would have taken the life of a less fit man. He pushed memories to the back closets of his brain from where they were sneaking out.

He turned into his street again. He was sweating now but feeling good. His house was only a hundred yards away, he stopped as it came into sight. In the driveway was a car, a black Toyota.

Kate felt the pressure of work lessen considerably. Terri was relieved of having to cope with the demands of two doctors, Sally had her own nurse to herself. She caught glances of them as Nick clerked in patients and Sally moved from exam room to exam room. They looked to be getting on well, each anticipating what the other needed.

At the end of the morning after dealing with their phone messages Nick White knocked on her office door.

"Excuse me Dr. Westbrook."

"Come in, what can I do for you?"

"Nothing, it's just that my predecessor has left some stuff in the desk, some of it looks personal. Is she coming back?"

"No, no, I don't think so. I'll ask Maureen to clear it out."

"Thanks." There was the smile again.

"How did your morning go?

"I really enjoyed it. Dr. Snooks is great to work with."

"Unfortunately she can only work for another week, we'll have to find a doctor to take her place."

"Oh, too bad."

Kate mentioned the contents of Angela's desk to Maureen and headed for the hospital. She would grab a sandwich in the canteen there and check on her patients too.

Jane Sommers was still worryingly sick. Dan Rule had increased the dose of her medications and had added another drug but she was noticeably short of breath. Flora Robbins was showing signs that her kidney function might be returning. That was good news and an indication that she could make a full recovery. There were no house calls scheduled for today so Kate returned to the office and a list of patient appointments. A call came through as the office was closing. Sally Snooks had just left and Nick White was on his way out of the office. Ruth at the front desk gave Kate the message. Kate recognized the name and guessed that the return phone call could take some time. She motioned to Ruth and Maureen that she would be here a while and that they should go. She had anticipated correctly and it was twenty minutes later when the conversation with her patient was ended. She put the phone down and dictated a note for the records.

Time to go home. As she reached for her car keys she remembered her instructions to Maureen. Had she cleared Angela's desk? Kate walked to the nurses' station and pulled open the drawers of the desk. Nick was right, they were full. Kate rifled through the contents of the first drawer, a mess of cosmetics, a nasal spray, combs, chewing gum, and various coupons offering discounts for a variety of goods. Another drawer was a jumble of forms and certificates that Angela would have used. Kate thought again how disorganized David's nurse had been. Angela had only been working in the practice for a few months and Kate wondered why David had put up with her for that long.

The final drawer contained scraps of paper with reminder notes, envelopes with what looked like personal mail in them, and a small notebook. Kate opened it and flicked through the pages. There were scribbled names and dates. There were telephone numbers and annotations that seemed some sort of code. Kate was puzzled, what was this about? She pushed the drawer closed but kept the envelope with the notebook. Something about it whetted her curiosity, she would take it home and read it more carefully.

They met in the Botanical Gardens off Barton Springs Road. The small man with mousy hair who looked like an older Buddy Holly and the man with the envelope. They were both strolling through the Japanese Garden. In the distance there was the roar of traffic from MoPac, all around were the tinkling sounds of the streams of water flowing in falls in the Garden. They didn't know each other although they had met before, not here of course this had to be a new encounter. The small man stood staring at the koi fish moving lazily through the water. The man with the envelope strolled by, squeezing past him on the narrow stone path.

"Excuse me," he said, and the envelope was exchanged in a swift, hardly noticeable, action. The small man continued to stare into the water then he slowly moved on, the envelope disappearing into one of his pockets.

FIFTEEN

Jack quickened his pace and began to run toward his house. The Toyota was moving now, backing out of his driveway. He was still some distance away when the car sped off. He couldn't be sure of the license plate number.

By the time he reached the house he was breathless. Who was in the car, had the house been entered? He reached in his pocket for the key. Pushing the door open he moved silently into the house. If they had broken in would someone still be here? That seemed unlikely but he was suspicious anyway. He listened for any strange sounds, a movement, a breath. There was nothing. He made his way to his study, it looked just as he had left it. He had closed the files on his computer, nothing had changed there either. Jack walked around the house checking on the other doors and windows, there was no sign that anybody had tried to break in. Before he took a shower he made sure the outside doors were locked.

The long afternoon went by quickly. Jack was totally engrossed in his work. By the time Kate arrived home he was almost ready to put his proposition to her.

As they gave each other a greeting kiss Kate's phone sounded. She touched his cheek and reached for the phone.

"Dr. Westbrook."

She listened then asked questions. "It sounds like a sprain," she said, "call the office now and make an appointment for tomorrow, if anything changes before that call me."

"Your patients are spoiled."

She shrugged. "They pay a fee, they expect service."

"They must think you are worth it."

"Well that patient has probably saved herself an emergency room visit, I know her and that is where she would have ended up tonight. And she knows she can always get hold of me and that will help her sleep more soundly."

"And can you be certain of a sound sleep?"

Kate laughed. "No, but I really don't get an awful lot of night calls."

Jack wondered if this was a suitable time to mention his plans.

"Jack, why don't we go and eat at the Canyon Café?"

Probably not.

"Sure."

The sun was setting as they drove down the hill to the village. A steady stream of traffic filtered on the main road through the town square. They found a parking space and walked to the café. The inside was dark and fiercely air-conditioned. There were several empty tables and they took one near the back of the room. The décor was country, oak beams in the ceilings, rough wooden tables, benches for seating. A twangy guitar accompanied a wailing singer through the loudspeakers on the wall.

A young woman in tight jeans and a tee shirt declaring that Texas is A Free State handed them menus and took their order for iced tea.

"So, how was your day?" said Kate sipping her tea.

Jack considered telling her about the black Toyota but decided against it. It would only cause more anxiety and he really did not know why it had followed him.

"Okay, worked at home, got some things done."

Was this the time to tell her his ideas? He drank some of his own tea. They caught each other's eyes as they drank and a look was exchanged that spoke volumes. Kate laughed.

"You have such a lecherous look when you stare at me like that."

"That's because you stimulate lecherous feelings in my deeper parts."

Kate rolled her eyes and pursed her lips. "Later sweetie."

The waitress returned and, against better judgment, being hungry, they ordered plates that came with gigantic portions of food.

It was dark when they left the restaurant and the streetlights were on. The evening air felt warm after the air conditioning. The distant sound of a country band floated around them. Jack opened the door to the truck and let Kate in. As he walked round to the driver's side he noticed two men hurrying across the parking lot. He paused and watched as they climbed into a car there. On the way back to the house he noticed headlights too close behind him. They followed them into the road leading to Middle Way Road. He drove into the driveway half expecting the car to follow behind. It did not, it merely drove on. Jack pressed the remote and the garage door slowly rolled open. Before it closed he glanced back at the road. It was empty. He was being super sensitive, the car had not been following, it was just a coincidence.

They sat on the decking and chatted comfortably, avoiding the stress of discussing work problems although each was aware of a dull background of static worry.

While Kate was preparing for bed Jack went around the house checking that the doors were all locked.

Just in case.

It was the next day when Kate came across the envelope she had taken from Angela's desk. She had put it in her purse and had forgotten about it. There was a gap between patients and she had a few minutes to spare. She sat at her desk and took out the envelope. Why she had taken it she did not know. Some instinct had made her do it on impulse. The envelope was large and contained numerous papers. Kate felt a tinge of guilt as she tipped the contents onto her desk, she was sorting through someone else's private property.

She sifted through the pieces of paper, reminder notes, telephone numbers, a small calendar. The calendar had stars marked on certain dates, Kate wondered what was the significance of this. Probably some recurring private event in Angela's life. There was the small notebook too. She opened it and saw a list of names. She flipped through the pages, more names, a list of symptoms, descriptions of various diagnoses.

Kate was puzzled. She closed the book and put it back in the envelope.

Terri tapped on her door, her next patient was ready. Kate slipped the envelope into her desk drawer, she would return it to Angela's old desk later.

Only one house call was scheduled for the day. A charming elderly lady whose arthritis made it difficult for her to come to the office. She needed to have her blood pressure checked and a general examination before renewing her medications. Kate enjoyed this ongoing relationship she had with long time patients. She spent some time talking to the lady before driving back to the office.

"I called Angela this morning and asked her if she would like to clear out her desk," said Maureen. "She came by just a while ago."

"Is she still here?"

"No. She didn't stay long. Dumped her things in a bag, rummaged around in the drawers for a while then walked out."

"Still upset I suppose."

"Suppose so."

They exchanged a look that required no words.

SIXTEEN

Michael Maloney was brisk and to the point, this meeting would not drag on, thought Kate. The weekly routine was a commitment that came with the job of Chief of Medical Staff along with other time consuming duties. It was not a good situation for her to be pressured by an overwhelming workload, merely caring for her own patients was enough to keep her busy. Sally Snooks would be gone in a few days and another locum doctor was to take her place. Kate just hoped that he or she would be suitable.

"One last thing," said Maloney and handed her a letter.

The page was headed with the inscription 'Regis Law Offices'. Kate read the letter that advised of the intent to sue the hospital for medical malpractice in the case of the wrongful removal of an eye. She guessed that the surgeon, and probably anyone else whose name appeared on the record, would have received a similar letter.

"It was inevitable," said Maloney. "The case is indefensible."

"It didn't take the lawyers long to start proceedings."

"No. I expected this but not for a few months."

Kate handed the letter back. "I'm sorry."

The meeting was over.

As Kate walked along the hospital corridor she thought of Donald Templer and her own malpractice case. Her lawsuit was not as clear-cut as the removal of a healthy eye, in fact she still was not clear as to the suffering of Donald Templer. They had not been able to contact him or his family and the law office had not responded to their calls. She tried to reassure herself that there was no case against her, that she had not done anything to harm her patient because she was unaware of anything she had done. But there was a gnawing worry in the back of her mind that something was hiding in the legal shadows, something that was threatening to leap into view.

Flora Robbins was recovering satisfactorily and a planned discharge was mentioned in the medical notes. Jane Sommers was not as fortunate. Her chart indicated that her condition was worsening. Kate checked on her lab and x-ray reports and read Dan Rule's comments. He was now suggesting that a heart transplant might be the only effective treatment left. Kate spoke with Jane for a few minutes but Jane found it physically difficult to keep up a conversation. Kate walked away from the ward in a mood of sad frustration. She wondered again if the delay in initiating treatment had worsened the prognosis in Jane's case.

Maureen was smiling again as she met Kate outside her office. She had arranged with the locum agency for another doctor to take over when Sally left. Kate was relieved that she would not be trying to cope with the patient load alone and hoped the new doctor was as good as Sally Snooks. For the short-term temporary locum help was okay but this boutique practice needed permanent doctors. Could she manage on her own? David had for over a year until she joined him. But she had built up her own practice now as well and the total number of patients was far higher than when David was solo. She would battle through the next few weeks and keep a look out for a possible partner.

Jack listened in silence as Kate repeated her daytime musings on the porch that evening. His day had been busy but productive, he had things to discuss with Kate. But first she had to deal with her problems.

"So basically you're overworked and need extra help in keeping up with patient care."

"To put it in a nutshell, yes."

"I don't know how you do it, and being on constant call."

"My smartphone helps a lot, I can take calls almost anywhere, and the computer in the office lets me access patients' records from my phone and I can dictate notes at the same time. It's not really being on call that's a problem it's finding the time to give to the number of patients we have. The practice is committed to giving special attention to each patient's needs."

"And that's what they pay for."

"And that's what they pay for."

The conversation lulled, insect sounds throbbed around them, a dog barked somewhere in the distance, an answering bark echoed across the valley.

"What if you could have something that did some of that work for you?"

"Like another doctor?"

"Well, not really. Something different."

"Meaning?"

"The drone I showed you. I'm not sure your patients are ready for that, they probably need your gentle hand on their brow when they request a house call, but think about it for the future. An automated home visit with diagnostic capabilities second to non and virtually cost free to you. Apart from the original purchase of course."

"No Jack, I really don't think we are ready for that."

"Okay, I get that. I have something else. The original robots we were working on were office based. I have several models ready for trial."

Kate frowned. What was he trying to say?

"Let me show you what they can do."

"What do you mean?"

"I can bring one to your office, set it up there and prove how it can save you time and money, and really impress your patients."

"You sound like a salesman."

"Sorry, I do a bit. But I really believe in this. It's the future, and to be honest, it's what I'm gambling on."

Kate felt suddenly tired. There were too many things happening, too many problems to solve, she did not want to be faced with any more major decisions. Jack had talked about his robots before and the magic they could do but it had all seemed to be related to a different world, one of the future, nothing that she could be involved with.

"Oh, I don't know."

"Look, you just told me how your cell phone makes things work for you. Think about a few years ago when you would have to carry a pager on your belt and have access to a phone to be on call. No caller ID, no computer access to patient records. You see how modern technology has helped. My robots are more of that."

He had a point, but she did not have the energy right now to contemplate it. She was exhausted.

"I think I'll go to bed."

She hoped he would be following her but he was not. It was much later and she must have fallen asleep when she was aware of him climbing into the bed beside her. He lay still for a minute and she heard his breathing slow.

Something was wrong.

The building was quiet, the staff had all left for the day, Kate leaned back in her desk chair and closed her eyes. The day had started on an uneasy note. They had not had a row but she sensed an atmosphere between Jack and herself. Nothing was said, they were politely communicative as they ate breakfast together, but somehow she sensed a distance between them.

"About last night," Jack had said.

"Yes."

"The idea of bringing one of my machines to your office. Is that okay?"

She remembered a conversation she had with David some months ago when he had asked what Jack did. "I think people need people not robots," had been David's comment, and she had agreed.

Was that correct? So much of modern life was involved with technology. But people did need people. She thought of the patients she saw each day and the interaction she had with them on a personal basis. That could never be replaced with machines. And yet computers, machines, perhaps robots, could reduce the medical mistakes that she was seeing almost every day. Was that true? Maybe. Perhaps she could use Jack's robots as an adjunct, an extension of what she was providing as a personal service. Jack was bright and compassionate, he would not be trying to substitute for human contact would he? He looked so appealing now, the clear gray green eyes, the expression open and honest. Before she could think anymore she replied.

"Okay."

They had agreed that Jack would meet her in the office this evening, he should be arriving any time now. There were still doubts in her mind but she was reconciled to the fact that she needed help and that this was an experiment that could do no harm and might, possibly, have a positive influence on the practice.

She heard a sound, a door being unlocked and footsteps in the corridor. Jack appeared in her doorway, he had a smile of anticipation, an eager energy.

"Thanks for this," he said, and kissed her tenderly. "I'll bring the stuff in."

For the next fifteen minutes Jack carried and wheeled his pieces of machinery from the pick-up outside into the office.

"Do you want any help?"

"No, thanks, I'm okay."

He spent another half an hour assembling and arranging what he had delivered.

"Okay, let me show you how this works." There was a tone of relief in his voice, an object achieved. Kate hoped that his demonstration was not going to be a disappointment.

"Now, I want you to be the patient. If you were a regular patient your photo would be in your record and the robot would use face recognition to identify you, and address you by name," said Jack pointing to a padded chair he had set up in Kate's office. "Take a seat."

Kate sat down and there was a soft whirring sound. A band flicked around her wrist, she could feel a slight movement from the seat of the chair.

"That's got your vital signs, pulse, temperature, blood pressure, and weight." He indicated the readings on the tablet he was holding. "Now the interesting bit."

In an exam room was an object that looked like a small Dalek from Dr. Who. Kate's initial impression was that it looked rather sinister.

When it spoke to her she was startled. The voice sounded sympathetic and friendly, a polite greeting and an inquiry as to what were her complaints.

Kate recited the symptoms of the diagnosis she had invented and was impressed when the robot asked relevant questions specific to her imaginary illness. She answered, feeling a little foolish talking to a machine.

"Thank you," said the robot's voice, "now please place a finger on the white pad on my top, I need a blood test."

Kate did as she was told. She felt a cold sensation in her finger, disinfecting alcohol she guessed, and then a pinprick.

"Thank you," said the robot again. "We are through."

Kate looked toward Jack, he was looking at his tablet and smiling. "Take a look," he said.

Kate took the tablet and studied the screen. Her history was recorded as she had told it but in a cleverly edited way. A list of possible diagnoses was printed. She scrolled down the screen, recommendations for further examination and lab tests had been made. The robot had made a diagnosis and had suggested an optional observation and a blood test to confirm what it had decided. She scrolled further and the result of the blood test was already there.

"That is impressive," she said, "I was deliberately vague with my symptoms."

"Which was why it asked you the questions."

"What if it can't make a diagnosis?"

"It will give a list of possibilities and what it needs to be certain of a diagnosis."

"And what about a physical exam."

"It will decide what is needed and the doctor will be consulted. Or, there is a camera and your body can be scanned. It's really good with rashes, it matches the photo with a library of pictures."

"Clever."

"It can do your nurse's job and take the patient from the initial chair into the exam room, it is mobile. It can also recommend treatment and send a message to the patient's pharmacy to call in a prescription although I'm not sure if that would be allowed yet."

"I doubt it, you need a license to prescribe in Texas."

"So, what do you think?"

There was a silent pause. Kate had been truly impressed with the robot, its capability, its speed, its accuracy. It could make the practice more efficient.

Jack waited, he had tried to persuade her that his modern technology was what the future held. His own future might depend on how she accepted this. He waited.

"Using robots could certainly make my work less time-consuming but part of the difference a concierge practice has is the fact that I get to spend more time with each patient. I don't know how some of my patients would react to talking to a machine, they like the human contact."

Jack fought back the urge to point out all the advantages of his robot, Kate had to decide this on her own. It wasn't that he wanted to take over the practice, just borrow some time.

"Of course they do, but people are becoming more used to reacting with machines."

"Like the bank's auto answer?"

Jack chuckled. "Touché. No, not like those annoying put you on hold and listen to this music systems. This is highly personal and can be programmed quite specifically. Its computer can be linked to your central computer so the robot has access to the patient's files. It can refer back to his or her medical history. It knows the names of the patient's children, their social likes and dislikes. It can chat away quite comfortably and respond to the patient's comments."

Kate smiled. She had always been fascinated that she could talk to her phone and get rapid responses to her questions or commands. This was merely an extension of the same thing. Like so many things in life she accepted them even though she did not understand how they worked.

"I don't know how you can work all this out," she said.

"It's what I do. You can sort out symptoms and figure out what is wrong with someone, and what is going to cure them. I wouldn't have a clue on how to do that."

"Hmm."

"Tell you what. I was hoping you might like to try this thing out, just to see. Think about it. Can I leave it here rather than taking everything apart and carting it back home? If you decide against using it I'll get it out of here straight away."

"No harm in that. Okay." She checked the time. "It's getting late, are you hungry?"

"Starving."

Kate turned off the light in the exam room and they headed toward the exit. The building felt oddly empty, she was used to people being around and signs of activity. As they reached the door, she realized she had left her purse in the office.

"I just need to get my purse," she said turning back along the corridor.

"Okay I'll get the truck and pick you up here."

Jack grabbed the handle and pushed open the door, then stepped back in surprise. A young woman stood there, she looked as if she were about to enter the building. She looked as shocked as Jack felt. There was a moment like a tableau when neither of them moved. Then the woman turned and began to walk away. Jack stepped after her and was about to call out to her. The blow came quite suddenly, he didn't hear or see his assailant. All Jack felt was an explosion in the back of his head; he lost consciousness before he hit the ground.

Kate found her purse and headed for the door. She left one light on in the corridor, took a key from her purse and opened the outside door. There was no sign of Jack's truck, he was bringing it from the parking area she thought. Kate fumbled with the key as she found the lock. She looked toward the parking spaces. A car was leaving in an apparent hurry. Kate couldn't make out any details as it disappeared. There was Jack's truck, it did not seem to have been started and she could not see anyone in it. A feeling of apprehension sent the skin of her scalp crawling. Then she saw the body lying in the shadows. Her heart froze as she recognized that it was Jack. Had he collapsed, had he tripped? She bent over him, feeling for a pulse.

"Jack, Jack," she almost screamed. There was blood coming from the back of his head. She felt around his neck, checked his pupils, and gently touched his face. She felt insulated from the world as she dialed 911, waited for a reply, and explained the situation to the responder. She had to force herself to stay calm, to handle this as if Jack was just a patient. When she terminated the call she noticed that her hand was shaking violently. The world was now very much around her. The reality was that Jack had been attacked and was in a condition that could be serious. She was very much alone at the back of the building and she did not know if the attacker was still around. She bent over Jack and felt his pulse again. He was still unconscious. Kate had a horrible premonition that something bad was going to happen.

The wait for the ambulance seemed to take hours. Kate was helpless to do anything but be near Jack. Was she watching his life drift away? She told herself not to be so melodramatic but she couldn't rid herself of her terrible anxiety. She heard the siren in the distance and soon saw the reflections of flashing lights. She watched as the EMTs examined and stabilized Jack with frustrating slowness. He needed to be rushed to the hospital, why waste time. She knew that they had to follow protocol and that they could do more harm by hurrying.

At last the ambulance set off with lights flashing and with Kate riding in the back with the still unconscious Jack.

By the time they reached the Emergency Room Jack was beginning to come to.

"Honey, I'm here." She whispered in his ear.

Jack mumbled something incomprehensible and his eyes flickered open. Kate squeezed his hand and waited. His eyes closed again.

The ambulance pulled to a halt at the ER entrance. With clinical efficiency Jack was wheeled into the hospital and was immediately taken over by the emergency staff.

Kate was just a spectator in the ER cubicle. She watched as strangers busied themselves around her Jack, attaching IVs and monitors, placing an oxygen mask, inspecting his wound. Jack was responding now. He seemed confused, staring at those around him, not recognizing where he was. Kate was afraid he might try to fight them off but he calmed and closed his eyes again. When he reopened them he was much more rational. "Where am I?" he said, his voice crackling and hoarse.

Kate hurried to his side, the attending medics looked perturbed but did not stop her.

"Jack, it's me. Someone attacked you, hit you over the head, do you remember?"

He looked at her and his eyes appeared not to focus immediately. "Uh uh. All I remember is." He struggled with recollection. "All I remember is the robot."

The curtains to the cubicle were drawn aside and a figure appeared. He swooped back the curtains and they were in a private space again.

"Hi, I'm Dr. Butler."

He was young, medium height, dark hair and teeth that were too white.

"Kate Westbrook," she said shaking his outstretched hand.

"Well, what have we here," he said turning toward Jack.

Kate took an immediate dislike to him and then she remembered the name. Butler, Mark Butler, the ER doctor who had misdiagnosed and sent Flora Robbins home. Mark Butler whose name appeared on an incident report.

She looked on as Butler examined Jack. She noticed that he asked no questions, only did a brisk exam and barked out instructions.

"We need to do some tests," he said as he turned away from Jack and addressed the cubicle in general.

"What tests are you suggesting?" asked Kate.

"Just things that we do in cases like this," he said giving Kate a look that suggested he was irritated by having been asked to explain something to someone who would not understand.

"I'm a physician. In fact I'm Chief of Medical Staff in this hospital."

"Oh." Mark Butler looked temporarily challenged, "well a CT scan of his head first of all."

"Good," said Kate.

Mark Butler nodded briefly and hurried from the cubicle.

Jack was fully conscious now. He winced as he turned his head to look at her. "What happened?"

"I don't know, you were lying on the ground when I came out of the clinic. Don't you remember anything?"

He frowned and she could sense his straining to recall. "I remember the robot and you and then it gets vague and disappears."

Concussion. Loss of memory of events before and after the injury. Given time some of Jack's recall would return, Kate wondered if he would ever remember the full details of what had happened. Who was the person responsible? She remembered the car driving away and tried to put together any details to the vehicle. It had been too far away and the lighting had not been good.

She walked beside the gurney as Jack was wheeled to get his CT scan. She waited outside the room while the scan was in progress. When Jack reappeared he was completely alert and irritated by the fact that he was confined to a gurney.

"I'm fine now," he said as Kate stood to meet him. "When do I get to go home?"

"We have to wait for the results of the scan."

"What does that show?"

"To tell if there's any bleeding into your brain, you had quite a bang on the head."

Jack pulled a face. Kate smiled, he was obviously getting back to normal. Jack became more restless as they were taken back to the ER and told they would have to wait for the result of the CT scan. It seemed to take an age but Kate was impressed at how soon Mark Butler appeared again.

"I looked at the scan and it doesn't show any intracranial damage," he said. "But you've had a nasty concussion and I think you need to be admitted to the hospital for observation overnight."

The look on Jack's face was one of disbelieving disgust. "What?" He looked at Kate seeking reassurance that he did not need this.

"Do you have a personal physician?" Mark Butler's voice had a tone of impatience.

"No." In theory David had been Jack's doctor although he had never needed him.

"I'll contact the physician on call for unassigned patients and get you up to the ward." And Mark Butler was gone.

Kate was given a cot in Jack's room. They talked for a while trying to figure out what had happened, and why. A young woman came into the room and introduced herself as the hospitalist on duty. Another aspect of modern times that made life easier, Kate would find it much more onerous if she had to care for her hospitalized patients as well as her outpatients. She watched as the doctor examined Jack and thought about her experience with the robot that evening.

They both found it difficult to get to sleep. There was a faint background noise of activity. Every hour someone came into the room to check on Jack's vital signs. Each time Kate saw this she wondered if Jack was still doing well. She could not help remembering Flora Robbins and the screw up by Mark Butler. Had he really read the CT scan himself? She remembered that he had implied that. If so, could that be a reliable opinion? She kept thinking about the statistics. Medical error being the third leading cause of death, or so some people said. Sleep did not fill her night.

Morning brought daylight and a stale start to a new day. They were given coffee and an unappetizing breakfast. The lady hospitalist – Kate could not remember her name – came and pronounced Jack fit to be discharged. As they were checking out Kate realized they had no means of transport, both their cars were at the office. She called Maureen.

As Maureen drove them to the office Kate tried to plan her day. Jack should not drive back to the house, he seemed okay but he had suffered a significant head injury. She would take him. She would not be available to see patients until she could drive back to the office. As if to accentuate her problems her cell phone sounded. As she spoke with the caller Kate was aware that she was more involved with her own affairs than with the patient's. Admittedly she, Kate, recognized the triviality of the caller's complaint but to the patient the problem was very real. Kate ended the call and worried about the day ahead.

SEVENTEEN

It was late morning when Kate got back to the office. Jack had insisted that he felt perfectly all right but she had noticed that he seemed slow to react and his speech was more hesitant than usual. She instructed him that he should take it easy and to call her if anything changed.

Maureen gave the chair in Kate's office a frowning stare.

"It's part of an automated exam system," said Kate, wondering how to explain what Jack had demonstrated the previous evening. An evening that seemed a long time ago now. And what did she think of his robot? Today she felt the noose of responsibilities tighten around her, robots were not her priority.

"I finally got a response from the lawyers in the Donald Templer case." Kate had almost forgotten about the malpractice suit she was threatened with, almost but not quite, it was part of the stew of problems she was involved with. Her instincts had been that there had been no question of malpractice. She had reviewed the records and could see no way she could be held accountable for whatever Donald Templer had suffered, and she was still not sure what that suffering had been.

"Apparently he had a stroke when he was in Houston. Quite a bad one, some paralysis, speech problems. They claim that his blood pressure was very high and that you did not diagnose that and let him drive to Houston."

Kate felt the breath taken out of her. A stroke was a devastating injury. How could she have foreseen it? She remembered checking the computer for his records. Had she missed that blood pressure reading? A feeling of panic gripped her, she turned to her computer screen and clicked away with the mouse. Maureen watched as Kate stared wide-eyed at the screen. How easy, thought Kate, it was to miss something as simple as this. And a simple error could have devastating results. She found what she was looking for and scanned through Donald Templer's medical record searching the details. She knew she was going to find that incriminating evidence, that blood pressure reading that would prove her guilty of malpractice and of causing harm to her patient. There it was, a reading of one twenty over eighty. A perfectly normal blood pressure. She went over the chart again to see if another reading had been recorded. Nothing.

Maureen was still watching as she tore her attention from the screen. "The insurance company wants copies of the medical records."

Kate knew that their lawyers, her lawyers now, would search the chart and try to find evidence to prove that she was guilty of any malpractice. From what she had just read she could not see anything that suggested it, and yet Donald Templer had had a stroke. She pictured the future, depositions with aggressive lawyers peppering her with questions, the constant uncertainty of a lawsuit hanging over her.

She rose wearily from her chair. A quick check of her schedule showed that the afternoon was busy, she had some catching up to do from her morning's absence. She also had three house calls booked. As she entered the first exam room an image of a drone robot flying over traffic and finding those three houses flashed into her head. It stayed hovering in the background for some time while she struggled to keep up with her afternoon schedule.

Sally Snooks reassured her that she could finish off the afternoon clinic on her own while Kate did her house calls. Kate left the office feeling grateful for the way the temporary locum had fitted in. She had a hint of trepidation at the idea of an unknown replacement coming very soon.

The late afternoon traffic was heavier than usual. The first two calls were fairly routine. She was on her way to the third and final visit when her phone sounded.

"Kate?" She recognized the voice of Dan Rule. The cardiologist sounded worried. Kate remembered that recent afternoon when she had been driving just like this to visit Jane Sommers. She guessed that the call was about her.

"I'm afraid it doesn't look good," said Dan Rule. "We are doing all we can but her heart can't make it. The only hope is for a transplant but whether we could find a donor in time is not very likely."

"I'm sorry. Thanks for letting me know."

There was a moment of silence. "I don't think she'll make it through the night," said Dan Rule.

Her third call turned out to be more complicated than the previous two. On the journey back to the hospital Kate called Jack to tell him she might be late getting home.

"Are you okay?" she thought his voice sounded strange.

"Yeah, I must have fallen asleep."

"Any headache, nausea, vision okay?"

"Actually no, apart from feeling muzzy I've been good."

"Are you sure?"

He chuckled. "Don't worry, I'm fine. Maybe I'll just have a nice cup of tea, and one waiting for you when you get home."

Was that a joke, was he really all right? Kate was sometimes confused by his British sense of humor, and there was that soldier toughness that kept things hidden. She parked and walked into the hospital. She knew she could do nothing to help Jane Sommers medically, that was her cardiologist's prerogative, she was here to add emotional support.

Jane's husband was sitting beside her bed. Kate was sure he was wearing the same old jeans and scruffy shirt he had on when she had first seen him. She shook hands and quietly murmured words of consolation. Then she turned to Jane.

She was propped up in bed, her eyes were closed and she was fighting for each breath. Kate noticed the blueness in her swollen extremities. She touched her hand and Jane slowly opened her eyes. There was a dull expression in them and Kate wondered if she recognized her, then a flicker of a smile touched her face and she closed her eyes again. Kate stayed for a few more minutes before leaving.

In the car she dialed Jack's number. It rang several times before his recorded voice told her that he was unavailable right then. Kate stared at her phone as if it were to blame for Jack not answering. As she drove she knew something was terribly wrong. What had happened to Jack? She worried about the head injury. Had the CT scan been read correctly? Even if it had shown no sign of bleeding into the brain last night it was still possible that something had happened inside Jack's head during the day. She recalled cases she had known when a delayed bleed had caused severe brain damage and death.

Kate realized she was speeding as she left the outskirts of Deep Wells and saw the police car parked in a side road. She braked and checked her rear view mirror. Her heart skipped a beat as she saw the police car pull out onto the highway. It speeded up to her and followed her closely but did not turn on its lights. Her mind rehearsed what she would say when she was stopped. She would explain that Jack might be desperately ill, or worse. She would emphasize the fact that she was a doctor. She would play the damsel in distress role.

But the flashing lights did not come on and after a few hundred yards the following car turned off the highway and disappeared. Kate breathed a sigh of relief and resisted the urge to speed up on her way home.

Then her phone sounded.

EIGHTEEN

The small man who looked like Buddy Holly checked through a list of names. Against each name was a date and a short annotation, in a margin on the right side of the page was a number ranging from one to ten. There were a couple of tens, he would like to see more.

It was a game of chance he was playing, the choice of victim was arbitrary as was the number each could merit.

He picked one of the tens and punched in a number on his cell phone. A voice answered after two rings, a man's voice that sounded guarded. Buddy Holly spoke softly and concisely. There was a short silence on the line as the other man digested what he had been told. "Sounds good," he said.

Another pause. "It is, it's worth the slight increase in my fee."

"How much?"

Buddy mentioned a figure. There was a sharp intake of breath.

"Okay." Buddy picked a name that had a five against it and described the annotation accompanying it.

"Not so good."

"You get what you pay for."

The negotiating was over, Buddy ended the call with a satisfied feeling. Only one ten left on the list, he needed more. He studied his contact file and picked a name.

"Is everything alright?" Kate saw that her caller ID showed it was Jack who was calling.

"Yes fine. I missed your call, I was in the bathroom."

Kate felt a mixture of relief that he was okay and anger that he had caused her so much anxiety. "I'm on my way, shouldn't be too long."

Jack was about to say something when the line went dead. Kate had sounded abrupt. Probably stress, and she must be tired. He filled the kettle and put two teabags in the teapot. He would have preferred a beer like in the old days but they did not keep alcohol on the house. Kate had told him about her father's drinking problem and the way he had died. She had vowed not to risk touching alcohol and even felt uncomfortable if she smelled it on someone who had been drinking. Jack had been okay with that, he was never a big drinker anyway. He had reverted to the British habit of treating any situation with a 'nice cup of tea' and, surprisingly, Kate had followed suit.

He stared at the kettle and thought, not for the first time that day, about last evening. He remembered taking the robot to Kate's office and had a vague memory of talking about it. Had he demonstrated it as he had intended? That was a fuzzy image. If he had, what had been Kate's reaction? It had been important to impress her but it was also important that she make her own decision and not feel forced into anything she might not want to do. His mind fought to recall what had happened. He was almost certain that he had demonstrated his machine, almost certain. Well that was an advance from this morning when he couldn't remember anything.

The kettle was starting to make faint spluttering sounds and whisps of steam fluttered from its spout. Jack waited for the water to truly boil before pouring it over the teabags. Then he remembered the adage; a watched pot never boils, and turned away. Almost immediately a hiss and bubbling told him the water was ready.

The tea had stood for a suitable length of time when Kate arrived.

She walked into the house, dropped her purse on the floor, and hugged him. He felt her body, warm against him, tremble. Then he heard the sobs and the spasm of her tears. For a while he held her and stroked her back.

"What's up," he whispered.

"Sorry, it's been a bad day. How are you, I've been worried."

He drew back and held her face between his hands. Their eyes met, her's blurred with tears, his moistening. He kissed her on the lips, softly at first and then with increasing passion. They held each other and let some of the tension of the day loosen. "Later," she murmured and he kissed her again.

"Nice cup of tea?" He smiled, and she could not help smiling back.

"Tell me about it," he said as they took their cups out to the decking.

"What?"

"Your day."

Kate's mind went back to what seemed an age ago. Was it just this morning that Jack was in the hospital? Then the struggle to keep up with the day's work.

"It's just that there is so much to do. If Sally Snooks wasn't there I couldn't cope, and she'll be gone in a few days."

"You've got another locum though?"

'Yes, fingers crossed that he's okay."

"Anything more on the lawsuit?"

Kate shook her head and brought him up to date on Donald Templer.

"But why would his blood pressure go up so much on a drive from Austin to Houston?"

"Doesn't make sense. Unless he had something like a pheochromocytoma."

"A what?"

"It's a tumor of the adrenal gland, in the cells that produce adrenalin. Very rare but one of the symptoms can be an intermittently raised blood pressure."

"Do you think that's what he has?"

Kate was completely mystified about the case. She had not considered this diagnosis before but now this rare possibility became a reality. Had she missed it? Could she be blamed for it? A missed diagnosis and a harmed patient, she could see a good lawyer proving a case.

Her phone sounded, it was Dan Rule. She listened, then thanked him for the call. Jack raised an eyebrow as she put down the phone.

"Patient with cardiomyopathy, heart failure, died this evening."

"Sorry."

Kate told him the story of Jane Sommers, the viral infection, the heart damage, the failed treatment. She mentioned the mix up over the chest x-ray.

"Would an earlier diagnosis have made any difference?"

"Probably not." But she could not help imagining an aggressive lawyer blaming her for Jane Sommers' death. She was becoming paranoid.

"You need more help in the practice, you spend a lot of time with each patient, you do house calls, you answer the phone twenty four seven." Jack wondered how far he had gone the last evening. Had he even mentioned drones?

"I need to find another doctor." It was as much a question as a statement.

"And how long would it take to find someone suitable, have you anybody in mind?"

Kate had thought about this and had not considered any of the local doctors she knew to be available or appropriate for this particular practice. She could continue to employ a locum, but that was expensive and the patients were paying to have their own personal physician available to them and might not like to have a doctor who was employed on a temporary basis. Long-term plans would take some time to formulate, in the meantime she was on her own.

"The robot you showed me last night, is it ready to use?"

So he had been persuasive enough. Jack felt a wave of euphoria flow through him.

"Ready when you are."

"I've been thinking, I can still give the office patients the attention they need if they don't mind reacting with a machine for some of the time. And you made a very good point about the accuracy of a computer generated diagnosis."

Had he? He still could not remember.

"I can get it all set up properly tomorrow."

"How long will it take?"

"I'll get started early, it should be functional by mid morning. There's a bit of training to get the staff familiarized and then Bob's your uncle." He remembered showing Kate the drone he had built in his study and her rather negative reaction to it. "Have you thought about the house calls?"

Kate had thought about this time consuming part of her practice, a service that was very much appreciated by her patients. Would they still appreciate that service being provided by a machine even though she would be communicating with them through the drone?

"Let's see what the office robot does first."

They ate a light supper. Kate felt a sense of relief that there was a possibility of easing some of her immediate problems. Jack could see the beginnings of a victory in his battle for control of Clinotics.

They made love in a bedroom bathed in the silver light of a half moon in the clear sky, and fell asleep to the sounds of night insects and the distant hooting of an owl.

Jack woke in the middle of the night, a dream had gripped him in a terrifyingly realistic experience. He came to with a gasp of air and a slight delay in realizing where he was, sweating, heart racing, tight airways. He slipped out of bed and padded toward the bathroom. For a minute or two he fought to control his breathing, afraid that the noise he was making would wake Kate. He flushed the toilet to disguise the real reason for his bathroom visit. Still trembling and with a dry mouth he returned to the bedroom. Kate rolled over in the bed and muttered something. He squeezed her hand and lay beside her. He fell asleep again just before it was time for him to get up.

NINETEEN

Brenda Carr stared at the strange machine in the room. She had been somewhat alarmed by the magic chair, as she had regarded it, which grabbed her wrist and vibrated and hissed softly and, with a little bleep, had apparently obtained information about her body that satisfied the blonde haired nurse who came to check it.

She did not know that Dr. Mansfield had passed away until she called to make her appointment. She was given the choice to see Dr. Snooks or Dr. Westbrook. Snooks sounded new and strange but she had heard of Westbrook and had therefore chosen to see Kate.

A tall good-looking man with short fair hair had led her to this exam room and explained that the machine would be collecting information from her. She could take as long as she needed.

"Please tell me what your problem is." The voice coming from the robot was female, soft and pleasant. Brenda was lost for words.

"Do you hurt anywhere?"

"No. Well, yes."

"Where do you hurt?"

"In my leg, but not all the time." She was getting used to this, it really was quite simple. The questions kept coming and Brenda enjoyed answering them.

"Please take off your shoes and place your feet on the platform with the arrow."

Brenda did as instructed, her feet and ankles were encircled by flexible bands which tightened. She felt a pulsation that was not uncomfortable and then the bands released themselves.

"Thank you Brenda Carr, the doctor will be with you shortly."

After a brief wait Kate entered the room. "How do you like my new assistant?" she asked.

Brenda smiled. "Very interesting."

"It's already sent information to me." Kate showed Brenda her iPad. "I just want to double check something in your feet." She bent and felt for pulses in Brenda's ankles and feet. The robot had detected some defect there. Kate was impressed that it was correct. She was also impressed with the detailed medical history and the analysis of the salient points of the 'conversation' that had taken place between it and Brenda.

She couldn't help rechecking some of them with Brenda. There was a list of possible diagnoses with suggestions as to what tests could be done to prove or rule out each one.

"I think you are suffering from something called intermittent claudication," said Kate, although she had to admit the robot had deduced that first. She was about to ask Brenda if she was a smoker but noticed the robot had already asked that important question. "It means that the muscles in your legs are not getting enough oxygen when you are using them, and that gives you the pain."

"Why would that be?"

"It means that the arteries to your leg muscles are not carrying enough blood either because there is a partial blockage or perhaps a spasm of the artery."

"Spasm?"

"Sometimes, in smokers, there is a condition when the artery contracts in response to the smoking and doesn't let enough blood through."

"Never touched a cigarette in my life."

"Good." Kate smiled. "We need to do some tests, an ultrasound scan to check the blood flow in your legs and then more tests to see if there is a blockage in the artery."

Kate gave Terri instructions to arrange the appropriate tests and went to the next exam room. She spent the next twenty minutes taking a medical history and examining her patient. She couldn't help comparing the consultation with the brief visit she had with Brenda. The same ultimate conclusion but in less than half the time. She vowed to check with Brenda Carr to see if she was happy with the way she had been treated.

Her next patient was a man who was obviously very happy with the robot – she must think of a name for the machine, it was so human it had to have a name – he was continuing a conversation even though his diagnosis was made and treatment had been decided. He, of course, did not know this for the machine kept responding to his questions although not asking any of its own, it already had the answers. Kate detected a faintly flirtatious tone to his voice as she knocked on the door and entered the exam room. He turned toward her and grinned, perhaps a little embarrassed. "I like your assistant."

Maybe she could call it Dolly.

There was one house call. As Kate waited at a red light she mused on the image of a drone doing this journey, but with no red lights, and communicating with the patient while she could do the final connection during a break between office patients. A toot from behind told her that the light had turned to green and the drone drifted from her mind.

Maureen brought the letter into Kate's office. It was addressed to Dr. David Mansfield and was a request to send copies of the medical records of Grant Lewis to a lawyer's office.

"I suppose Dr. David's problems are now your problems," said Maureen.

"Suppose so." Kate looked at the letter and wondered how a lawsuit against David would involve her. She was not personally involved in the treatment of Grant except for his allergic reaction in the office. The prescribing of a medication to which he was known to be allergic was difficult to excuse and even though Kate did not have anything to do with the prescription she had no doubt that the practice, which was hers now, would be sued.

She read the dry legal verbiage and experienced a heavy sinking in her stomach. Would she be involved in dispositions and questioning regarding this case? She knew she would be attacked by Donald Templer's lawyers and she wondered too if she might be involved, as Chief of Staff, in the hospital's eye surgery suit. She anticipated having to find time to fit it all in. Hopefully she was looking into a fairly distant future from what she had heard of the speed of legal proceedings. But how long had Grant Lewis taken to consult an attorney? Not long at all, in fact it had happened in a remarkably short time.

Maureen took back the letter that Kate handed her. "I wonder what we should do with the things in Dr. David's desk," she said. "Nobody has contacted us."

"I'll go through it later." Kate did not look forward to sorting out her old partner's personal belongings. David had never been unfriendly but had always been a secretive man, she knew very little about his private life. From what had transpired it seemed that he had no close family. His ex wife had not made any attempt to contact them.

It was late in the afternoon when Kate had time to go into David's old office. There was little sign that it was now being used by Sally Snooks, she was a tidy person who kept things neat, a surprise considering her appearance. Kate felt a tinge of regret that Sally would be leaving very soon. She heard the back door close as the last of the staff left for the evening. She was alone in the building.

She had no idea what she would find in David's desk. He too was a neat and tidy person so she expected to find carefully arranged drawers. Not so, the first drawer she opened was a mess of pieces of paper, pens, paper clips, and assorted junk. There was nothing that Kate imagined could be important. She dumped the lot into the trashcan.

The second drawer was much more organized, with forms and notepaper arranged in orderly fashion. Again there was nothing that needed to be kept. Kate went through each drawer

121

and systematically emptied them. The final, bottom, drawer she reached with a sense of relief. She had not looked forward to this task, sorting through a dead man's possessions, with any joy. She had anticipated discovering articles that needed to be disposed of and the decisions she would have to make. But there had been no difficult problems, all she had found was filed trash, and unimportant papers. She pulled at the drawer handle. It was locked. She tugged again, it was still locked. Her own desk was identical to David's and it had a lockable drawer. She had never needed to lock it but she did have a key. Would that fit this desk?

Kate stood up from bending over David's desk. A crick in her back told her that she had been at this job for some time. She checked her wristwatch, it was time to go home, this could wait until tomorrow. But something made her walk back along the corridor to her own office. She was aware of the silence in the empty building. The hum of the air conditioning, the insulation from the world outside, the fact that she was alone and would have to open the door to leave the building and get to her car. She remembered the attack on Jack, and her spine tingled.

She tried to remember where she had put the key to her desk drawer. It was one of those items that she should keep available but not one to which she needed instant access. Top drawer right, stuff she filed to remind herself in spite of her smartphone, just in case. But also, keys. She found what she thought was the one that fitted the desk drawer, tried it in her desk. The lock clicked shut. Walking back along the silent corridor she felt a strange sense of the danger of an imminent discovery that almost made her turn and not use the key to the lock in David's desk.

Her hand trembled as she fitted the key into the slot. She turned it and it did not budge. She jiggled it and twisted again. No response. So David had his own key to the locked drawer. Where was it? If he wanted to keep the contents of the drawer secret he would not make the key easy to find, if not it should be readily accessible. Kate did not feel like searching, she was ready to go home.

Again she walked the silent corridor. At the exit she punched in the code to the alarm system and pushed open the door.

TWENTY

Kate had a feeling of apprehension throughout the day, partly because of what seemed like a multitude of problems jostling for position in her mind but also the fact that this was the last day that Sally Snooks would be working in the practice. They had not really socialized in the two weeks Sally had been there but somehow the locum instilled a sense of stability that Kate found reassuring. She and Nick White worked well together and patients liked them. Kate hoped the new locum would fit in as well tomorrow.

She checked her iPad and saw that the next patient had been vetted by Dolly. She quickly scrolled down to the robot's conclusion, she was beginning to trust that the machine would usually get the correct diagnosis, she hadn't been wrong yet. She paused outside the exam room as the idea of her redundancy hit her. Could machines really take over the practice of medicine? People need people, David had said, and it seemed obvious to her that was true. As she pushed open the door it occurred to her that this was the people part of the interaction, Dolly just took some of the routine work out of her timetable. The patient, a middle aged lady, was still talking to Dolly when Kate entered the room. She had noticed this before, this apparent communication between patient and robot. She greeted the patient and was very conscious that she should justify her role as a human contact.

At the end of the morning Kate checked on communications from specialists she had referred patients to and from the hospital regarding test results. She scrolled the computer screen and noted that the arterial biopsy on Olga Bebb showed that she did in fact have temporal arteritis. She would ask Terri to call her for a progress report later. Why Olga had not received the prednisone prescribed for her was a mystery, as was the fact that she had reported an improvement in her symptoms which she did not remember. She made a note that Olga would need a referral to an ophthalmologist to get her eyes checked.

Kate had two patients in the hospital, a young woman recovering from pneumonia and an elderly man with cellulitis of his leg. The young woman was improved enough to be discharged home, the infection in the man's leg was looking worse though. Kate worried that he might be victim to one of the dreaded antibiotic resistant bugs. She entered a request for consultation with an infectious diseases specialist.

In the hospital cafeteria where she called in for a quick sandwich she saw Dan Rule sitting at one of the only tables that had empty seats.

"Mind if I join you?" Kate did not wait for an answer, she sat down and unwrapped her sandwich.

"Hi, yes, of course." Dan Rule took a sip of his iced tea. "Your patient, Jane Sommers, so sorry, we tried everything."

"I know. Sometimes it happens."

Rule snorted an unmirthful laugh. "Strange thing, the hospital got a request today for copies of her records. Can you believe that?"

"Lawyer?"

"Of course. Don't see what they think they can sue for, straightforward case of bad luck, no question of malpractice."

Kate remained silent, wondering.

"You don't doubt that do you?" Dan Rule was on the defensive.

"Of course not, what more could you have done?"

"Right."

Kate knew the matter of the mishandled chest x-ray would soon emerge.

Jack called in to the office in the afternoon. He was pleased at the smooth running of his robot, he was equally pleased at how much Kate was accepting it.

"Dolly still behaving?"

Kate grinned, "Very well, I wonder if we could do with two of her."

"Now that's an idea."

"Oh Jack, there's a locked drawer in David's desk and I can't find a key. You any good at picking locks?"

"I'm ashamed to say I am."

Sally Snooks was in David's office studying the computer screen. "Sorry, Kate wants me to get into a locked drawer."

"I'm just leaving, got patients to see." She smiled at Jack as she got out of her chair and left the room.

Jack found the locked drawer, checked the others for a key and, not finding one, turned back to the lock. It took him a short time and with the help of a bent paper clip, to turn the lock and open the drawer. Inside was a pile of papers. On top was a square card. Jack picked it up and turned it over. It was a photograph of a woman, an attractive auburn haired woman with a pouty sensual expression. In one corner of the photo was a penciled drawing of a heart. Jack stared for a moment, there was something familiar about the person. He had never met her but she reminded him of someone he knew. He racked his brain but could not make a connection. He replaced the photo and closed the drawer. Kate could sort out the contents later.

He checked that the robot was communicating with the main computer in the office and was satisfied that it was. All the information it was acquiring was stored and accessible on line. He was almost ready for the confrontation he was anticipating.

He heard the signal from his phone on the journey back home. It was notifying him of a received message. It was not until he had arrived and parked in the garage that he dared to read it. When he did he saw that the confrontation was closer than he had realized. Would he have what he wanted within the next forty-eight hours? He needed it if he had a hope of keeping his share of the business. The euphoria he had felt about the success of Dolly began to evaporate as he realized how close he could be to losing it all.

***

Graham Burett reminded Kate of a praying mantis. He was tall and lean and had long thin fingers that seemed ready to pounce and grasp. His hair was a crispy wave, his expression one of self- importance. She was missing Sally Snooks already. She reminded herself that her first impressions of Sally had not been favorable but somehow she did not feel comfortable about Graham.

"What is this thing?" he said with an aura of disgust when he saw Dolly.

Kate explained the robot's function, restraining herself from emphasizing that she was in charge here and he was an employed locum.

"Well!" was Graham's comment, the one word saying quite a lot. He decided that he would rely on his own skills and not use 'the machine'. "If you don't mind."

"Of course," said Kate. "Let me explain the philosophy of the practice and we can get to work."

She enjoyed outlining the way the practice worked, the emphasis on patient satisfaction, the extra attention each patient should be given. She was not convinced he understood, or wanted to understand, what she was implying and they parted ways to see their own patients. Kate had doubts as to whether Graham Burett would fit in.

Her morning went smoothly, patients were seen on time, Dolly behaved impeccably, and there were no real problems.

She did notice that Nick White did not seem his normal relaxed and happy self. She once caught his eye as he was ushering a patient into an exam room. She did not like the message his look gave her.

Graham Burett finished seeing patients before Kate and had disappeared for lunch before Kate came out of her last exam room. She checked the computer to see if the locum had a full list of patients or whether his morning had not been completely booked. All the appointment slots were full. Why had Graham finished so early? She checked her own appointments, a full afternoon and three house calls. There were two empty appointments in the locum's schedule but Kate did not feel comfortable moving two of her own patients to see him instead. It would be a late afternoon again.

She had time to think on the drive home after she had dictated the details of her last house call. She had bad feelings about the new locum, his attitude seemed inappropriate. Kate was surprised to realize she felt defensive about his implied criticism of Dolly. In spite of her initial doubts she was now convinced that the robot had a place in the practice and patients were accepting it. She thought about the time consuming house calls, they were an essential part of this practice, patients expected them to be available.

By the time she arrived home and had accepted the cup of tea that Jack had brewed she had made up her mind.

TWENTY-ONE

The first patients of the afternoon were arriving when Kate found time to look at the newly unlocked drawer in David's desk. She picked up the photograph and stared at it, puzzled. Then she sorted through the rest of the contents of the drawer.

"Can I help you?" His tone was possessive and condescending, Kate again had to resist the instinct to remind Graham Burett that, even though he had use of this office, this was her practice and she paid the rent.

She was proud of her self control although she found it impossible to act like her naturally friendly self. Graham seemed not to notice. Kate guessed he did not encourage a friendly response in too many people. She took the papers to her own office and put them on her desk. There were several letters written in an untidy scrawl. Other papers were in a tidy pile. She flicked open a diary and recognized David's neat handwriting filling almost every page. Then she picked up the photograph again and began to wonder.

Kate had arrived home late again. Jack worried that she was becoming over stressed with her timetable. He had spent the afternoon in his study double checking his system. Forty-eight hours was a very short time. He wondered how far he could push Kate without breaking his own rules of not involving her directly in his own problems. The events of the night of his concussion were still a little vague, he was not sure how far he and Kate had gone in discussing things. He was almost completely recovered from his injury, the dull headache he had today was due to the tension he was under, he convinced himself. Patches of memory of the evening kept appearing although there were still gaps of vacant recall.

Kate vented about her day, the busyness of it, her doubts about the new locum, her fight to fit it all into a limited number of hours. To Jack there was a solution but he was not going to approach the subject directly. To his surprise and relief it was Kate who suggested it.

"Is that drone of yours ready to go?" she asked.

"Well, yes."

"All legal?"

"I think so."

Kate hesitated before putting her thoughts into words. "Graham Burett was kinda insulting about Dolly, and I was offended by it. She is working out fine. Then I get these house calls and have to spend an hour on the road. The drone could have done them, with me in constant touch, in a fraction of the time. I know people need people but your machines are not depriving my patients of that. This is a practice that departed from the regular way medicine is provided, David took risks when he started it. How do you know if patients will buy into something new? Well they did, and I think they will accept machines."

Jack got up from the chair he was sitting in and kissed her on the mouth. "Thank you," he said.

"Is that just for saying nice things about your machines?"

"Well yes, and I like doing it anyway."

"So do I. Repeat?"

He had spent most of the morning setting up his drone. He arrived at the office in the early afternoon. Kate was in an exam room with a patient. Jack took the drone into her office, he noticed Nick White staring at him with an inquisitive look. Maureen was in her office, Jack explained what he was doing and instructed her on how to maintain contact with the drone and match it up to the main computer in the office.

"It can do all that?" said Maureen in a tone that suggested she did not quite believe what he was telling her.

Jack smiled and nodded. He waited until Kate had seen the last of her patients and dealt with telephone messages. "Do you have any house calls?"

"Just one. A man who says he's hurt his back."

"Come on then let's try this thing out."

Kate called the patient's number and explained that a drone would be arriving soon and would ask him questions. "I'll be in close contact and if you are not happy I can drive out and see you myself."

"A drone, who would have thought," said the man. "Okay."

Jack showed her how to program the drone. "You can type in the address you want it to go to or you can speak to it." He said the patient's name. Roy Blake, and address. "It will connect with your office computer and access Roy Blake's records before it reaches the house."

They carried the small machine to the outside of the building. Jack pressed a button and the drone whirred into action, gently rose to a hundred feet above them, and headed off into the distance. In less than ten minutes it signaled that it had arrived at the Blake's house. Kate had instructed them to leave an outside door open. The drone camera showed a surprised looking Roy Blake staring from the monitor screen on the office computer. Kate was about to speak to him, Jack held up a restraining hand. "No, wait, let it do its job."

They listened, fascinated, to the conversation between the robot and patient. Kate was amazed at the way the machine analyzed Roy Blake's answers to the questions it asked. His complaint was of sudden back pain earlier that afternoon. The camera showed him wincing as he described his symptoms. Kate had already made a preliminary diagnosis from the medical history although she knew a physical exam would be expected to confirm it there was little doubt as to what was wrong with Roy Blake. The drone asked Blake to perform several movements which he did. They watched his reactions. The drone asked one more question. Then a message showed on the computer screen, and a flashing red signal. A list of possible diagnoses included the back strain that Kate had assumed was the correct one but what got her attention was the line highlighted by the flashing light. Her mind raced, this could be urgent, she tapped a key and connected with the drone. "Mr. Blake, I think you need to go to the hospital. I'm going to call an ambulance right now."

There was a shocked silence. "What's wrong doctor?"

Kate explained what the drone had told her and then called 911. If the drone was right then Roy Blake's life could be in danger, if wrong then it was probably curtains for the drone. Jack was thinking exactly the same thing.

Kate called the Emergency Room and told them to expect Roy Blake and what the suspected diagnosis was. She omitted to explain how the diagnosis had been made. How was she going to broach that subject? And if it, and she, was wrong how was she going to justify using the drone on a house call?

"So, what's going on?" Jack had seen the monitor but he was not sure of the terminology or significance of what it signaled.

"From the medical history, and your machine did a brilliant job of asking the right questions by the way, and presumably the information it could access from Blake's records in the computer, it figured out a list of the possible diagnoses. Back pain can be a symptom of several things. It's easy to take the patient's word for it that he hurt his back, and that would be the most likely cause of pain. But the drone calculated the odds and a dissecting aortic aneurysm was high on the list of possibilities. That's not for certain of course but it's one thing you can't wait and see so it puts out a warning." Kate could see the logic of what was happening, it was a question of how correct the drone was.

"An aneurysm, that's a weakness in the wall of the artery, right?"

"Yes, the aorta is the main artery that takes blood from the heart to the rest of the body. If it is damaged then blood under pressure gets between two layers of the wall of the artery and splits it."

"What would cause damage?"

"Several things could. High blood pressure, arteriosclerosis, some genetic conditions."

"And the treatment?"

"Surgery, if it's not too late."

"That bad eh?"

Kate nodded.

The camera on the drone was still working although Blake had left its field of view. They could hear scuffling sounds from somewhere in the house as he and presumably his wife prepared to meet the ambulance.

Then the sounds of a siren, becoming louder. The arrival of EMTs, the questions and instructions. Jack pressed a button and they saw the camera pan back as the drone floated out of the house. They heard a voice as it began to rise. "God damn, look at that thing." Then it was on its way home.

They left the clinic door open and in a short time the drone hovered near it and slowly drifted back to its home.

They drove back to the house in their separate cars. Jack was satisfied that his machine had done what it was intended to. There was a doubt in his mind that it might have overreacted. It was programmed to scan through all the information it had available and to make a judgment, an infinitely more rapid process than could be achieved by a human. It had picked the possibility of a serious condition in

Roy Blake, was it being too sensitive? If so it would lose credibility and his plan would be in ruins.

Kate was worried about her patient. If he did indeed have a dissecting aneurysm he was in a precariously delicate position. If the wall of the artery should burst he would hemorrhage internally and death would be rapid. A memory of her father and the room filled with blood sneaked into her mind and she felt a wave of nausea as she almost smelled the sharp scent of stale blood. Would she have made the same diagnosis as the drone? Would she have thought to ask the relevant questions? She didn't know and she wondered if she had panicked in sending for the ambulance.

They arrived home together as the sun was setting. The house was quiet and still warm from the heat of the day. They sat on the decking and sipped hot tea. Each was restless, a great deal was resting on the news they were expecting from the hospital. Kate checked the time and considered calling the ER and asking about Roy Blake. What if she had been wrong? She would look like an over zealous amateur who had panicked because a machine had lied to her.

They went over what had happened, voicing their doubts and fears. Time seemed to drag on. Kate checked the time again, they should have an answer in the Emergency Room by now.

Her phone sounded. Her hands were trembling as she connected.

Jack watched as she listened. Her expression did not tell him what the news was. For the patient's sake he hoped the drone was wrong but what would that do for his future?

Kate asked some questions, their meanings were ambiguous. Then she terminated the call. They stared at each other in silence for a few seconds.

"Well?" Jack's throat felt dry.

"It's an aneurysm, he's on his way to surgery."

Jack felt a guilty relief. The patient was really sick and in danger but his drone had been right, it had proved itself.

"Will he be okay?"

"It's major surgery, but he's in good hands." She smiled and moved toward him, putting her hands on his shoulders she kissed him. "You have a very clever machine."

"Thank you." The next twenty-four hours would tell how clever.

TWENTY-TWO

The letter had come in yesterday's mail, Maureen had only just opened it. Kate had a feeling of déjà vu, this was becoming too frequent an occurrence. She read the familiar wording requesting the medical records, this time of Jane Sommers. She had anticipated the chest x-ray mishap would come to light sooner or later, especially as the hospital had received notice that a lawyer's office was interested in the case. But this was far too much sooner than later. Had Mr. Sommers with the jeans and scruffy shirt been more attuned to what was going on than was obvious or was this just a fishing net action on behalf of the lawyers involved? Kate had heard that in a medical malpractice lawsuit the lawyer might investigate anybody named in the medical records of the patient in the hope that they find some vulnerability.

Kate had never been sued in her life - was it because she was lucky, or perhaps because she was still young? Talking to her colleagues it seemed that being sued was something to be expected, sometimes for purely financial reasons. An obstetrician she knew had been sued by the mother of a teenaged boy because she claimed the circumcision performed when the boy was newborn was not done properly. It was clearly a ridiculous suit but the amount claimed was for only twenty thousand dollars. The insurance company would have to pay much more than that to defend him so they settled and paid up. He found out that the woman needed twenty thousand dollars as deposit on an apartment and this was an easy way of getting it.

Kate wondered if she were opening herself to liability by using the robot and drone. She imagined a clever attorney making the use of machines to treat patients seem lazy and greedy. In the very short time and the little experience she had so far she was impressed by the robot's performance. But what if a mistake was made? She was always around to double check of course, she would have to be careful that she did not cut corners and relax her vigilance. She pushed the negative thoughts from her mind. Terri had ushered a patient into an exam room to be interviewed by Dolly. She had a few minutes before she was needed. Kate pulled open a drawer and took out the documents she had fetched from David's desk. She opened the diary and studied the pages, something clicked but she was not quite sure how. She put the calendar and notebook from Angela's desk beside David's diary and compared dates and annotations. There was definitely a connection, but what? She looked at the photograph again and searched her memory for signs of what she was thinking.

Terri tapped on the door and told her the patient was ready. Kate put the papers back in her desk drawer and made her way to the exam room.

There were requests for two house calls. Kate decided to test the drone again. With the help of Maureen she programmed the machine, called the patients to tell them what to expect. An added incentive to them accepting this unorthodox delivery of medical care was the fact that they would get attention much sooner than if they waited for Kate to finish her office appointments. She touched the button and watched the small shape hover away.

The cases were not complicated. Kate monitored what was happening while Dolly was dealing with her office patients. She found it easy to slip into an exam room and then back to her office computer and give each patient her attention.

At the end of the afternoon she checked the computer for the records of the patients the drone had seen. Each had a perfect description of the symptoms and complaints, recommendations for any tests or examinations, a list of differential diagnoses, and a suggestion of treatment. Jack had mentioned that the drone could also contact the pharmacy and prescribe but she was sure this would not be approved of. She called in the medications herself.

"Good news, bad news," was Kate's reply to Jack's, "How was your day?"

"Which comes first?"

"The good news is that your machines are working fine."

"And the bad?"

"Could be another lawsuit." She told him about the request for the records on Jane Sommers.

"But what did you do wrong?"

"Nothing, but the records don't look good. There was an abnormal test result that wasn't noted. There was some lack of communication. And the patient died. Lots to try to explain."

"And this was David's patient?"

"Doesn't let me off the hook. The practice can get sued as well as the individual physicians, and that's me now."

"You said the machines worked well. Did you use the drone today?"

Kate told him how the two house calls had gone. Jack smiled.

The aging Buddy Holly man parked his car near to Trader Joes in the Arboretum. He strolled casually around the corner to where the Starbucks tables spilled out onto the sidewalk. The photo chromic lenses had converted his heavy framed glasses into darkened shades. On his head was a red baseball cap. His contact today was new, he would be recognized by the blue t-shirt he would be wearing. Buddy ordered a latte and sat at one of the outdoor tables. He sipped his coffee and glanced around, he was early but not too early, he could relax for a few minutes. Today the payment was for a pair of fives, not something he was prepared to turn down but nothing to compare with the big ten he anticipated in the not too distant future. His plans for another ten were being formulated, another big one might make it possible to quit, or at least move on. He was getting the impression that the market was becoming saturated, that his clients were a little too greedy. Ah well, he would milk them while he could.

He checked his watch, his contact was late. Old Buddy had no patience for tardiness, he would be gone in a few minutes and the price would go up accordingly. He had no doubt that what he sold had a ready market, the amount of money he was making proved that.

He took a final drink of his latte and prepared to leave. Could it be they had decided to cheat him? It was possible but unlikely, this was a small deal, if they wanted to cheat they would pick a ten. Like the big ten he was expecting. There was always the chance that he could fail to collect, he had only a small leverage although they did not know how small. He relied on greed and fear to maintain his business.

He almost bumped into a man in a blue t-shirt as he was about to leave. He was hurrying and looked flustered. He hesitated as he recognized the small man's red cap. He caught his eye, gave a slight nod, and went into the coffee shop. A few minutes later he re-emerged with a cup in his hand and took a seat at an empty table.

The switch went as planned. The package left on a chair, a casual exit, a subtle pick up, and the man who looked like Buddy Holly was strolling toward his car. He smiled to himself as he started the motor and drove away.

TWENTY-THREE

Jack spent the morning on the phone. By the time he had finished he had made twenty-one calls. The responses he received were mixed. Without the evidence he had he realized he would have been in a much more vulnerable position. As it was he was not sure he had persuaded enough of the board to vote for him.

The meeting was to take place this afternoon. Tom Windle was confident that this would be the final step leading to his acquisition of Clinotics. Jack hoped the work he had done this morning would help block that ambition. It was not a meeting to which he looked forward, he disliked the unnecessary conflict involved and the avarice that had initiated it, although he had to admit he had used the greed instinct as a tool of his persuasion this morning.

The traffic was heavy as he approached downtown Austin. He had allowed time for any possible delay but was beginning to feel anxious as he looked for somewhere to park. The room was full when he arrived, men and women sitting round a table. At the head was Tom Windle. He looked up as Jack entered. He was a big man, broad as well as tall. His fair hair was too long, his chin was heavy and full. He had a smirk on his face. Jack felt a sharp dislike for his former colleague.

There had been a low rumble of conversation but now there was silence as heads turned to observe Jack's entry.

He sat at the opposite end of the table from Tom. The two men stared coldly at each other.

"Thank you for coming here today," said Jack. "We have a few things to decide and I think we can do so in a reasonably short time. I spoke to most of you this morning and you know what my position is. I believe Tom has his own ambitions."

Tom had looked perturbed when Jack mentioned his conversations of this morning. Jack knew Tom felt confident that he could rely on the backing of the group of investors who would vote this afternoon.

"I sure do," began Tom. He proceeded to list reasons he believed should give him the right to take over control of the company. When he finished he smiled with a self-satisfied expression.

"Of course if Tom wants to pursue this project on his own then he can. If you want to continue investing in him that has to be your decision. There are some things you should know though Tom. As I pointed out to several of you this morning, I would also be continuing on my own and would hope you would back me. The advantage to you is that I happen to own the patents to some of the specifics of the robot workings, I also have the patents for a medical treatment drone which has been used successfully with several patients. Tom will not have access to anything involving these patents of course."

Tom was staring at him, his mouth beginning to gape open. Jack had guessed correctly that Tom was not aware of some of the background work he had done on this project.

There was a pause as Jack allowed the meaning of his words to sink in. "So," he said, "is there any discussion before we vote on the subject?"

There were several questions regarding the legal status of the present situation. Jack was fairly confident that he was sole owner of vital parts of the robot systems. He hoped that the investors were persuaded enough to reject Tom's challenge and continue to support him.

"Jack is lying to you," said Tom when there was a pause. "I have full control over the company." Jack could see that he was blustering. There was a silence as faces turned toward him.

"Well then, time for a vote."

"No, wait," said a man sitting halfway along the table. "I think we should clarify the situation here. I propose we delay making any decision until that is done."

A middle-aged lady across the table from him raised a hand. "I agree," she said, "We have invested in an idea, a business plan, but we are also investing in the technology that will make this plan work. If we make the wrong decision then we could be tied up with litigation for months or years."

"And maybe time is something of an essence," said Jack. "As I mentioned I have a working drone with a proven record. It would take the company headed by Tom a long time to catch up with that. I take it the vote has been postponed." There were nods and murmurs of affirmation.

He rose to his feet. "I will leave you now, let me know when you are ready to meet again." He glanced around the room. "And please make that soon."

Outside the sun was bright. He felt the adrenaline still coursing through him. It was up to the investors now, he hoped he had persuaded them that their money was in better hands if they stayed with him. If they decided to go with Tom then Jack was left with some great ideas but without the finances to develop them. He would have to wait and see.

Kate left the hospital room and removed the paper gown and the gloves and mask she had been forced to put on before entering the isolation ward. The patient's leg infection had become worse, the swollen flesh bursting out of his skin. The infectious disease specialist she had consulted had suspected resistant bacteria and had ordered the isolation. A surgeon had been called in too. It was likely that the man would need an operation to relieve some of the pressure. Kate thought it was more likely that amputation of the leg would be necessary. If the man survived. As she drove the short distance to her office she considered the rapid advances in the medical field and yet now some simple infections were incurable. No matter how clever we are we are always playing catch up with bacterial and viral diseases or the appearance of new ones.

In her office Kate opened her desk drawer and took the papers out of it. She had been thinking about what she had found and the strange connection between what had seemed personal records of David and Angela. She read through them again and wondered what the coincidence of dates meant. She would check the computer later and find out what was happening in the practice on the days in point.

There was a knock on the door, Nick White was standing there. He apologized for disturbing her before coming into the room and closing the door behind him.

"I need to tell you something," he said. He had a sad, serious expression.

Michael Maloney went through the printouts of the evidence. Somewhere prior to Diana Bond's surgery the records had substituted her right for her left eye. There was no indication as to who was to blame. He had personally interviewed every member of the surgical team present that day and had not come up with a clue. There had to be a reason that this happened, this was an accident that should be anticipated and avoided with as many safeguards as were necessary. The image of the blinded young woman flashed into his mind and he tried to force it away. He wondered how a jury would react to her. He knew how. And so too did the Regis Law Offices. The letter he had received today offered to settle the case for a multi- million-dollar amount, the threat was that if the case went to court then the claim would be for a much higher amount. It was a decision that was hard to make. The hospital was covered by insurance but there was a limit to the amount it would pay. The insurance company may not want to gamble the legal fees involved and then the possibility that they would still be liable for the maximum of their coverage. The hospital might be forced into accepting a settlement instead of making itself liable for any payment over what the insurance covered.

He put down the papers and rubbed his eyes. The outcome was indisputable, the blame was a mystery. But there was no doubt that Diana Bond had come to the hospital with a good chance of being cured of her cancer and had left with the removal of both her eyes.

"Shit." This was not good news. And there was the request for the records of the woman who had been sent home from the Emergency Room and had to be admitted later that night. He had spoken to the surgeon who had operated on her and to her own doctor, Kate Westbrook, and it seemed that the ER physician had made an error of judgment. Would the consequences of that error be enough to justify a lawsuit?

He picked up the first letter from the pile of today's mail. As he read it he had a feeling of déjà vu. What was happening?

"Sit down, please." Nick White sat on the chair to the side of Kate's desk.

"I'm sorry," he began, "but there are things you need to know."

A knot of anxiety tightened in Kate's gut. What had gone wrong now? Possibilities raced through her mind, some stupid, some frighteningly realistic. She let him continue.

"It's about Dr. Burett. I hate to be critical but this is your practice and I think he might not be good for it."

Kate had guessed there was some tension between the two men, Nick's body language had suggested that. As for Graham Burett she could see how he could irritate. But Nick had suggested that he had done something to harm the practice.

"In what way?"

"Well, he has his own way of doing things. He is the doctor and it is up to him to make clinical decisions, but sometimes they seem to be, well, strange. But then he saw a patient who had seen Dolly."

"I thought he had refused to use the robot."

"He had but this patient had been put in the room already. Anyway Dolly's report came through and he looked at it and just sort of snorted. He said some rude things about machines and lack of brains and prescribed for what he decided was wrong with the patient, which was not what Dolly had diagnosed."

"Which was what?"

"Lumbar ligament strain. It looked like that, a typical back sprain to me, but – ." He held his hands out and shrugged.

"And what did Dr. Burett decide?"

"He said the patient had a urinary tract infection and prescribed antibiotics. Bactrim."

"Reasonable choice, if that was the diagnosis."

"Not really, the patient was allergic to sulphonamides."

Kate's mind was mulling around back pain and drug allergies and the recent cases she had been involved with that connected with both.

"And?"

"He changed it to Cipro."

A powerful drug, not without serious side effects, for an unproved diagnosis. Not the careful medicine she wanted her patients to experience.

"Nick, I do appreciate you telling me this. We do try to keep up a high standard of care and it is a team effort. Thank you."

She stood and held out her hand.

He took it and smiled his smile.

Kate had some decisions to make.

TWENTY-FOUR

Jack drove the short distance across downtown to his office. He had not been here for what seemed an age. He parked his truck and walked to the office building. He could feel the hum of the city all around him, the steady roar of invisible traffic, the occasional horn and siren. He climbed the stairs to his office, the elevator was notoriously slow and he felt too impatient to wait for it. He was still affected by the stress of the meeting, still working over in his mind where he was with the investors. It was with a feeling of apprehension that he unlocked the door and entered his office. He had the same sensations as he had the last time he was here, that someone else had left a presence, almost as if there was somebody lurking in a corner spying, or preparing to pounce. He remembered the black Toyota and wondered again who were its occupants, and what was their intention.

He locked the door behind him and turned on the computer. As he waited for it to boot up he double checked the closets, feeling a little silly as he did so.

As expected he found that the computer had been used by someone else. He had been careful to not leave any information on it that could have been useful to Tom, who was quite entitled to use the office, he was still a partner in the company.

Jack knew though that he had the technological skills that Tom did not although, he had to admit, Tom had a certain expertise in marketing and persuasion that was very impressive. After today's meeting he marveled at how Tom had managed to sell his takeover scheme to the investors. He hoped that his explanation of the logic of the situation would be successful.

He stayed in the office for a few minutes letting the quiet and seclusion calm him. The work he had done here, the excitement of discovery, the collecting of investors, the thrill of expansion and success, just memories now. But there was a future, of what he was not certain.

He locked up and headed for the stairs again. On the ground floor a man was waiting for the elevator, he turned as Jack descended the stairs. Jack noticed a brief surprised expression before the man turned his back on him.

He walked out into the sunshine and the city. He wondered if he would be coming back to this building or whether his days with Clinotics were over. The thought of that possibility made him more determined to fight it.

He paused at the curb and glanced back toward the building he had just left. The man at the elevator, he had seemed vaguely familiar and his reaction to seeing Jack had been odd. Jack now realized where he had seen him before. He hurried back to the office building.

The foyer was empty, the lights showed that the elevator was at the first floor level. Jack stepped into it and pressed the floor button. The door slid closed with a frustrating slowness. A slight pause and he felt a gentle elevation before the soft bump of a stop. Jack stared at the doors waiting for them to move.

He stepped into the corridor, there was no sign of the man. Jack was fairly certain he knew who he was. He had seen him before climbing into the black Toyota parked in his driveway. He had been some distance away but Jack's eyesight was good. He wondered now if this mystery person might have disappeared into his office. If the pair who had followed him were connected to Tom that would make sense.

Jack moved toward the closed door of his office. He could feel his muscles tensing, his mind plotted what he would do next. If the man was unarmed he had no doubt he could overpower him. If he had a gun then his fighting skills would be more challenged. He slipped the key into the lock and turned it slowly. As he felt the door loosen he pulled it open with a quick jerk and stepped sideways. If he was facing a man with a gun he did not intend to be an easy target.

There was an eerie silence. Jack stood still, listening. He moved slightly and peered around the doorway. There was no sign of anyone. He moved inside. There was a hidden space behind one of the desks, it was unlikely that he would be hiding there. But unlikely things can do the unsuspecting a great deal of harm.

He made sure the office was empty and turned back toward the open door. He stepped out into the corridor, it was empty. There were several other office suites leading into this corridor, could the man be visiting one of those? Or had he recognized Jack and decided to leave the building?

For the second time Jack locked the door. He took the stairs down and walked out into the sunlight. He had the impression that somebody was watching him. There were no pedestrians visible on the street and it was empty of vehicles. Jack stopped and looked around. He could feel eyes on him, but where were they? And who did they belong to?

Graham Burett was either in an exam room or had already left for lunch. Kate did not have the time to find him although she would have liked to get this business over with. She checked the time and accepted the fact that she would be late for the monthly meeting of the hospital surgical department. The meeting had just begun when she pulled open the door to the room and took a seat at the back.

Richard North was the current Chief of the Surgical Department. He was the surgeon consulting on her patient with the leg infection. He was a much better surgeon than he was a speaker. He had a shy demeanor when he had to stand up before an audience and he was now hesitatingly opening the meeting. He managed to get unanimous approval of the minutes of the last meeting and stumbled through mundane old business. Then he addressed new business and his manner changed. As he described the case of Diana Bond he became more animated. He was clearly moved by the tragedy of the woman's fate and for all those involved in the incident. The meeting's attendees, mostly dressed in surgical scrubs but some, too, in smart suits, listened in silence. Most had already heard of the case via the hospital rumor mill. Richard did a good job of describing in clinical detail what happened and what had so far been found out. That turned out to be very little. In some way the wrong information was entered into the records. The two words, right and left, had been mixed up, and a young woman was blinded for the rest of her life.

Kate could sense the mental shudders of the surgeons in the room. It was a nightmare to each of them that an operation could go wrong. There were always risks of course, there was no such thing as simple surgery because surgery involved cutting and destroying as well as repairing human tissue. Finding and identifying vital nerves and blood vessel, avoiding damage that might result in permanent injury, these were all part of a surgeon's life. But to make the basic mistake of removing the wrong organ, that was the unthinkable nightmare.

Kate had time to talk to Maureen before she went into the first exam room of the afternoon. Burett had not yet arrived and she did not have the time or the opportunity to confront him all afternoon. By the time she had finished her busy day he had left. The termination of his employment as locum tenens was easy, Maureen had taken care of that. Kate had instructed her that, regardless of whether she could get an immediate replacement, Graham Burett was no longer welcome in her office. She felt that she should talk to the man, tell him why she did not appreciate the way he had dealt with her patients. It was a closure, more for her own sake than for his. She could imagine his reaction to her criticism. Maybe it was better that she never had to meet him again.

Before leaving the office Kate took the papers she had found in David's and Angela's desks and stuffed them in her briefcase. She would study them at home this evening.

***

In a room that was buzzing with activity during the day Liz felt strangely alone at this late evening hour. The desk chairs were unoccupied, there was an unnatural silence, the computer screens were dark. Except her own. She scrolled and clicked, aware that she was breaking all sorts of rules. She knew she could bluff her way through any discovery of her presence here at this time of the day but she still listened for a sign that there may be someone else around. Her recent success had stimulated her efforts, she was looking for something that might equal or surpass that achievement.

She'd had moderate results before, in more intimate and risky surroundings, but here the pickings were rich indeed. She searched. She had found some possibilities but she was not going to stop until she hit the big time.

A rustle or a creaking sound caught her attention. She stopped her search and concentrated on the sound. It was not repeated, possibly the air conditioning. She returned to her hunt. And then she found it.

TWENTY-FIVE

They were both hungry, tired from the day, and so comforted to have the evening together. They exchanged accounts of the day's events while they made meatballs and mashed potato. The aroma made each realize that this was the first food they would taste since early this morning. They ate mostly in silence, the food being the prime topic of interest.

"How's Dolly doing," Jack said after swallowing his last mouthful.

"She's doing very well."

"And the drone? You need to find a name for it too."

"How about Homer?"

Jack laughed. "Good one."

Kate began to clear the plates. "Didn't you have a meeting today?"

Jack grunted a reply.

"Did it go okay?" Kate was still fuzzy on the details of Jack's business, partly because she did not understand the intricacies of computer workings and also the fact that Jack was secretive about what was going on. She knew he was only trying to protect her from any problems he might have. She did tend to worry more than Jack, seeing the possible downside of things whereas he was, in her opinion, over-optimistic. She watched him now, helping her with the plates, and wondered if his neutral expression was hiding something from her.

He turned on the kettle and put tea bags into the pot.

As they carried their cups out onto the decking Kate's phone sounded. She didn't recognize the caller ID name, Nathanial Blake.

"I was trying to reach Doctor Mansfield," he said.

"I'm afraid Doctor Mansfield passed away."

There was a stunned silence then a strangled, "Oh."

Kate asked what she could do to help and Nathanial Blake described what was troubling him. She felt comfortable in giving telephone advice but insisted he make an appointment to see her in the morning. Something about the patient's story made her curious. She tapped a number on her phone and connected with the office computer. She found the medical record of Nathanial Blake and scanned through the entries. There were questions she would have to ask Nathanial tomorrow.

Jack raised an eyebrow. "Okay?"

"Yes, okay." She sipped her tea. She had intended to check the office computer tonight for what had happened on certain dates she found in the diaries. She could do that now but this moment together was to be savored, she would do it later.

Jack watched her as she touched the cup to her lips. The sun had gone down and the moon was just visible, low in the sky. Her face was partly shadowed and in silhouette, her hair dark and thick, her eyes looking down at the cup. And then they glanced across to him. He was captured by them, as he always was. His smile came instinctively, hers followed. He put down his own cup and moved to her. Her lips were warm and tinged with the aromatic taste of her tea. He touched her neck, her breasts. Her body felt smooth and firm, his kiss deepened.

The moment had happened quite naturally. Her mind was vaguely on other things and then there was a glance, a spark of eye contact, and he was beside her. She felt his touch, felt him harden, felt his desire. And they were moving toward the bedroom.

Afterwards they lay side by side, their bodies touching. She let the atmosphere nestle her and sank into a mood that was totally relaxing. Sleep must have come for she woke some time later. The day's realities skipped around in the background of her mind, things she had meant to do this evening. Jack was breathing slowly beside her. She closed her eyes, things could wait until tomorrow.

Nathanial Blake was a man of sixty-two with a thin worried face. His thinning hair was gray, his skin sun-wrinkled. Last evening he had noticed some numbness in his left hand and had panicked. "They say it's a sign of a heart attack," he had said. Kate had taken a history, yes, he had been doing some unusual activity, yes, the tingling was confined to his pinkie and ring finger.

"You have irritation of the ulnar nerve," Kate had reassured him. "That's the nerve that crosses behind the elbow, the funny bone, and it carries sensation from those two fingers."

Today she wanted to examine him to confirm her diagnosis. There was something else that had sparked her interest. "You saw Doctor Mansfield a few weeks ago, for a physical."

"Yes, he said that everything turned out fine."

"And he ran some blood tests?"

"Yes, they were fine too."

"I'd like to recheck some of the tests. It means drawing more blood."

"I've eaten this morning."

"Doesn't need to be fasting."

Terri collected the blood sample.

"What's it for?" asked Nathanial.

"Just to check your prostate."

"Funny, that was okay last time."

"I'll call you with the result."

Graham Burett had not turned up for work this morning, no doubt he had been told by the locum agency that his session had been terminated. His replacement was not able to start until tomorrow, Kate had her hands full today. She was very thankful for Dolly but still found herself running late as the morning progressed. She regretted not having been able to speak to Graham before he left, it would have been good to have told him why he was being fired, for her own sake certainly and possibly for his own improvement too. Although somehow Kate doubted that. Busy as she was she felt more in control of the office. Terri and Nick worked well together, and Dolly did her fair share of work. By the time they finished the morning's work it was almost time to welcome the afternoon patients. Kate checked with the hospital by phone. The man with the infected leg was not doing well, as she had guessed Richard North was now considering amputation as being inevitable. Kate knew that this was not necessarily a cure as the risk of this highly resistant infection spreading to the rest of his body was high.

A request for a house call came halfway through the afternoon. In between seeing patients Kate programmed the drone, now known as Homer. She pressed the action switch and waited for the machine to buzz into action. Nothing happened. She double checked that she had done the right things and touched the switch again. Still nothing. A feeling of frustration bordering on panic began to flow over her. She was conscious of activity going on all around her and waiting for her attention. She glared at Homer and punched the switch again. She gave up and hurried from exam room to exam room to see her next two patients then shut herself in her office and called Jack.

She listened to the sound of dialing which seemed to go on for an age. He answered on the fourth ring. She explained what had happened and he asked her some basic questions. She had done all the correct things to send the drone on its way.

"I'll come in to look at it right away," said Jack. He hoped Kate could not detect the worry in his tone.

He drove quickly, his mind working over what could be the problem with the drone. His plans relied a lot on the success of the machine. It was early and its use was strictly speaking still experimental, a failure now could be catastrophic.

He let himself in by the back door, he could sense the busyness of the place, there was a murmur of voices coming from the waiting room. Kate's office was empty, as expected. Homer was sitting there, inactive. Jack bent over it and checked power and connections. He noted that it was already programmed and should be ready to go. He picked up the remote and tapped in signals. As he did so the cause of the problem became obvious.

"Who could have done that?" said Kate. She had listened to Jack explain why Homer had not performed as expected. It was a relief to know that it should be functional in a short time but it was worrisome to think of what had happened.

"Anyone could have done it. The thing is why? Why would somebody deliberately change the settings and then not do anything with them?"

"Was somebody trying to disable the drone do you think?"

Jack scratched his head, staring at Homer. A light flickered on the machine. "There, it's powered up enough to do at least one house call. Shall I set it to go?"

"Please."

They watched Homer flutter into life and float toward the door. There was a moment of tension as it rose into the sky outside, a pause in its ascent as if it was about to plunge back to earth. Then a flock of doves appeared and flew overhead. Homer continued its climb.

Jack grinned. "Just what it's meant to do."

They walked back into the clinic. "I think someone was just playing with it," said Jack. "If whoever it was intended damage then it would have been easy. Unless they wanted it to fail on a call."

"You mean harm its reputation?"

"Something like that. Perhaps I'm paranoid."

"But who could it be?"

"Someone in the building, a patient, staff."

Kate frowned. "It's unlikely a patient could stay alone in my office for any length of time. And who on the staff would do a thing like that."

"Have you heard anything from your failed locum?"

"Graham? No. Do you think - ?"

"Did he have his own key?"

"I don't think so but I'll check with Maureen."

"Look, I'll hang around here and keep an eye on what the drone is doing."

"Okay, there are still patients to see. Let me know when I need to check in with Homer."

Jack sat before the computer screen and connected with the drone. He checked its position, the distance to the destination was further than he had estimated. He watched the landing and listened to the conversation with the patient, an elderly lady. It was time to get Kate to the screen. He tapped on an exam room door and she opened it, apologized to the patient she was seeing, and walked with him to the office.

"Here's the history and findings," he said as the screen showed the print out. "And here are the drone's recommendations."

Kate studied the screen and nodded. She clicked with the mouse and was able to transmit her voice through the robot. In a few minutes she had arranged for a prescription to be picked up and had instructed the lady on how to proceed. "Please call me if you are worried or if anything changes. My nurse will call you in the morning to see how things are going."

The patient smiled gratefully. "Thank you doctor," she said.

Jack could not help but feel impressed at the robot's performance. Kate obviously was happy with the diagnosis and treatment plan and the whole house call had taken a fraction of the time it would have involved if she had to drive to the house herself.

Kate touched him on the arm and hurried back to the exam room. Jack focused his attention back to the screen. A message flashed across it. "Damn," he whispered.

He had miscalculated the amount of power the machine would need to complete the mission. It had calculated how much was required to get back to base and was warning that it could be a very close thing. If it ran out of power before reaching the office it would make an emergency landing. This would be risky as it could put itself in a dangerous situation, or it could land in a place that was difficult to access. How close a thing was it? Jack had to make a decision. It took him seconds. He spoke through the drone and informed the lady that he would be arriving soon to pick it up. Then he left a message with Terri to give to Kate.

As he was leaving he noticed a man he did not recognize rummaging through the drawers in what had been David's nurse's desk. He paused to watch for a second and the man glanced over toward him. For a moment there was a guilty expression of being discovered on his face and then what looked like an embarrassed smile. He stood and slammed a desk drawer closed.

Jack entered the house address into the truck's GPS and followed its directions.

What had happened to the drone? Well he knew what, but why and by whom? His instincts told him that the interference with the machine had been accidental, something that might happen if someone was playing around with the remote. But what if was not accidental, what if whoever it was had been trying to program it for some specific purpose and had failed? His mind veered onto the possibilities of abusing the drone's talents. Like so many advances that benefited the human race there was the risk that misuse could do so much harm. He let these thoughts drift as he listened to the mechanical voice of his GPS guide him to his next turn.

After what was a long and meandering journey he was almost at his destination. His GPS told him it would be half a mile away on his right. He was in a street lined by low houses with small windows, an older neighborhood. He slowed the truck and checked for house numbers. His GPS told him he had arrived at his destination. He parked street side and climbed from the vehicle. The house was ordinary, brick faced, curtained windows. He saw something move in the corner of one of the windows and ducked defensively. A sudden recollection hit him. He fought the urges that welled up and closed his eyes to blot out the image.

Then the dizziness, the fighting for breath, the chest pain. Jack held onto the truck, willing himself to stay upright. He could feel the blackness descend around him, his legs were weak, his heart thumped.

The door of the house opened and an elderly lady stood there. 'Took you a while," she said.

Jack sucked in a deep breath and took an unsteady step forward.

TWENTY-SIX

It had been the house, Jack realized as he loaded the drone into his pickup. He waved goodbye to the lady who was staring at him in a worried way. His breathing was returning to normal and the tingling in his limbs was fading. He glanced in his rear view mirror and the sight of the house almost brought it back to him, as if a switch had been flicked on and lighted up a hidden memory. He focused on the road before him and headed back to the clinic.

He checked the drone and plugged it in to charge. He would give the remote to Kate to keep in a locked drawer, just in case. Again he wondered who was responsible for what had happened, hiding the remote would make it more difficult for someone to interfere with Homer again.

Jack was about to leave when Kate appeared. "Just got a few telephone messages and I'll be through." She walked to Terri's desk and they went over the calls that had come in during the afternoon. There was an end of the day atmosphere. The electric buzz of activity that had pervaded the place earlier had gone, exam rooms were empty, telephones were silent, computers were clicking as the day's balances were calculated. Terri was on the phone when Kate came back to the office.

"Maureen will lock up. I'm done. Time to go home."

Jack thought she looked tired. Hardly surprising, she'd had a busy day taking on the workload of two doctors and then the drone problem. He hoped she was not over-stressing herself, she was tough but everybody had their limits.

Kate followed Jack's pickup out of the parking lot. Evening traffic was not too bad, she was glad she did not have to cope with Austin roads every day although Deep Wells was starting to suffer from the overflow of the burgeoning suburbs. As they drove out toward Mill the roads quieted. Kate could feel the tensions of the day loosen. It had been a good move to settle in this village which was just far enough away from the city to stay almost peaceful. It was quite a commute for Jack though, when he did go into his downtown office. He had worked from home recently and seemed happy with that although it was sometimes difficult to tell with him, he tended to hide his feelings behind a stiff upper lip. He was stressed today she thought, there was an expression that he found difficult to disguise behind his smile. She put it down to the problem with Homer. Thank goodness that was solved. But was it?

The sun was low in the sky when they arrived home. "There are steaks in the refrigerator, do you mind cooking?"

"Not at all, I'm rather hungry."

Kate had to admit that she was more than rather hungry as she had missed lunch again. She turned on the oven ready to put potatoes in to bake. "Give them an hour. You can fire up the grill in a while."

Jack put the steaks on a platter and seasoned them. They would warm up from the fridge in the next forty-five minutes or so and by then the grill should be flaming hot. His mouth was watering in anticipation.

They sat and watched the sun setting. The sky turning a deep orange and then a dark blue, the underbellies of clouds tinged with crimson from the hidden rays of the now invisible sun. Evening insect sounds buzzed around them.

"I saw a guy rummaging through David's nurse's desk today."

"Tall, older guy?"

"Yeah."

"Nick White, the new nurse."

"Of course. It didn't click. Must be getting paranoid about people messing with my drone."

"You think he was messing with your drone?"

"I was suspecting everyone. Guess I was wrong."

"Nick is okay. It was he who warned me about Graham."

A synapse connected and Kate remembered she had not yet had a chance to check on the diary she had from Angela's desk. She would do that later, after the steaks. Unless? Her mind went back to last night and her good intentions.

"Did you check if your locum had a key?"

"Maureen said he did not. She had her doubts about him from the beginning."

Jack put the steaks on the grill, the sizzle was just right. The smoky fumes drifted in the soughing breeze carrying mouth-watering aromas of cooking meat.

They ate at the outside table, a moonlit location and a perfect way to end a day. Although the day had not yet ended. Their evening tea lasted into two cups. Kate reluctantly dragged herself indoors to find the diaries she wanted to look at. Jack disappeared into the study to "look into a few things".

Kate spread the documents on the kitchen table and opened up the calendar and diaries. She checked dates and scribbled notes as she did so. There were names and diagnoses in Angela's diary too which did not seem to make sense. The dates that coincided did fit a pattern though. Did this mean what she thought it did? She took out her laptop and signed into the clinic computer network. Each date had the records of patients seen, telephone calls recorded, prescriptions called in, and telephone advice given. Kate tried to connect any of these pieces of information with what had been written by David or Angela. She checked a few of the dates and decided to rest until another day. Her mind was over stimulated. There was something that would make sense though and it was a possibility that shocked her. Why had she not suspected it before?

Kate had wanted to talk about it last night but had fallen asleep before Jack came to bed. This morning had been the usual routine rush and did not seem the time for a prolonged discussion. She arrived at the office having spent the journey mulling over what she suspected. Could David's suicide be connected? She wondered how.

The first person Kate saw as she let herself in was dressed in a flowing robe with her hair hanging loose. Kate felt weirdly disorientated. What was Sally Snooks doing here? Sally answered that question herself.

"My other assignment got cancelled and I heard you needed someone."

Kate grinned with delight. She had been concerned that the locum agency might send another Graham. Sally had already proved herself so that worry was put to rest. And indeed the morning sped by smoothly, in contrast to yesterday's session which had been a constant game of catch up. There was time to grab a sandwich in the hospital cafeteria before checking on her patients.

The progress of the man with the leg infection was not good. The sepsis had spread throughout his body and was now affecting his vital organs. There was not an antibiotic available that would kill the bacteria. There was no way of saving him. Kate did not go into his room. The poor man was comatose and would not be aware of her presence. She would not be adding anything to his treatment and she would be risking contact with the dangerous bacteria and an unlikely possibility of spreading it beyond his isolation room.

She got back to her office with a heavy heart just before the afternoon session began. Along the corridor she saw Nick White searching for something in his desk drawers. She remembered Jack mentioning seeing Nick doing the same thing.

"Is everything okay Nick?"

He looked up and smiled. "I like to keep notes of interesting cases, jot them down and read up about them in the evening. Never stop learning do we? Anyway, I thought I left my notebook in one of the drawers here and I can't seem to find it." He shrugged. "No problem, I can always get another one."

Kate checked her computer for the latest correspondence. A lab report caught her attention. It was the result of the PSA test she had ordered on Nathanial Blake. Her heart sank when she saw it. She went back to his previous records. This did not make sense, no sense at all.

Kate sent Homer out to do the one house call requested that afternoon. She would check back in her office in between seeing patients in the exam rooms. She was startled to see him sitting there when she entered her office.

"Jack, what are you doing here?"

"Just passing by, thought I would check on the drone. It's gone missing though."

"Working for a living." Kate clicked her computer and tuned into what Homer was doing. A summary of the patient's complaints and suggestions as to treatment appeared on the screen. Kate studied the screen searching for anything that might be an error. She could find nothing that she did not agree with. She spoke to the patient through the drone. "I'll call in a prescription," she concluded, and turned to Jack. "Pretty good?"

"Yea, pretty good."

Kate thought she detected a tone of relief. Was he worried that his machines could have a problem? She had to admit that she examined every contact between the robots and her patients, ever afraid of mistakes being made. The recent lawyer letters had made her sensitive to the fact that errors can occur. A little to her surprise she had been impressed with the accuracy of Jack's machines and marveled at the mysteries of modern technology.

"So your locum didn't have a key, nobody on your staff is a suspect, who else has access to the building, cleaners, maintenance?"

"Well, yes."

"Can you check on who has been in the building in the last few days?"

"I suppose so. Why is that so important?"

"As you know Tom is trying to take over the company."

"Is something happening, I thought that was at a stalemate."

Jack had understated the seriousness of his battles with Tom, he had seen the stress she was under and did not want to add to that.

"The board is going to vote and I've got a lot resting on the success of the robots."

"And they are working just fine."

"But if they were not, if somebody could figure out how to program them to make mistakes they could do a whole lot of damage."

"Is that why you came in today, to check them?"

The computer bleeped. "Good timing, better let Homer in."

They opened the outside door and the drone hovered in, coming to rest in Kate's office. Jack immediately examined it and looked satisfied that all was well.

But there was something wrong, Kate was sure. They needed to talk.

TWENTY-SEVEN

It had to be done at night, the place would be too busy in the daytime. She was fortunate that her looks were indistinctive, people did not seem to recognize or remember her. She was wearing a surgical cap and mask anyway so it was easy to remain anonymous.

She walked confidently along the empty corridor. The lights were dimmed now, there was a strange silence, the hospital was asleep. Or so it seemed, but Liz knew that in the background machines were monitoring, charts were being updated, patients were healing, or dying.

A nurse came hurrying along the corridor toward her. Liz nodded but the nurse barely acknowledged her presence. Liz turned into the ward and checked the numbers on the patient room doors. She found what she wanted and, ignoring the instructions regarding entering the room, pushed open the door and stepped inside. This had to be quick. She already had on rubber gloves, she took out a handful of gauze swabs and a Ziploc bag.

The man lying in the bed was unconscious, dying, his medical records had said. His leg was infected with a resistant organism. Liz stripped back the bedclothes and was overcome with the putrid odor of decaying flesh. She fought the gagging that started in spasms from her stomach. The leg was oozing pus and blood. She held her breath as she mopped the diseased limb with her swabs. Carefully she put the swabs in the Ziploc and sealed it. She pulled the sheets back over the patient and let herself out of the room, dropping her gloves in the disposal bin outside the door. The whole episode had taken less than two minutes and she was confident that she had not been observed.

The next part of her plan would be more difficult.

She took the elevator to the next floor and walked toward the closed door of the ward. Opening it she saw that the lights were turned down low, this was a time when sleep was encouraged. Two nurses were at their station chatting quietly. She could walk past them in the corridor and they may not notice her. She hoped that the main ward beyond was empty of staff. The corridor was lined by windows looking into the nursery. Here were rows of small cots, most of which contained a tiny newborn baby. In a separate room further along the corridor was the intensive care unit, if any nurses were working on a baby it was there they would likely be.

Liz paused at a window and made sure there was nobody in the nursery except the babies. She slipped on rubber gloves, opened her Ziploc, and pushed through the door.

There were soft sounds of infantile breathing, snuffling and faint snoring. A whimper came from a corner of the room. Liz held her breath waiting for the whimper to change into a full throated cry. It did not. Quickly she moved to the nearest cot. A pink faced baby lay on its back, legs spread-eagled, its eyes were closed and lips were pursed as if in thought. Liz did not have time to absorb any feeling for the child, she had her job to do. She took the pus sodden swab from the Ziplock and smeared it across the raw stub of umbilical cord. The baby stirred and she moved to the next cot and repeated the procedure. She managed two more before cries began to sound. It was time to go. She flung the contaminated swabs into a trashcan and moved out into the corridor. She could hear sounds of activity as the nurses started to respond to the cries. They did not seem to notice her as they left the nurses' station and she headed back along the corridor to leave the ward.

That had gone better than she had anticipated. Time to go home and get some sleep, the morning would come soon. Liz felt a thrill of excitement as she waited for the elevator.

Nathanial Blake did not feel it was necessary for him to come into the office to be told the results of a blood test. He had sounded quite irritated when Terri suggested it, after all he had been reassured that everything had been okay after his physical. Kate had a rule that she should not communicate bad news over the phone but rather in a face-to-face interaction. But this needed addressing urgently and Nathanial left her no alternative.

He answered his phone on the third ring. Kat introduce herself. "I have the results of your blood test," she said.

"I know, and I don't have to take the time to come to the office to be told everything is normal." His blustering tone did not quite disguise the fear he was trying to hide.

"I'm afraid it was not normal."

"What do you mean?"

"Your PSA test, the prostatic specific antigen test, showed a level of over twelve, the normal level should not be more than four point five."

"Does that mean I have cancer?"

"No it doesn't, but your free PSA is very low –"

"Well that's good."

'No it's not good. A high total PSA can be caused by several things but combined with a low free PSA then the possibility of prostate cancer is increased."

"There was a silence while Nathanial digested this unsavory information.

"So what do I do?"

"I'll refer you to a urologist, you will probably get an MRI to scan your prostate, if that shows anything then you might need a biopsy."

"How come this has happened so soon after the normal blood test?"

This time it was Kate who had to think before speaking. "Your previous test was not normal, your level then was ten point seven."

"Then why -?" Nathanial left the question unfinished. Kate did not have an answer but she was beginning to develop suspicions.

***

She had intended to ask Jack's opinion last night but she had first broached the subject of what was stressing him. His initial response was one of reassurance but she pressed him to confide his worries. He told her in more detail than he had before what the conflict was between him and Tom and, indirectly, the board.

"So they could vote you out of the company?"

"Yes."

"After all you've done?"

"They call it business, who can make the most money. My only weapon now is that I own the patents for the robots, and so far they are working well."

"But can't they use your ideas and build their own machines?"

"Yes they can but that would take time and meanwhile I have the machines. I could take legal action to try to stop them but that would cost money."

"And you need money to build more robots."

"Precisely, money I don't have, I would have to sell my ideas to another group of investors."

"Back to square one."

He had nodded and smiled a mirthless smile that she knew hid the hurt he was feeling. The look had melted her heart and they had kissed, and she melted some more. The bedroom did not seem the appropriate place to discuss what had been bothering her and they had drifted into a post coital sleep. They would talk tonight.

"So you think David and Angela were having an affair?"

"Something was going on between them."

"Why would they keep it a secret?"

"Perhaps Angela didn't want her husband to know."

"That would make sense."

Kate could think of nothing else to explain what she had discovered in David's and Angela's desk drawers. "What if she had finished with him and he decided to shoot himself?"

Jack frowned. "Or maybe Angela's husband found out about them and it was he who shot David."

Kate stared at him. 'You have a wicked imagination."

Jack shrugged. "We don't know so all we can do is imagine."

"One thing I do know is that Angela must have been very distracted. These lawyer requests for medical records all involve mistakes made by her, or perhaps by David."

"I thought that one case was your patient."

Donald Templar, of course, he was Kate's patient and it was she who had seen him that day. Had she or Terri been distracted too? "Yes, can't blame Angela for that one."

"Can I take a look at the papers?"

Kate handed them to him. The photograph fell and fluttered to the floor. Jack picked it up and glanced at it. He put it down and then picked it up again, staring at it.

"What's the matter, you've seen Angela's picture before?"

"Yes but I've never met her. Or so I thought."

TWENTY-EIGHT

Gail Morgan had waited a long time for this day. It had taken many months of trying before she got pregnant. Then there was the bleeding that would not stop, the bed rest to try to prevent the miscarriage, and the devastating hemorrhage that ended the pregnancy. It was more than a year before her first missed period and the joy of the positive pregnancy test. The first few months went by with no threatening bleeding and the rest of her pregnancy had proceeded with no problem. Little Tim had been born after a labor that was easier than she had expected and today she brought the wrapped bundle that was her long awaited baby home. Her husband, Ken, beamed like a new father should as he helped her through the door. Tim was already taking from the breast and Gail felt such an overwhelming love for this tiny infant as she felt the lips search and suck.

They had put the cot in their own bedroom and they both laid Tim in it after his evening feed, looking down at him as his eyes fluttered closed and he slipped into a peaceful slumber.

"Good looking kid," said Ken.

"Takes after his father." She squeezed his hand and he kissed her lips.

Tim took another feed before their bedtime and then it was time to turn off the lights and begin to share the night with their son.

He woke sometime in the night and Gail sleepily held him to her breast. He made hungry snuffling noises as he fed and finished in a shorter time than she expected. He whimpered quietly when she turned off the light and tried to get back to sleep herself. After a few minutes Gail picked him up and patted him on the back. A loud burp sounded and she was relieved that his discomfort had been so easily relieved.

She fell asleep knowing that he would wake her for feeding in too short a time. When she did wake she was amazed that it was daylight. For a moment she felt as though she had been in a dream, the flood of joy, the overwhelming love she felt for her long awaited baby, the almost unreal feeling of achievement.

She allowed herself to drift out of sleep. Her breasts began to ooze milk as she anticipated the hungry mouth on her nipples. Then an uneasy alarm crept into her mind. It was too quiet, the silence sounded ominous.

Her thoughts were frozen as she climbed from the bed, she was unaware of Ken stirring behind her, her eyes were focused on Tim's cot. He was lying quite still, his face looked pale. She felt as though she was wading through quicksand as she walked the few steps to the cot. Her legs were numb and heavy. Her mind screamed a desperate "no". And then, as she touched his pale forehead and felt the coldness, her voice echoed with a whispered and anguished "No".

TWENTY-NINE

Jack concentrated on trying to recall what had happened that night. Details floated in and out of his memory like ghosts in a fog. He would grasp at an image, hold it firmly and then find it had disappeared without a trace. But one memory kept recurring and it was beginning to stay. The meeting with the woman as he left the office and just before he was attacked and knocked unconscious.

"Yes, that was Angela, I'm pretty sure."

"Pretty sure?"

"That means almost certain."

"But not quite?"

"If it was what does that mean?"

"It means she was planning to get into the building."

"And she would have a key. Why didn't I think of that?"

"You think she may have messed with the drone?"

"Somebody did." Kate thought for a moment. "But she wouldn't have known about Homer or Dolly before seeing them, why would she want to come back to the building?"

"Do you think she might have left something behind that was important?"

"Like a diary?"

"She wasn't alone, somebody banged me over the head. If that was her husband then would she have told him of her secret affair with David?"

"We only assume that they were having an affair but what else can we assume?"

"We are assuming that it was Angela you saw that night."

"I'm pretty certain."

"If it was then she must have been after something, and she didn't know about the robots. And somebody did get into the building later and messed with Homer. And, I've just thought, Nick was missing a notebook."

"So, she came back one night, found a notebook she thought might be hers, saw a weird machine, fiddled with the remote, and then went home."

Kate shrugged. "Should we do something about it, after all you were attacked?"

"I doubt the police would be interested, Angela could easily deny being there and I'm probably not a great witness."

"Even if you're pretty certain."

Jack snorted. "Even if I'm pretty certain."

The man who sometimes looked like Buddy Holly saw the message and had mixed feelings about it. A definite ten if it worked but how could he track what was happening? He would have to do some careful research, but he was used to that. It could have been made much easier for him. He smiled to himself, he was becoming too accustomed to having it the easy way, not like the old days when it had all been up to him, now he had others to do the work. He leaned back, staring at the computer screen, his mind estimating the rewards he was expecting and those that were already guaranteed. His previous ten had brought him a hefty advance and there was promise of much more to come. The latest was still uncertain but he had high hopes of another windfall. Soon he might have to ease off on local work and spread his wings further afield. There may be some reluctance from his helpers and he may be forced to recruit others. That was always a risk. Perhaps he could delay the decision for a while.

Kate rummaged in her purse and took out the remote for Homer. She kept this with her now since Jack had warned her that anyone could activate the drone if the remote was available. Only one house call this afternoon, not much information as to what was wrong with the patient, she hoped Homer could continue with its so far successful diagnostic skills.

Her desk telephone buzzed. It was Ruth at the front desk, "Mr. Mahoney is on the line."

Kate was puzzled as she waited for Ruth to switch the call through to her. The hospital CEO rarely called her, most of their communications took place either through e-mails or during the weekly meetings held at the hospital.

"Hi Michael, what can I do for you?"

"Got a problem you need to know about." Mahoney was never one to waste time with pleasantries. Kate waited for him to continue. "Several cases of sepsis have been admitted in the last few days. The lab confirms that the same bacteria is the cause in each."

Kate could feel the hairs at the back of her neck tingle. This was obviously a serious infection or he would not be calling her.

"Three newborns have been readmitted, two with umbilical infection and one with septicemia. Infection control has confirmed that these cases are caused by the same bacteria carried by a patient who recently died."

"My patient."

"Yes, your patient."

"Completely resistant to all antibiotics."

"Yes."

"So the baby with sepsis is in bad way."

"So they tell me."

Sepsis meant that the infection had spread through the bloodstream into the baby's body. With no drugs able to fight it the infant had to rely on its own immature defense system to survive.

"There was another baby in the nursery at the same time as these three who died in its sleep. Thought to have been a sudden infant death syndrome."

"Could have been sepsis too."

"An autopsy is planned."

"Do we have any idea how the infection was spread?"

"We're looking into it. I'll send out e-mails to the staff to keep them informed. I've called an emergency meeting of the Infection Control Committee tomorrow lunchtime, I'd like you to be there."

"Of course, I'll be there."

Kate put down the phone. This was a nightmare situation, a vicious and deadly infection threatening to spread throughout the hospital. She recalled the comatose dying man and imagined the poison killing him being transmitted to other unsuspecting patients. Michael Mahoney had the unenviable job of solving the problem and of trying to prevent the news of his hospital's contamination being broadcast to the general public. News like that is not good for the reputation of a hospital in this highly competitive healthcare field. Kate also wondered about the tone of Maloney's voice when he had confirmed that the dead patient had been one of hers. Was he somehow blaming her for the spread of the infection? She had been in his room but had taken all the precautions. And she had not been in the nursery for some time. She was being paranoid she told herself. But the niggling worry remained.

Jack was frustrated. He sat on the decking and sipped from his mug of tea staring out across the valley to the village. Distant vehicles crawled like ants along the narrow ribbon of road leading through the small collection of buildings. The scene acted as a bland backdrop for the activity in his mind. He was at a roadblock, until the board voted he could not plan for the future. Even if the news was going to be bad he wished it were done with. He pushed those negative thoughts away, concentrating on how he would proceed when the company was his to manage. The behavior of his machines in Kate's clinic was a great encouragement, certainly a plus in his fight with Tom. He had confidence that they would continue to succeed but there was always a risk that a mistake could be made. Just as there was with human medical practice. He closed his eyes and let the sounds of nature soothe the worry. But the conversation they had about Angela kept creeping into his memory. The concussion had blocked all recall of the event but recovery had drawn back the blinds. He still could not accept the arguments they had both presented last night. Why was she there? What was she looking for? And why did someone hit him over the head so hard?

An affair with David was plausible but did not explain her subsequent behavior. And it certainly did not account for David's apparent suicide. Something was missing.

He opened his eyes and a reflected flash of sunlight from a car windshield dazzled him. Such a long way away and yet so powerful.

He went back into the house, rinsed his mug and left it to drain in the sink. Then he went to the bedroom and opened the drawer in Kate's bedside table. He had guessed right, this was where she often kept books or magazines she was reading. He pulled out the diaries and calendar that had come from David's and Angela's desks. He took them to the desk in his own study smoothed out a blank sheet of paper and began to jot down dates and names from what David and Angela had recorded. There was a pattern, or possibly two patterns. Donald Templer did not fit in but that may just be a coincidence. He tried to recall what Kate had told him about the mistakes that had occurred in the clinic, the names and diagnoses were a bit blurred in his memory. He folded the paper with his notes and put it with the diaries into Kate's bedside drawer. Something nasty was going on in the clinic, and Kate was the victim.

THIRTY

They ate cheese and tomato sandwiches out on the decking that evening. Jack was pouring their second cups of tea when he broached the subject.

"I've been looking at the notebooks you brought, David's and Angela's."

"Have you figured out what they all mean?"

"Perhaps. There are a series of dates that coincide with what look like code names, possibly referencing meeting places."

"An affair?"

"Presumably, can't figure out why they would meet secretly otherwise."

"You think there's more?"

"Yes, I do, and I don't think it's good news."

Kate stared at him, her eyes dark and probing. "Go on."

"We assumed that Angela was incompetent, or distracted, whatever, we assumed that she was making mistakes."

"Well, she was."

"What if she wasn't? What if she was screwing up on purpose?"

"Why would she do that?"

"It could only harm the practice, do you think she had something against you?"

"Not that I can think of, I really didn't know her that well, and we never had any falling out."

"What about with David?"

"You mean a lover's quarrel, a woman spurned, that sort of thing?"

"Well it's a possibility."

There was a silence as they both digested the theories.

"And David's suicide, the ultimate spurned woman's revenge?" Kate asked the question with raised eyebrows.

"That's pushing it, could Angela overpower David and fake him shooting himself?"

"Maybe with some help from a muscular husband."

"Who also had it in for David. But who was not pleased about Angela's part in the affair either."

"Now we're really getting complicated." Kate finished her tea and put down the cup.

"Sometimes life can be complicated." Before Jack smiled and shrugged Kate saw a look in his eyes that told her he was serious.

The meeting room was full, there was a somber atmosphere. Kate nodded greetings to various staff members who made up the Infection Control Committee, representatives from nursing, pathology, surgery, and a man she did not recognize who introduced himself as being from central sterilization.

Michael Mahoney opened the proceedings in his usual no nonsense manner and quickly introduced the subject matter that had prompted the meeting. He explained the situation as he had to Kate the previous day.

"We have confirmed that the bacteria infecting three newborn children are the same strain isolated from a man who recently died of sepsis." He paused and looked around at the sea of serious faces. "Another child has died, quite possibly from sepsis."

"Do we have any idea how this infection could have spread? Is there any connection between the patient who died and the nursery?" The surgeon asked the question with a tone of aggression.

"We have obviously looked into that," said Mahoney in a voice that demonstrated a suitable hint of sarcasm, "There is a development since I first contacted you all though. The video from the surveillance cameras in the nursery shows a person in the ward who is not identified for certain."

Kate frowned a question.

"The lighting was not good and there is no shot of her face. The staff are not certain that the image is one of them but there is certainly some doubt as to who she is."

"So, what does that mean? What was she doing?" This time it was the man from central sterilization.

"It's not clear, she seems to be touching the babies in several cribs."

"Touching?"

"Yes. It's all very quick, as if she's in a hurry, then she disappears."

The head of nursing raised her hand. "There is one thing, although we can't be sure, but it looks as if the cribs she was touching were the cribs the infected babies were in."

There was a general discussion. Who was the woman? What was she doing? Did she accidentally spread the infection, and how?

"The main objective we have now," said Mahoney, "is that we ensure there are no more cases in the hospital. We also need to identify how this could have happened and make sure it cannot happen again." He brought the meeting to a close and thanked everyone for being there. He left the room and walked quickly along the corridor toward his own office.

Kate walked down the same corridor, one of her patients had been admitted through the ER last night and had his appendix removed. She would make a courtesy call. She saw Michael Mahoney turn off the main corridor. She felt sorry for him, he really tried to run the hospital as well as he was able, to have something like this infection happen was catastrophic. She thought too of the lawsuit involving the poor woman who had lost both her eyes. And her mind switched to her lawsuit and various other of her own problems. She recalled the discussion she and Jack had had last evening. Her jumbling thoughts suddenly fell into place. Jack had spotted a pattern of unfortunate events in the office and they all involved Angela, and David's patients. Except for her patient, Donald Templer. Kate had a flash of memory as she pictured the day she had seen Donald Templer and had advised him to go home instead of driving to Houston. She had been busy that day, busy because David was not there and, she remembered now, Terri was on vacation. Angela was working as her nurse in place of Terri. There was the final connection that fit the pattern.

The young man was recovering well from his appendectomy. He wanted Kate to authorize his discharge from the hospital. Kate explained that the physician in charge of his case was the surgeon who had operated on him and that the decision as to whether he was ready to go home would rest with him.

On the way back to her office Kate thought about Angela and decided that she was convinced the nurse was guilty of something, whatever that was. She needed to contact her, she needed to clear up what they suspected. By the time she reached the clinic building she knew what she must do.

THIRTY-ONE

The phone number was unavailable. Kate tried it three times. There was an e-mail address, she sent a message. The reply came back that it was undeliverable. Kate checked the address and tried again with the same result. So Angela had disappeared. But Kate still had a street address from the information on Angela's employment records. Her instincts were revving up, something was just waiting to be discovered.

The afternoon clinic seemed to last forever, she wanted to get away and investigate further. She finished going through the telephone messages with Terri and walked out to her car. The sun was still high in the sky and she could see the road was filling with end of the day traffic. She entered Angela's address into her GPS and headed in the direction it instructed.

Her mind had been focused on the need to talk to Angela, to get answers to the questions she had, to end the guesswork. As she drove now the simplicity of her intentions became clouded with possible complications. What if Angela did not want to talk to her? When she thought about it that would seem to be a logical choice if Angela had been involved in something illegal. She pushed that nagging doubt to the back of her mind as she listened to the GPS directions. What if Angela, and perhaps her husband, became aggressive, was she heading toward a dangerous situation? She remembered Jack's injuries and felt a shiver travel along her spine. She should have let someone know where she was heading. She used voice activation and her phone called Jack. His voice-mail answered and she left a brief message and the address she was headed to. This was listed as a number on a county road which, Kate guessed, was out in the country somewhere. Her guess seemed to be accurate as she drove west of Deep Wells and into the Hill Country. Her GPS took her off the main highway and onto a quiet narrow road that led through meadows and undulating countryside. An occasional mailbox at the roadside was the only evidence that there was human habitation here, where was she heading?

Another turn along a rough and dusty lane with cedar trees overhanging from either side. She could feel them scrape her car and decided that she had come far enough, this was a foolish venture and would gain her nothing. But where could she turn? She drove slowly gritting her teeth at the sound of branches scratching at the paintwork of her car.

"You have reached your destination." The voice of the GPS had an ominous sounding finality to it. Kate found herself next to a pathway that led from the road and disappeared into a mass of vegetation. There was just enough room for her to inch her car along it. After a few dozen yards she spotted the house. It was small and looked uncared for. There was something about it that made her feel uncomfortable. She looked around her, there was no sign of anybody else. She turned off the motor and there was a deep silence. She felt very much alone. Her ears strained to pick up a sound that might connect her to the rest of the world. A distant cawing of a crow hardly broke the silence. A pair of vultures floated in the sky high above her.

She climbed from the car, the crunching of her feet on the gravel path seemed over-exaggerated. What if she was not alone? What danger lurked in this isolated place?

A fluttering sound close by startled her, then the clattering of the pigeon's wings as the bird flapped its way to a height that just cleared the trees lining the path. Kate stopped, her heart beating as rapidly as the bird's wings. She should not be here, a voice inside screamed at her, this was a foolish mission. And yet she had to know, had to have some clue as to what Angela had done.

She walked toward the house as if by rote, the warning bells in her head drowned out by the need to know.

There was a bell by the door to the house. She took the rope attached to it and the loud clanging echoed into the surrounding foliage and died there. No sign of movement, inside or out. She clanged the bell again, and waited. She glanced back at her car standing in the narrow path, trees and bushes around it, hidden from anybody's view. She turned the knob on the door and was surprised to find that it opened.

The house was dark and smelled musty, she sensed that it was empty. "Hello," she shouted and her voice sounded small and strange, swallowed up in the hidden space around her. She moved forward, wanting to turn and rush out of this place but feeling compelled to explore further.

The drapes in each room were drawn and the house was dimmed to twilight level. Kate bumped against a chair and let out a soft cry of alarm. She found herself in a small kitchen, there were dirty dishes in the sink. The house gave the impression that it had been abandoned in a hurry.

The door leading outside from the kitchen was unlocked. It led into a dark space and what Kate assumed was a garage. There was an odor of oil and gasoline, and another more powerful smell. Kate felt for a light switch. She stepped into the darkness and reached along the wall until she located the switch. The light revealed an empty garage with a row of shelves against one wall. As her eyes adjusted to the light Kate saw something lying near the door. Then she recoiled as she recognized what she was seeing.

Angela was lying supine, her head flung back, her half-open eyes staring unfocused toward the ceiling. Her arms were spread. Around her head there was a pool of blood, black and clotted. Kate could see the movements of hundreds of tiny insects. The smell of decomposing tissue drifted up and she felt a wave of nausea.

Quickly she raced back through the house and out of the front door. She took a deep breath of the fresh air.

Her reflex was to get into her car and drive away from this nightmare, her doctor's instinct was to calm down and take charge. She pulled out her phone.

THIRTY-TWO

"What happened?"

"Long story, give me time."

Jack hugged her. He could feel her heart racing, the slight tremble of stress rippling through her body. He could guess what she was feeling.

It was late, they sat on the decking under the moon and Jack listened. Kate had called the police and waited for them to arrive. She had watched the drawn out proceedings as they followed protocol, taping off the scene, taking photographs and video, searching the area around Angela's body. She told her story to an officer who took laborious notes. Finally she watched as the body was loaded onto a gurney and wheeled away. She was told that a detective would be in contact with her.

Jack took her hand. "You've had a hell of a day."

"I was really scared at that place, I don't know why but there was something weird about it. And then, - then when I saw her lying there." Kate took a deep breath. "I remembered seeing you the night you were attacked at the clinic. Only you are still alive, and she is dead."

There was a silence, they both saw the connection. It was Jack who asked the question. "You think her husband was the one who did it?"

"It makes sense."

"Sure does. But why?"

Kate shrugged. "And to just leave her there."

They sat in silence, night sounds surrounding them, and then, wearily, they headed for the bedroom.

Kate could not sleep. She would drift into a drowsy pre-sleep and find herself alone in a musty dark house where strange and threatening creatures hid in every corner and she waited for that inevitable blow to her head. Then she would be wide wake sweating and trembling. Morning came as a relief.

There was a somber atmosphere in the clinic. The news of Angela's death shocked them all.

It was mid morning when Terri told her there was a Detective Lopez on the line. She remembered fuzzily that she had been told a detective would be contacting her. They arranged to meet in her office at lunchtime.

Troy Lopez was in his early forties, dark hair cut short, tidily dressed in slacks and sports shirt. Kate shut the door to her office and invited him to sit down. He started by thanking her for her co-operation last evening and apologized for taking up her time today. Kate appreciated his politeness and his soft, non-threatening tone.

"The victim was an Angela Bone. I believe she used to work for you."

"She worked for the practice. She was nurse to my late partner."

"Late?"

"Yes, he committed suicide several weeks ago. His name was David Mansfield."

Lopez scribbled a name on his notepad.

"When did you last see Angela?"

Kate hesitated. There was so much about Angela, their suspicions, the fact that Jack saw her on the night he was attacked. "There's quite a story," she began.

Fifteen minutes later she thought she had covered all the facts and theories involving Angela. She felt drained, the combination of lack of sleep and the emotional effort of recalling and recounting Angela's story had been a strain.

Troy Lopez was still jotting in his notepad. He stopped and looked at her.

"So you think her husband may have done it?"

"Just a theory."

"Angela didn't have a husband. There was a man she apparently lived with and we are trying to find out more about him. But what interests me Dr. Westbrook is what you told me about the mistakes Angela was making. You seem to think these errors were committed deliberately, why was that?"

"I can only think it was to harm the practice and particularly David."

"Why would she want to do that?"

"If they were having an affair and something went wrong."

"Your partner, Dr. Mansfield, committed suicide. Can you tell me about that?"

Kate told him what had happened on the night of which she had vivid recollection.

"No suicide note?"

"No."

"Did you know they were having an affair?"

"No."

"We are obviously treating this as a homicide and as is usually the case family members, or close acquaintances, are possible suspects. We will be looking very hard for Angela's companion. Thank you Dr. Westbrook for your assistance, you have been a great help. I may need to ask more questions later if that's okay."

Kate was again impressed with his politeness, there was no way she could imagine refusing to answer more questions.

"I would like to talk to your staff if you don't mind. Try to maybe learn more about Angela."

"Of course."

THIRTY-THREE

Michael Mahoney was working late. Something was wrong and he had to make it right. The eye surgery debacle and now the spread of the dangerous infection. Problems that he knew were harmful to patients, that was still his main concern, but were also damaging to the hospital. He was in charge, he was responsible, he felt a personal blow when bad things were allowed to happen. There was not just the hospital's reputation, there was a financial component too. Medicine was a business, a competitive business, and reputation mattered. There was also the regulatory body that certified that a hospital was performing well enough to retain the right to remain open. Mahoney felt a prickle of sweat on his forehead as he contemplated the possibility of losing that recognition.

This evening he was reviewing recent adverse events. The eye surgery was something that could not be defended, well, it could be defended with enormous legal costs and with so much harmful publicity and a very good chance that the hospital would lose the case, that the matter would be settled out of court for the multi million dollar amount Regis Law Offices had demanded. There was still no explanation as to what had happened in the operating room that day. The infected babies seemed to be the result of a deliberate act. The latest reports indicated that the infants were in critical condition. There had been a couple of complaints about the emergency room doctor,

Mahoney checked the name, Mark Butler. He had talked to the CEO of the company that employed him, it was planned to discuss his status at their next meeting, a full two weeks from now. There was a problem about terminating his contract without definite cause, they had been sued in the past for trying to keep their reputation clean. Mahoney could empathize but wished they could get on with it.

His mind went back to the sick babies. Could the hospital be held responsible if it was proven that they were victims of a deliberate act? What if the perpetrator was an employee of the hospital? Who would know where to find deadly bacteria, and what to do with it? He mentally listed the sort of employee who would have that source of knowledge. Not too many.

Then he remembered something Kate Westbrook had mentioned to him and his mind took a different direction.

The man who looked like Buddy Holly was worried. There were several projects that promised to bring in a moderate amount of income, although they were over concentrated around one source. Shouldn't be a problem if he was careful.

The idea that Liz had suggested was alarming at best. She had worked well, whatever risks she had taken, and with excellent results but this latest was really pushing things. Typically she had been resistant to his cautions and this was what worried him. She stood a fair chance of getting caught and then what would happen? He thought he had taken adequate steps to distance himself from any traceable contact with her but there was always that danger. She would do what she wanted to and he made plans to make sure he was at a suitable distance from her.

There was also that creepy ER doctor. He had been little more than useless, unimaginative, ineffectual, investment-wise a waste of time. Buddy had suggested to him that perhaps his value had outlived his presence. Mark Butler had promised he would do better.

He was mystified by the sudden disappearance of Angela. She had been depressingly dependant but had provided smaller fodder, enough to justify her participation. He gathered something must have happened to scare her off but was puzzled that she had not contacted him for the pecuniary rewards he had promised.

He may have to disappear himself, evaporate and re-invent himself somewhere else with new contacts and new victims. He had done it before and had, sadly, left several people to take the blame for what he had paid them to do. That was business, not everyone was a winner.

In the near future though he was anticipating a substantial return on his investments. He hoped that would occur before the possible catastrophe that Liz could precipitate.

Dr. Mark Butler was nearing the end of his shift in the Emergency Room. He was still stinging from the communication he had received from his contact. God, he had done his best and it had all gone unappreciated. He really needed something big to justify the risks he was taking, something spectacular. His imagination was a stagnant pond, he found it hard to invent events, he merely played along with what was happening. Each patient he had seen in the last few hours had been a challenge. Was there something he could do? Nothing clicked.

He left the hospital, his head bursting with frustration. He needed something big. As he walked to his car he was unaware of his surroundings, his own world was all-consuming. Could he gamble and risk it all? No, he forced himself to say, it was gambling that had got him into this situation in the first place. His debts were enormous, and dangerous. The threats were getting more ominous, he would have to make some sort of payment soon. His contact had made it sound so easy - risky, but easy - after all he was a physician who made decisions that could affect a patient's survival. He could be sued for medical malpractice but he had insurance for that, his other payment would more than cover the damage to his reputation.

He gunned his way out of the parking lot. The traffic light ahead was changing from orange to red. He bet he could beat it. He slammed his foot down on the gas pedal.

THIRTY-FOUR

The day was weighing heavy. The emotional trauma of the day before, the lack of sleep, the interview with the detective, and the continuous flow of patients had drained Kate of her energy. As the afternoon dragged on she was grateful that she did not have to drive out into traffic to any house calls, today was quiet in that demand. She was within an hour or so of finishing her workday, although she realized she was never totally finished, she was on continuous call. But the real physical, and mental, challenge was the day long contact with patients in the office, the constant fear that she might make a mistake, a wrong diagnosis or a missed diagnosis. The recent flood of lawsuits had made her slightly paranoid, she had never before been so worried about her ability to practice good medicine. She could dismiss some of what had happened as a result of what Angela had done, but how many other people were involved in the care of her patients, who could she trust? Kate could feel her brain seizing up as she left an exam room and prepared to go into another to see her next patient.

"Got a message from Sylvia Lee." Terri was standing the corridor. Kate's heart sank. Sylvia was one of those people who could make a problem out of nothing, and yet it was difficult to dismiss it as nothing.

"Yes?" Kate could actually feel her muscles slacken and her mood slip down into a deeper depression.

"She's having one of her turns," said Terri with a raise of her eyebrows.

Kate was familiar with Sylvia's turns, a mixture of symptoms that did not immediately make sense but contained enough warning signs to warrant urgent attention. She summed up the situation. She was running a little late and still had several more patients to see in the office. She would hit heavy traffic if she drove out to see Sylvia later on. She would try to persuade this, sometimes-unpersuadable, patient to meet Homer. Terri was given the task of explaining how the drone robot could help Sylvia.

Kate dealt with her next patient and, as she emerged from the exam room, was confronted by Terri. Terri shook her head. "She doesn't want a machine. Sorry."

Kate felt a surge of annoyance verging on anger. Sylvia was a manipulator, a demanding hysteric who had caused a considerable amount of worry and concern in the past. Her symptoms today did not suggest a serious emergency but there was still the possibility that something bad might be going on. Kate picked up the phone and got through to Sylvia. The familiar whining voice answered. Kate responded with a reassuring tone and explained that the drone was very efficient and could be at Sylvia's home in a short time.

"But I really want you to come and see me."

Kate pointed out that she would be delayed in doing the house call and that she wanted to avoid the necessity of Sylvia needing to be referred to the Emergency Room. It was her trump card, a drone visit was far more comfortable than a trip to and a wait in the ER. Kate allowed Terri to program Homer and went to the next exam room.

It was only thirty minutes later that she was in communication with the drone and Sylvia Lee. As usual the robot had taken a thorough history, although taking more time than the average. There were several suggested diagnoses, the top of the list was a stress reaction to an event involving an altercation with her husband that morning. Homer had also mentioned the vague possibility of a couple of more serious conditions. Kate took some comfort in the fact that the, so far, infallible computer had found this patient almost as difficult as she had. She called in a prescription for a small dose of a tranquilizer and promised to contact Sylvia in the morning. She sent a message for Homer to return to the office and settled down to wait for it.

Should she rely so much on the drone? Would it have been wiser to send Sylvia to the ER to rule out those two alternative diagnoses? Kate realized that the computer on board the drone had access to millions of pages of medical publications and could calculate the chances of a diagnosis being correct in seconds. But, was anything perfect? Her mind browsed the events that had happened in her practice, almost entirely precipitated by Angela. Then she thought of the tragedy inflicted on the poor defenseless babies in the hospital. Another deliberate act.

A synapse of revelation. Kate felt a sudden chill shiver through her. Could what she was imagining be true, and, if it was, what was behind it?

Michael Mahoney came to a conclusion. Well, not really a conclusion more a hint of an explanation. The unfortunate events at the hospital he had put down to human error and bad luck but now there was evidence that there had been a deliberate act that was harming patients. This was not human error, this was human intent. Kate Westbrook had hinted that there had been one of her office staff who had made a series of errors that resulted in patient mishaps. Could there be a connection? It seemed very unlikely, what had Kate's practice in common with the hospital? She was Chief of Staff, she did admit her patients to the hospital. But why should any happenings in her office be related to what was going on in the hospital? If there was a common factor in the attempt to harm patients what was it? A group of psychopaths? How and why should there be a correlation?

And then something else Kate had mentioned popped into his mind. It didn't make sense but it was a common factor.

Liz sat in her tiny cubicle, the clicking sounds of a multitude of computer keyboards echoed around her. This was a crowded place but she had her own secluded space. She also had access to so much useful information. It had been so easy. The eye case had needed some careful manipulation but had turned out fine. The infected babies had involved a risk but the results were turning out to be quite satisfactory. Her next project was even more ambitious and she was still working out the details of how she would pull it off. There would be a great deal of suffering, and a great deal of publicity if she could time it right. But that was the aim of the game, wasn't it? She smiled as she tapped her own keyboard. Just a few more details and she would be ready to go.

There was a lingering worry about Sylvia Lee in Kate's mind as she drove home. The day had been exhausting, she was dead beat. She had relied on the drone's diagnosis but she still remembered the mention of other possibilities. Conditions that could be serious. Had she done the right thing? By the time she drove into the garage and climbed from her car she had forced the doubts from her thoughts. She entered the house and could feel the tranquility of the place. A foreshadowing of a peaceful evening with Jack and an early bedtime sent a comforting buzz along her nervous system. He smiled a greeting and they kissed. The buzz felt a little more comfortable. Until her phone sounded.

It was as if she had been doused with a bucketful of cold water. She knew before she checked it that the caller ID would show the call was from Sylvia Lee, and she dreaded to hear what the problem was. She was wrong, it was another patient and his complaint was easy to deal with. Kate ended the call and found her way back into Jack's arms.

"Busy day?"

"Kinda. Good to be home. And you?"

"So so."

"Any news of the business?"

"Not yet, still early days."

Kate knew Jack was much more worried about things than he was prepared to show. She wished he would confide more in her. When she felt angry that he did not she reassured herself that he was only trying to protect her from concerns that could stress her. She was about to say something to that effect when Jack spoke.

"About the business. I'm really quite worried at the time it's taking for the board to reach a decision. Maybe I'll give them a couple of days longer, then I'll have to do something."

"Like what?"

Jack shrugged. "Not sure. That's what's so frustrating. I might find I'm on my own and looking for money."

"But the robots belong to you."

"The patents do but there are people who could make machines just as clever without impinging on my ideas, it's just a matter of time."

Kate sensed his concern. She sometimes suspected that he tended to keep his feelings hidden, a reassuring dismissal of any real problem, but now he was opening up, if only slightly.

"How bad is it?"

His familiar smile, reassuring. Then a shrug. "Could be worse."

"But could be a lot better?"

"Yeah. A lot better."

She moved toward him and they held each other in silence. How near was he to a financial crisis? He had never before confided a possibility of failure, he exuded strength and a positive attitude. He was still trying to shield her from the stress he was under but he had allowed a glimmer of light to escape from the opaque curtain that surrounded his feelings. Kate felt a surge of love for this man in her life. They kissed and their world became condensed into an experience of contact and shared pleasure. For a while they were able to ignore their problems and worries and lose themselves to each other.

They drifted into a post coital slumber, it was dark when her phone sounded from the living room. Kate stumbled from their bed and reached the phone just after the call had been routed to voicemail. She could feel the grip of concern tighten as she checked the caller ID. She had almost forgotten about Sylvia Lee.

THIRTY-FIVE

Troy Lopez checked through the notes he had made. It seemed obvious that Angela Bone had been murdered and that her boyfriend was the number one suspect. Why he had killed her and whether it was a premeditated act he did not know. The first priority was to find him. His initial assumption was that it was as simple as that. But he had learned that to assume something unproven could be a big mistake. Several years ago there was a case of a self inflicted gunshot death that he assumed was a suicide, until another member of the same family committed suicide in the same way. He discovered a complex family situation that had resulted in the two murders. If he had not assumed the suicide then he might have prevented the second killing. It was something that had plagued him ever since. He doubted Angela's case was that complicated but there were questions about her behavior in the clinic and what he had learned from talking to the staff there. He forced assumptions from his mind and let the doors of curiosity open wide.

He was in the unusual position of having time to concentrate on this case, two other cases he was working on had suddenly and unexpectedly solved themselves. Troy knew that this luxury would be short lived, there was always more work than there were people like him to deal with it. He took a clean sheet of paper and began to make lists. This was his way of doing things - lists led to ideas (or was it that ideas led to lists, he could never quite figure that out), but a list gave him a pathway, a direction in which to take the next step.

In a few minutes the paper was covered with scribbled names and phrases. He took a fresh sheet and chose from the jumble of words the few that he considered important. Something was beginning to emerge from the information he had recorded in his notes. Was it relevant to what appeared to be a murder case? Perhaps. He jotted down a short list of what he needed to do next.

Jack took his tea mug and put it down next to the computer. He stared at the screen for almost a minute while his mind was on other things. He was worried about Kate, she had left the house in a distracted state this morning. He had sensed her stress when she arrived home last night and felt guilty that he may have aggravated it by mentioning his own problems. And then there had been the phone call in the night. A patient Kate had sent the drone to do a house call on. He had heard her side of the telephone conversation and she was clearly concerned that Homer's diagnosis had not been accurate. Her clipped instructions and the tone of her voice as she communicated with the hospital emergency department reflected the alarm she must have been feeling. Afterwards she had told him about Sylvia Lee, a hypochondriacally-inclined patient who had described some puzzling symptoms. A brain tumor or stroke had been on the list of possible diagnoses.

A call later in the night from the emergency department brought the good news that a scan of Sylvia's head had been negative for disease. Another call was not so reassuring. Geraldine Glade, a neurologist, had been called in to consult and she had questioned some of the results and had ordered a bunch of further tests. Sylvia was admitted to the hospital, her diagnosis and prognosis uncertain.

Jack closed his eyes and took a deep breath. If they found something seriously wrong with Sylvia Lee then his drone robot had failed. Not only would that put Kate in an embarrassing and vulnerable position it would diminish the value of his product and the leverage he was hoping it would bring to his retaining control of the company.

"Fuck," he muttered as he slammed his fist down on the desk. The computer screen did a little flicker and he pushed away from it. He waited for the frustrated panic he could feel building began to calm. He took a sip of tea, it was cold. What was he going to check on the computer, e-mail, Facebook? He didn't know, and didn't care. Things were getting out of his control and that was eating at his nerves. He needed action, something he could wrestle with, not the cloudy intangible ghosts of lurking problems that were now haunting him.

"Fuck," he said again. And, in the empty house where there was no one to hear, he shouted "Fuck."

***

Sylvia Lee's hospital room was empty. Kate had studied the records at the computer station, the full history recorded in a manner that reflected the confusion the emergency room physician must have felt last night, the normal scan results, the neurologist's consult. Her vital signs had remained stable in spite of reports of bizarre symptoms. Kate could understand the ER doctor's puzzlement at such a difficult patient.

She pulled open the door and stopped in her tracks, aware as she did that she had taken a deep breath before entering the room preparing herself for a challenging conversation. She let out that breath now with a palpable feeling of relief. An initial stab of alarm that something bad had happened to Sylvia was calmed by the realization that she was away from the room undergoing one of the battery of tests the consulting neurologist had ordered. As Kate left the empty room she could not help thinking she had made a mistake, she had relied on the robot and not listened hard enough to the doubts in her own mind. She had to fight back an anger toward Jack that he had let her down somehow. It was unfair, she knew, he had always been so supportive, but after this case and after Jack's admission of his business worries last night she felt maggots of doubt nibbling at the flesh of her confidence.

She drove to her office with a worrying sensation of impending doom. Maureen was in the corridor near her office door. Kate offered a distracted "Good Morning" and then noticed the expression on Maureen's face. Something was wrong, and in her present mood Kate knew something was very wrong.

"He's in your office."

"Who?" Her mind was a whirl of possibilities.

"Detective Lopez. He just turned up and asked to speak to you. I tried to put him off but he was really pushy."

Kate wondered what his was about, she felt her heart rate increasing as she hesitated outside her closed office door. Then she pushed it open.

Troy Lopez had been sitting in one of the armchairs in the room. He got to his feet now and held out a hand which Kate shook.

"I'm sorry to bother you and I won't take up much of your time."

Kate was not in the mood to be questioned again, she had enough going on to keep her mind occupied. She sat in the chair behind her desk.

"I just wanted to touch on some of the problems that seemed to be connected to Angela," began Lopez.

He asked a few simple questions which Kate was sure she had answered before. Her thoughts were drifting to the patients waiting for her attention in the exam rooms outside. Then something Troy Lopez said caught her interest.

"Why do you say that?" she asked.

"Because, Dr. Westbrook, the reasons for Angela's behavior may not be what we have assumed."

Kate frowned. What did he mean?

Lopez continued in a calm voice. Kate listened as he listed off possible scenarios. When he had finished she realized that her own imagination had been sorely lacking. She was good at solving the niceties of a tricky diagnosis but the detective's mind worked in a very different way. Nothing was as simple as it sounded, or had he explained that sometimes things are more simple than one assumes? Nevertheless she was given a view from a different angle, and it made her shiver.

"So what do we do about it?"

Lopez smiled. "We, or rather I, check the facts on every aspect I mentioned. Then we weigh the evidence. Then we act."

After Troy Lopez had left Kate sat in her desk chair for a minute or two. Her mind was buzzing, she had been confused and puzzled before this conversation but now she felt buried in a quagmire of possibilities that threatened to drown her completely. A soft knock on her door preceded Terri's voice informing her that the exam rooms were all occupied. She rose and set out to start her day's work.

THIRTY-SIX

The man who looks like Buddy Holly paced the room. The message from Liz had disturbed him, she was showing signs of really losing her mind. Her plans were bizarre, reckless, dangerous. Granted she had been lucky so far, and very profitable. But she was threatening to expose the whole program, to destroy a scheme that was keeping him in financial heaven. It had always been a gamble, what was not in today's competitive market? But he had managed to insulate himself from the front lines of where the action was, it would be difficult to trace him as a responsible party. The problem was that left him with less leverage power than he would have liked. Anonymity had its price. He sensed now that he should cash in on some of his investments before Liz, or one of the others, screwed things up. He picked up one of the disposable cell phones from the drawer in which he kept them.

His call was answered by the familiar voice, a tired female with a Texas accent.

"Mr. Feather," he said, almost interrupting the routine greeting the receptionist was reciting.

"Who shall I say is calling?"

Buddy gave his usual alibi.

"Hold on."

He had to wait only a short time before a rather breathless Ernest Feather came on the line. If Buddy had been the slightest bit interested in Dickens he would have seen the name and the situation through a very different lens, but he wasn't. Without preliminaries he spoke.

"I need something for the big one."

Feather cleared his throat. "The funds are not yet available."

It was as Buddy expected. "An advance, to show good faith."

"It's too early."

"No, it's not. The money is on its way, you and I know that."

There was a pause. Feather's tone changed. "You are asking a great deal, and before the matter is settled. As far as we are concerned we could consider the account settled."

This was what Buddy had feared, a reneging on their agreement. He had very little leverage and a lot to lose. Liz would expect her cut, as would the other people. He felt an anger bubble inside him.

"Now look, we have an agreement, you owe me."

"We had an agreement, we can change that at anytime."

Buddy was enraged, words came without the control of forethought.

"I have other clients who might be more interested in co-operating with me. Perhaps you would rather I dealt with them."

The silence lasted for longer than was comfortable. Then Ernest Feather said. "So be it." And ended the call.

Buddy took a deep breath. Things were getting out of his control. He had to maintain a momentum, his threat had been made unwisely but now he had to follow it up. He checked a number and punched it into his disposable phone.

"Burton and Butt," the answering voice sounded so much like a machine that Buddy wondered if he should actually say something.

"Hello, Burton and Butt." It was a real person.

"Could I speak to Neil Smart."

"And who shall I say is asking?"

Buddy gave his usual pseudonym and waited on hold for a minute. He had met Neil Smart some time ago and had been of the impression that he could be receptive to the sort of deal Buddy was able to offer. It was a gamble, but what did he have to lose? That was a thought he did not want to pursue.

"Smart." The voice suddenly appeared, Buddy thought the man must love that name. He introduced his pseudo self and began the sales pitch. Neil Smart listened in silence then shot some relevant questions, a good sign considered Buddy, he was interested.

"I'll have to get back with you after I've talked to Mr. Butt."

Another good sign, Buddy was beginning to feel better about what he was doing.

Two hundred and fifty miles south of where Buddy Holly was negotiating his future Port Aransas basked in a late spring sunshine. The long wide beach was almost empty, a few cars crawled along the sand, windows open to the brisk sea breeze. Police sergeant Oliver Grant parked his car outside the Sea Dolphin café and strode across the parking lot to the beachfront building already filling with lunchtime guests. The inside was air conditioned cool. He walked through to the open decking that looked out onto the beach and the rolling sea. There was an empty table in a corner. He sat down not bothering with the menu, he had been here many times and knew what he wanted. The waitress, Mary, was well acquainted with Officer Grant's tastes. "The usual?"

"Yes Ma'am."

He waited, sipping on the iced tea she brought and thinking of the fried shrimp with French fries and ketchup and tartar sauce and buttered bread roll that would soon be coming to his table. It had been an easy day and promised to remain so. Port Aransas was not a hive of criminal activity, Oliver Grant was not overworked. He gazed now at the lazy Gulf of Mexico waves washing up against the long beach, he could hear the gentle sough of the water, feel the balmy touch of the sea air, smell the salt. Life was good.

A man came through from the main building, a big man but with nothing more to distinguish him from any other. Oliver Grant watched as he selected a table and sat down. His training and instinct rang a reluctant bell. Curiosity, he told himself, he was just a big man coming in for something to eat. But there was something else, the shifty look, the glance around that spelled defense. His observations were interrupted when Mary brought his huge plate of shrimp and fries, the mouthwatering aroma drifted to his nostrils, he couldn't wait to sink his teeth into the succulent meat and crispy fries. And then he glanced over to the big man again. There was something about him that drew his attention. The man was looking around as if searching for someone. His glance caught Oliver's eye and a startled expression flashed briefly across his face. He rose to his feet and walked toward the exit trying unsuccessfully to appear not to be hurrying. Oliver had a vague recollection of where he might have seen that face. What was he wanted for? Something violent. Oliver left his table and the hot shrimp and followed the big man out into the parking lot. He must have run from the building for he was already in his truck and was making a tire scrambling exit toward the highway. Oliver rushed to his own car and followed with lights flashing and siren sounding. He punched the button on his radio, reported what he was doing and requested backup.

Big man was in a hurry, it would get him nowhere. He was heading into the small community of Port Aransas and there was no roadway out in this direction, only the ferry. Oliver Grant hoped he would slow down, he was driving dangerously fast on this normally quiet highway. A voice came over the radio, the road ahead was covered. A fleeting vision of his shrimp and fries came to mind as he followed the speeding truck. That image vanished completely as he saw the SUV creeping from a side street and into the path of his fugitive.

Big man's truck swerved into oncoming traffic, the SUV slowly entered the highway. Big man clearly decided it was safer to rear end the SUV than to risk a head on collision. His brake lights came on as he swerved back to the right side of the road. There was no way he was going to slow down enough to miss the crawling SUV. There was a grinding crunch of metal, the SUV lurched forward, surprised at the impact. Big man's truck snaked onto the edge of the road and then back again, hitting the ailing SUV one more time. It tilted and seemed to balance on two wheels for seconds then gently the SUV toppled over and skidded on its side to a road-sparking halt.

Big man's truck appeared to regain some life as it accelerated away. It was limping though, Oliver guessed a tire or two had blown. He was right. The truck wobbled to a stop and its door was flung open. The big man glanced toward the police car and then took off running. Oliver followed sprinting as hard as he could go. The big man was fast and seemed to be getting away. The wailing sound and the flashing lights of the backup car which suddenly appeared seemed to slow him down as he decided in which direction to flee. It was enough for Oliver. He hit the man hard and forced him to the ground. He felt an elbow hit him in the ribs and leaned heavily to try to subdue the man. The big man was strong and Oliver was struggling to hold him. Just as he was afraid he was losing his grip he felt another body beside him and heard the metallic click of handcuffs being applied.

Michael Mahoney walked into the newborn nursery. He stopped at the nurses' station, to go further he would have to don a gown, cap, and protective paper shoes. He nodded a greeting to the two nurses tapping at their computer keyboards. He stared up toward the security camera and then back down to ground level. The shadowy images he had watched so many times of the figure shifting into the nursery and inflicting so much harm came to mind. Why had that happened? Who was the responsible party? He shuddered as the thought of how much suffering had been caused in the hospital he was helping to run and which was meant to relieve pain and suffering. Could this happen again? Not if he could help it. But what could he do to guarantee that? He pictured the shadowy images from the camera recordings and wondered that the person seen on them had not been identified. It had been with some reluctance that he had reported what had happened to the police but he envisioned the results if, or when, the story broke and it came to light that he had not reported a possible crime. The investigating officer was convinced that the person was an outsider, someone who would not be recognized by the hospital personnel who had been questioned. Mahoney was not so certain, whoever it was had knowledge of hospital events that an outsider would find hard to obtain. But who was the mystery person?

He left the nursery and strode along the corridor toward his office. His mind was buzzing with the uncertainties that plagued him, he almost collided with Kate Westbrook as she walked toward him. She looked as distracted as he felt.

"Hi Kate."

"Hi. How are things?"

"Fine," he lied. "And you?"

"Fine," she said and he knew she was lying too.

Kate was on her way to visit Sylvia Lee. She had heard nothing about her progress all through the day and was dreading the news that the tests she was undergoing might bring. Why had she allowed the robot to overrule her own instinct? Medicine was more than just science, she should have trusted her knowledge and experience.

The elevator ride and the walk along the corridor to the medical ward seemed to take a long time. Kate could feel a dryness in her throat as she walked up to the central station and sat before a computer screen. After logging on she drew up the medical chart of Sylvia Lee. She skimmed through it as quickly as she could, the initial history was familiar to her but she studied the hospital record more carefully. Dr. Glade's list of possible diagnoses mentioned some very serious diseases. The investigations ordered were many and comprehensive. Kate checked the results of the tests already reported on, they all were normal. That was a relief. She went over to Sylvia's room. The patient did not look to be suffering although she had her usual 'I'm hurting' expression.

"I want to go home," she said in a sadly pathetic voice.

"I know." Kate reached out and touched her hand.

"Will you let me?"

"Dr. Glade will decide if you're well enough."

"What about all those tests?"

"Most of those are normal."

"Most?"

"All the ones that have come back."

Sylvia looked disappointed. Kate found it difficult to understand the hypochondriac mentality, a fear of and yet a desire for a serious illness.

"We'll see," she said and gave Sylvia's hand a squeeze.

226

They chatted inconsequentially and then Kate left the room. She closed the door behind her and turned to come face to face with Geraldine Glade.

"How's she doing?" said the neurologist.

Kate shrugged. "Surprisingly well. What do you think?" She waited to hear the bad news.

Geraldine Glade shrugged. "We've got results on all the tests."

Kate waited for what she knew she was about to be told.

"As you know it was important to rule out some of the metabolic conditions that might be causing Sylvia's symptoms but we had to investigate the possibility of a neurological cancer."

So that was it, brain cancer, and she had allowed the robot to persuade her to accept the diagnosis of a stress reaction.

"I've just seen the report of the scans we did today." Geraldine shrugged again and the action seemed an ominous sign. "Absolutely normal. We've pretty well ruled out any pathology. It might be a good idea to get a psychiatric opinion but it looks like a reaction to a stressful situation at home."

Kate smiled and had to force herself to stop from bursting into laughter. The drone had got it right in the few minutes it had needed. Was this a freaky accident? From Homer's history it apparently was not. She could feel herself sending waves of apologies to Jack for the doubts she had had, although she had not openly voiced those doubts. Had her body language betrayed her? She hoped not.

THIRTY-SEVEN

Troy Lopez welcomed the arrest in Port Aransas as a perfectly timed event. He had the time and now it appeared he also had his man. The suspect had not tried to conceal his identity or his relationship with Angela Bone. The prisoner would be transferred to a unit nearby but Troy was anxious to question him as soon as possible.

The drive to Port Aransas took him less time than he had anticipated. He checked in at the motel he had booked and then drove to the jail in which Marvin Barnet was being held. Barnet was a big man with a shaven head showing few day's growth. He wore a tee shirt that bulged with the muscles it covered. Troy was reassured that an armed officer stood guard in the interrogation room as he sat at the table across from the man he was about to interview.

Barnet glared at him with an expression Troy recognized, a stubborn aggression that hoped to inhibit the questioner. Troy responded with a friendly smile and greeting. He studied the other man's face as he gently led into his interrogation. When he sensed he was being too searching he backed off and let Marvin Barnet relax his guard. It was much easier than he had expected. Some of his questions must have seemed irrelevant to the prisoner but Troy had his reasons for asking them. At the end of the session he stood and held out a hand. Barnet was confused, he hesitated and then, instinctively, thrust out and shook the offered hand. Troy held back a smile of satisfaction.

Later that evening Troy returned to the jail. "Just a few more questions," he explained. Barnet was puzzled, what did this cop want now? As the interview continued he was even more puzzled. He felt that the focus had been taken off him and his so-called alleged crime. He relaxed a little, until he realized the path he was being taken on. And the final question to which he did not have an answer.

Troy Lopez ate fresh fish from the Gulf with fries and coleslaw, washed down with a glass of cold beer. The day had gone well. He recited to himself what he had suspected and what he was certain he had discovered. He slept well that night.

Early the next day, as the sun was still low in its rising, he drove to the short ferry and left Port Aransas. The flat coastal plains eventually became the rolling countryside that would lead to Austin and the Hill Country beyond. Troy had plans for the day.

THIRTY-EIGHT

It was a short session in the office, Sally Snooks was not seeing patients on this Saturday morning but Kate finished way before lunchtime anyway. Kate still felt the relief of the drone robot's correct diagnosis and the guilt that she might have doubted Jack's machine. She had also been concerned that she would become the target of another malpractice lawsuit. On impulse she looked up the number and dialed the Regis Law Office. All the requests for patients' records had come from this law firm and Kate remembered that the same firm was involved in the threatened hospital lawsuits. She had asked Maureen to try to contact the lawyers to find out what the complaint was against her but the telephone was constantly put through to voicemail and there had been no initial response to the e-mails she had sent. It had taken several days of effort to get a brief e-mail mentioning the stroke her patient had suffered.

There was a click on the line and a voicemail message came on. Kate was curious. This must be a large law firm judging by the number of cases they seemed to have but she had never heard of them. Although why should she have heard of them, she had never had much contact with lawyers before? Until now. She checked the address and Googled its location. It was this side of Austin not far from Deep Wells.

Ruth was walking toward the rear exit. "See you Monday," she said as she passed Kate's office.

"Thanks." Kate followed her and they left the building together.

Instead of turning right toward home Kate drove in the opposite direction. She had entered the Regis address into her GPS and followed its instructions. She drove out of Deep Wells past the grocery store and the gas stations on the edge of town and onto the main highway into Austin. There were residential developments spreading on both sides of the highway with an occasional commercial strip on the roadside. She was directed down a narrow road that did not seem to lead anywhere and to a small building which, she was told, was her destination. She parked in the limited space at the front of the building. It was of red brick, the only door visible was colored a dull blue and was in need of a coat of paint. Kate guessed that this had been a private house at one stage and had been converted into office space. Although space was difficult to equate with the size of the building. She climbed from her car and walked to the door. She knocked on it, not expecting a response, then tried the handle. It was locked.

She was conscious of the fact that she was so near the town of Deep Wells and yet she felt as if she were deep in the countryside, miles from anywhere. When this house was built it probably was miles from anywhere, how quickly the population growth was eating into the empty spaces surrounding it.

Kate walked around toward the back of the house. There was a shallow porch with two worn wooden chairs that looked as if they had not been sat on for a long time. They faced a weed-infested yard which faded to an overgrowth that stretched into the distance. There was an eerie silence, Kate felt as if she had been transported into a different world. She took out her phone and walked back to the front of the house. It was strange that this decrepit building could house a law firm, a law firm that was busy enough to request the records of several of her patients. She selected camera mode and pointed her phone at the house.

The noise startled her. A car had appeared suddenly along the narrow road. It looked as if it would turn into where Kate had parked her car. She stepped back but the vehicle swerved and headed along the road, accelerating as it did. Kate was vaguely aware of the driver, a youngish looking man with dark hair, looking surprised and alarmed at the sight of her before changing his mind. It was quiet again, just the chirping of insects and the occasional birdsong, and the imagined beating of her own heart. Why did she feel so anxious? She was in enemy territory, she told herself, Regis Law Offices were not her friends. And she was alone in an extremely isolated location. She climbed into her car and backed out onto the road, then headed back toward the main highway and home.

It was not until she reached the familiar road leading to Deep Wells that her hands stopped trembling and her racing heart slowed.

Jack was not home when she arrived. He appeared, dressed in running shorts and sweating, a few minutes after she got home.

"Hard day?"

"Needed some exercise." He headed for the shower stripping his shirt off as he went. Kate noticed the muscles of his back rippling under the shining skin and felt an urge to hold him. She smiled as she heard the shower start, it was a weekend after all.

She made sandwiches which they ate on the decking. Jack poured their second cups of tea.

"I finished early today and drove over to the Regis office."

"A grand place, like Fado's?"

"Not at all." Kate described what she had found and the strange incident of the young man who seemed to have changed his mind about driving into the office parking area.

"That's odd," said Jack. "From the number of clients they have you'd expect they'd office in some fancy building."

"How do we know they have a lot of clients?"

Kate finished her tea and put down the cup.

Jack was about to reply when they heard his phone sound from in the house. He reached it on the fourth ring.

"Jack?"

"Yes." Jack did not recognize the voice and the caller ID indicted that this was an unknown number. He was about to end the call which he guessed was some sort of sales message when the caller introduced himself as one of the Clinotics investors.

"I've been talking to some of the other board members and I think we can solve our problems."

Jack listened with a gradual feeling of relief that the wait was going to end soon.

"Can you meet me at the lake in thirty minutes?"

"Why the lake?" Jack was puzzled.

"I want our meeting to be absolutely private, that's important."

"What about at my house."

"Too obvious, you don't know who may be watching."

Jack recalled the black Toyota, he had subconsciously pushed the memory of it and its implications to the back of his mind. Who was responsible for it? Maybe he would find out at the lake.

"Business?" Kate was bringing in the teacups.

"Yeah, one of the board members, wants to meet me."

"Is that good news?"

"Could be, he said he had worked out how to get round the stalemate we are in. He wants to meet at the lake in thirty minutes."

"The lake?"

"Wants to keep it secret."

"My, aren't we in the mystery thriller mode today." She kissed him on the lips and he kissed her back. "Thirty minutes?"

He grinned. "It'll take twenty minutes to get there. But I'll be back soon."

She kissed him again. "I'll be waiting."

Jack drove out of Middle Way Road and down to the highway. He would have to drive through the village of Mill and into the Hill Country beyond. Mill Lake was not a large body of water but was surprisingly deep. Formed many eons ago when the upper sections of the aquifer collapsed and opened up a massive underwater cavern. It now was used by fishermen and by swimmers. The country road that led to it was quiet today. Jack caught the sight of water glinting in the sunlight as he descended toward the lake's edge. He and Stan Moss, the board member who had called him, had decided to meet at the far side of the Lake, a spot less frequented and with little risk of their being observed.

Jack felt as if he were becoming involved in something that stretched the bounds of logic. This secret meeting seemed a gross over-reaction, like something out of a spy novel, but the whole episode of what Tom was trying to do was somewhat incredible. If this could settle things then he was prepared to play games.

He parked in a deserted lane that looked down at the water. It was clear and clean, reflecting the blue sky. In the distance a fisherman stood on the opposite bank, Jack saw no sign of another person. He climbed from his truck and strolled to the water's edge. The air was cool and dry, he could smell the moisture from the lake. The sky above was blue and clear, a pair of vultures floated and soared.

Jack checked the time. They had arranged to meet ten minutes earlier. Perhaps Moss had been held up in traffic, Jack did not know where he was driving from. He went back to the truck and turned on the radio, switching from a news channel to one that played country and western music. Several songs later and still no sign of Moss. Jack checked his phone, perhaps he could call him back and find out where he was. Then he remembered the call did not show any ID, he would be unable to call back.

It was now over thirty minutes since their scheduled time. Jack figured that they had somehow miscommunicated where they should meet. He started his motor and set off to drive round the lake.

The journey took a little over twenty minutes. Jack saw nothing that could have been Stan Moss. There was a car in a small parking lot but when Jack drove alongside he saw it was occupied by a middle-aged woman who gave him a frosty stare as they made eye contact.

Jack drove back toward home seething inside with a mixture of feelings. There was the frustration of not having achieved anything for the effort he had put in, the anger of being stood up, and the worry that something serious had delayed Moss' arrival. There was also the background sensation that there was something unreal about the situation.

Kate wondered if Jack would find his trip to the lake beneficial. She sensed the stress he was under and wished it could all be over with. Her thoughts turned to her own problems. She was still oddly disturbed by her visit to Regis Law Offices. It was such an unlikely building to house a respectable business, and in such an unusual location. She wondered about the significance of the driver who seemed to change his mind. Had he just made a mistake or was he intending to stop there and was put off by her presence. If so why?

She swilled their cups in the kitchen sink and dried them. She checked the refrigerator and decided what their evening meal would be. Picking up a copy of American Family Physician she took the magazine out onto the porch, sat back in a chair, and began reading it. This was one of the ways she kept up with what was happening in the medical world, magazines, lectures, seminars. She flicked through the pages but found that her thoughts blocked her concentration. She closed her eyes and felt the gentle air moving around her. A bird sang with enthusiasm from somewhere on the slope to the valley.

A scampering sound made her open her eyes in alarm. The squirrel was perched on a low branch of the live oak overhanging the decking. It was staring at her with its shiny dark eyes. Then, with a shake of its head, it took off into the tree. Kate watched it as it explored the branches. She did love the peace of their home, it was worth the drive out of town to be able to escape the urban bustle and to breathe fresh country air. There was no total escape though, she was still slave to her phone, to the contact she had promised her patients. She had left it inside the house, would she hear it out here?

She put down the magazine and reluctantly left the chair and walked into the house to retrieve her phone. Outside again she put it beside the chair and relaxed again. How she relied on modern technology, she imagined the "good old days" when it would require a pony ride to summon the doctor and the limited tools he had available to treat a patient. The smartphone had become an accepted and necessary part of life's communication. She was beginning to see how Jack's robots would soon be what was expected in a medical practice. But not quite yet. She was ahead of the curve. Would the machines turn out to be as unreliable as Angela had been? From experience that did not seem to be the case but Kate had all sorts of uncertainties buzzing through her mind.

Why did she expect the phone to sound? The peace of her surroundings had evaporated, her problems, Jack's problems, had eased themselves into her consciousness, stirring disturbing thoughts and brewing worries. She slipped the phone into a pocket, wandered back into the house and poured herself a drink of water. She noticed a shadow in the glass of the front door. Someone calling? The mailman?

The doorbell sounded, she went into the foyer and opened the door. A man stood there, sports shirt and jeans, a stranger. Behind him another man, tall and thick. Kate felt an uneasy sense of being threatened. Their safe country home was immune from the rest of the world and yet now she sensed an invasion.

"Yes?" she said.

"Excuse me Ma'am, it is Dr. Westbrook?"

"What can I do for you?"

What happened was sudden and unexpected. The stranger moved with surprising speed. Kate found herself being pushed violently into the house. She felt arms encircling and confining her. The door was closed and she was trapped with the two men in her own home. The scream of defense was choked by the man's hand across her mouth. Nothing was said, she felt her arms being tied with some sort of rope, a gag was stuffed in her mouth and held there with a cloth wrapped around her head, a blindfold was applied roughly. She was helpless.

They pushed her forward and, when she resisted and sank to the floor, half carried her. She was outside and then being bundled into a car. She was vaguely aware of a brief muttered conversation as the car started. And then there was silence apart from the sound of the engine accelerating and the wind noise as she was taken away. To what?

THIRTY-NINE

There was a group of cyclists and a line of cars waiting for an opportunity to overtake them on this narrow road. Jack waited impatiently for his turn to be next in line. Then a clear road in sight and he gunned his truck and headed home. He was not in a good mood and he had been uncharacteristically annoyed by the cyclists. Usually he was quite willing to share the road, after all they had every right to ride where they wanted to, but today he was short tempered.

He turned off the main highway and headed up toward Middle Way Road. His mood improved as he left what he considered the rest of the world behind him. He looked forward to the peace and comfort of their house. He anticipated Kate's greeting kiss, and what may be beyond. Perhaps they could go out to dinner this evening. His mind dwelled on pleasant thoughts about the near future. By the time he drove into his garage he was smiling.

From the moment he opened the door to the house he knew something was wrong. An instinct told him the place was empty, there was an inaudible echo that indicated a vacuum. He sensed too an atmosphere, like an electric charge, that suggested recent trauma. His reflexes and training took over. As he carefully inspected the house room by room his mind was working. Kate was not here, there was no note to tell him if she might have been called out. There was no obvious sign of a break in or a struggle. There were questions and any answers boded unpleasant news.

Jack was still wrestling with what he should do next when his phone sounded. The caller ID showed an unknown number.

"Yes."

"Jack?"

"Yes."

"Listen carefully, I am only going to say this once. I want you to agree to transfer the patent rights to your machines to Tom Windle. There are papers we have that are ready to be signed. You will be paid fifty thousand dollars for the sale of your patents. Do you understand?"

Jack could sense what was coming next but answered anyway. "I don't think I want to do that."

"I thought you might say that Jack, well let me give you some incentive. Your charming lady friend is now our guest. If you want to see her alive again I suggest that you agree to my request."

The stabbing jolt in his chest merely confirmed what Jack had anticipated. "You can't get away with murder."

There was a silence on the line. Jack waited.

"Let me explain Jack. She will be dead. If they ever find her body then there will be enough evidence to show that you are a prime suspect in her killing. You are screwed Jack, but at least you will be fifty thousand dollars richer. A fair deal don't you think?"

"I'll get back to you."

"No, you won't. I will get back to you. You have twenty-four hours to make up your mind. Oh, and by the way, if you attempt to contact the police Kate is dead and gone."

The phone went silent.

Jack's head was buzzing. He had no doubt the caller had meant what he said, Kate was in serious trouble. He pictured her being held captive, possibly injured or in pain and had to force himself to push the image from his mind. He couldn't lose her, he could not see life without her. He would give up anything to save her but he searched for an idea that might save his business and not put Kate in harm's way.

The caller had said there was evidence that would put the suspicion onto him if Kate were killed. The computer in his Austin office could have been interfered with, possibly loaded with incriminating searches. He thought about his drive around the lake today, if they intended to dump Kate's body in the water there would his actions seem suspicious? The idea of Kate being thrown into the lake sent a wave of nausea through him.

Where had they taken her? He had no idea. Twenty-four hours he had said, not very much time and yet a timeless age to live through. Where to start? He thought of the black Toyota, could that have anything to do with this? Maybe, but how many black Toyotas were on the streets? Was Kate being held in a house or a building or was she being driven around? He felt his fists clench as he thought of anyone laying a hand on her.

Having gone through possible answers Jack came to the conclusion that he was helpless to do anything for Kate except to do as he was told. He would have to wait for the caller to contact him again and then he would give him what he wanted. The idea made Jack very sad, and very angry, he did not like to be beaten. He would not risk anything happening to Kate but his mind was racing to find an alternative.

The journey had been uncomfortable. The confining ropes had hurt where they dug into her skin, she felt choked by the gag they had forced into her mouth. Unable to see she could not anticipate the movements of the vehicle and felt herself being tossed around as they drove on what appeared to be a winding road. Kate still felt the effects of the motion sickness.

How long had she been here, and where was she? The men had remained silent until the vehicle had come to a halt, and then only uttered instructions in short sentences. They had bundled Kate out of the vehicle and pushed her forward. She stumbled as she tried to maintain a balance with her hands tied behind her. She considered resisting but she could feel the strength of the men and realized it would be futile. She heard a door open and felt the chill of air conditioning. Another door opened and she sensed being pushed into a room. The sound of the door closing and a lock turning, and silence.

Kate shuffled across the room until she touched a wall. Moving slowly her shoulder struck something solid. She moved along, came to a corner and continued until she had walked around the small room. There did not seem to be any furniture, she could not tell if there was a window. She was alone and locked in a room. Kate felt a moment of panic. Up until now she had experienced the adrenaline rush that came as a defense against her attackers. Now she was left to realize that she was a helpless victim of some unknown danger. Who were the men who had brought her here, and why? People were kidnapped for a reason, she couldn't imagine anyone would think they were wealthy enough to afford a big ransom. She couldn't help remembering the Regis Law Offices and the startled young man who had almost parked beside her there. But how could that be connected with what was happening now, it did not make sense.

She slumped to the floor, leaning back against the wall. A wave of nausea welled up inside her. She fought the urge to vomit, the gag in her mouth would make her choke if that happened. Taking small breaths through her nose she struggled to control the reflex that threatened to regurgitate her stomach contents. A panic overwhelmed her, breathable air just didn't seem available, she felt her lungs start to expand and her head fill with the pounding pressure of her overworked heart. She slid down the wall and fell to her side. The spasms from her stomach started and she felt the bitter taste fill her mouth and dam against the gag that prevented the choking liquid escape from flowing back into her lungs.

Jack decided that the bottom line was that he would do what they demanded. He would lose his business but he would not lose Kate. But he instinctively wanted both, he was a fighter, he did not like to lose. How to find Kate? How to rescue her from wherever she was? His mind raced, his thoughts tracked along computer guidelines and military tactics. That had been his experience but then Kate was not part of the pattern. He could take his own risks but he was not going to put Kate in any danger. Although she was already in danger. A chill shivered through him as he recalled the telephone call. It had been cold blooded and precise, no maybes, no idle threats. He had no choice unless he could think of some way of finding Kate.

Did she still carry the remote for the drone? If so the drone would be tracking her position. Jack walked to the bedroom, Kate would have the remote in her purse but would she have the purse with her? For a moment a flare of hope lightened his mood. Then he spotted it and his hope spluttered into nothing. The purse was lying on the chair where Kate must have put it when she arrived home. He picked it up and searched through its contents. There was the remote, he held it and stared at it as if willing it to be with Kate, the only thing the drone would be able to tell him now was that the remote was here in their bedroom.

Jack sat on the edge of the bed. He closed his eyes and let his mind work on a solution. But there was no solution, he kept coming to a dead end, he could feel time drifting away, precious time that he was not using to any great benefit. His brain felt full and overactive, he told himself to calm down, relax and try to think clearly. But when he did it seemed even more obvious that he could not think of a way to help Kate. Except to comply with the demands made of him. He let his thoughts travel in this direction and pictured what the future might hold. As his imagination drifted he saw a scenario he had not yet envisioned and he felt as though he had been stabbed in the chest.

Kate did not want to die like this, or to die at all. A panicky instinct of survival took over her total bodily functioning.

The regurgitating contents of her stomach would choke her, she knew that. She managed, with supreme effort, to inhibit the threatened retching. She concentrated on using her restricted airway to take short breaths that allowed her to maintain her blood oxygen in a survivable range. She felt bad, waves of nausea, dizziness, the verge of losing consciousness, all threatened to overcome her. She waited, breathing slowly, swallowing the liquid that had built up in her mouth. Pain returned, the ropes burned, her muscles ached, her head pounded.

Kate felt the hardness of the floor under her force its harshness into her body. She shifted her weight to let other parts of her anatomy share the punishment. She stopped. There was an extra nudge of hardness. Her telephone, she had put it in her pocket at home and they had not noticed it. She let her mind calm and tried to decide what to do next. If she could somehow get enough movement into her arms and hands maybe she could reach into her pocket for the phone. A call to Jack, or to 911, would be enough. A shaft of hope shone through the clouds of suffering. But the shaft dimmed as she tried to fight the tightness of the ropes. There was no way she was going to reach her phone. Could she wriggle against the floor and force the phone free? She tried. No way. And what if she had been successful? As soon as she had started talking, if she could with this gag in her mouth, they would have heard, surely. Perhaps not. She started to work on another plan.

Then a sound that set her heart racing and her nerves on edge. She waited for what she knew was about to happen.

What if they had already harmed her, what guarantee did he have that Kate would be released if he did comply? Jack rose to his feet, a spark of an idea was developing. He grabbed Kate's purse again and rummaged through it. The remote had been in it but he had not seen her phone. He rushed through into the living area. Her phone was nowhere to be seen. He found his phone and dialed Kate's number. He listened for the sound that would locate the phone if it were in the house. The only sound was the ringing in his own phone. The call went on to voicemail. So Kate might have her phone with her, but was not answering it. Jack balanced the possibilities. The phone may have been taken away from her, or she was not able to access it. He hoped she had not lost it before reaching the destination she was now at. He remembered the way her office computer was set up, it kept track of her phone via its GPS so that her whereabouts would always be known when she was out on house calls. He knew that these records were stored for a short time. There would be no reason that on this, a weekend day, the records would already be erased. It was a long shot but he should be able to get into the computer and find out the latest position of the phone and, hopefully, Kate.

He drove carefully, time was valuable and he did not want to waste it by being involved in an accident or being stopped for speeding. The journey to Kate's office seemed to take an age, the early evening traffic was slow and clumsy.

Jack drove into the parking lot and stopped his truck outside the rear entrance to the office. He unlocked the door and entered the silent building. He could feel his body tensed for action, adrenaline flowing. But he had an objective, a target to aim for, his training kept him alert and focused.

He walked along the corridor past Kate's office and the room in which David Mansfield had died. The main computer was in the back office. As he pushed open the door he wondered if it had been shut down for the weekend. That would make his hopes and his journey useless. He mentally crossed his fingers until logic made him realize that the computer was never turned off, it was Kate's contact with her office files, her way of getting patient information when she was out of the office. But he still had his doubts as he entered the room.

The light on the machine was glowing, there was a faint hum, something was working. Jack sat at the desk before the big screen. He knew the passwords and clicked the mouse until he was in the location program. Something was blocking him, he tried again. There must be a way to view the position recording. Jack clicked and searched with frustrating negative results. He paused, thinking, working out what he was missing. He started again, forcing himself to concentrate, to ignore the pressures of time, to keep the fountain of hope flowing.

The screen rewarded him with a map of where the phone had been. He connected his smartphone to the computer and synced the location to its GPS. Then he checked the time of the record. Almost an hour ago. What was the guaranty that the phone, or Kate, was still there? There was no certainty, but it was his only hope.

Kate first felt the vibration from the phone in her pocket, and then the sound of its ring. It seemed loud in this empty room and she knew it would be heard all over the house she was in. She was helpless to stop it, she could only hope for it to stop. She heard the door opening and the sound of someone approaching. She felt a hand slip into her pocket and the phone being taken.

"What the fuck, why didn't you take this?" The voice was not one she recognized from the two men who had attacked her.

"Uh uh," was the reply from whoever else was in the room.

There was a silence and Kate sensed she was being inspected. She waited for the blow to fall, the punch or the kick, or worse.

"Take off the blindfold, and the gag, she looks better without them," the original voice said.

Rough hands complied with the order and Kate took a deep unrestricted breath. She screwed her eyes as she felt the blindfold dragged from her face. She recognized the tall man who had stood behind the man on her doorstep, he had subdued her with ease then and looked as if he would like to do the same again. The other man, she assumed he was in charge, was thin with a face like a weasel and eyes that gave her the creeps. He smiled now, an action that was more like a grimace and made her feel even more uncomfortable.

"Yea, she sure does look better without all that." He reached out a hand to touch her cheek. Kate cringed and tried to shrink away from the fingers that made contact with her skin and his eyes flared with a mixture of sadistic longing and a warning against rejection.

"Who are you and what do you want?" Her voice sounded hoarse and trembly.

"Well now, that all depends." The thin man was not smiling now and Kate felt a chill of fear track along her spine. For a long few seconds she held his gaze then he turned away, grabbed her phone from the other man who followed him out of the room. She heard a key turn as the door was locked from the outside.

Kate could feel her body shaking. What was all this about? Who were these men? She could breathe properly now and that was a relief but the ropes still tied her hands. And she could see too. A thought occurred to her and a blaring alarm seemed to explode in her head. They had made no attempt to hide their faces, she would be able to identify them at any time when this was over. If they intended to let her go they would have made sure she would not be able to recognize them later. The chill of fear became a deep freeze as she contemplated what that meant for her future.

Jack followed the directions as the female voice issued instructions from his phone. He drove back toward Deep Wells and through the town's outskirts heading west. His mind was busy. What would he find when he reached his destination? Would Kate still be there? Would she be unharmed? How was he going to rescue her from who knows how many captors?

His phone's GPS told him there were only a few miles until he reached his destination. He was driving now on a narrow country road, Jack estimated that he was heading for somewhere near Mill Lake. He remembered the journey he had made there earlier in the day that seemed a lifetime ago.

The light was dimming, evening stars were beginning to appear. Shadows in the road deepened, live oaks and cedars lining his way were close and dark. Almost there. Along the way a mailbox placed roadside indicated a hidden dwelling behind the vegetation. Jack felt very alone, about to confront an unknown enemy, perhaps to save the woman he loved. If she was still here, if she was still alive. He was aware of his military training and of the experiences he had been exposed to, he had been in much more dangerous situations. But this was different.

His GPS told him he had arrived at his destination. He drove into the narrow path that led beside the mailbox and switched off his lights. He stopped the truck just off the road and killed the motor. How near was the house, had anyone heard his approach? This he would find out. He took his phone and switched it to silent. There was a nocturnal quiet with a background of buzzing insects and the waking sounds of creatures of the night.

Jack wondered how he could arm himself, he was not a big believer in carried handguns but this was a moment when he could be converted. He searched the toolbox in the back of the truck and selected a heavy wrench and a screwdriver. As an afterthought he shoved a Swiss Army knife into his pocket. Not much defense if he was confronted by an armed assailant but he had no choice.

He climbed from the truck and walked carefully down the path. It curved gently, the lights of the house gradually came into view. His phone showed that he was at the place that Kate's phone had last been detected. He stepped off the path and into the woods. A twig crackled under his foot. He stopped and stood perfectly still. There was no sign of activity from the house. He moved forward.

He could see the building clearly now although it was draped in shadows. His heart lurched in his chest as the familiarity struck him. It was almost identical to a house in a very different land, a house that held memories he wished he could forget. He forced those memories from his mind as he moved closer.

A sound came from the side of the house. Jack froze again. Another sound, a door closing, followed and a figure appeared from around the building. Jack saw a flash of light and the illuminated face of the man as he lit his cigarette. Then the intermittent glow from the tip of the cigarette as he sucked on it. The man was standing apparently staring out into the trees.

He was facing away from Jack. There was cover up until a few yards from where the man stood. If Jack could take him by surprise he was confident he could subdue him. Subdue, that old euphemism for a possible outcome that too often had been the case. Jack moved slowly, concentrating on staying silent. He was within ten yards of his target and at the edge of the trees. The man had his back to him, Jack prepared to rush. The man took a drag of his cigarette and then threw it to the ground. Turning to stamp out the butt he stared directly toward Jack. He was quick. He crouched into a defensive posture as Jack sprinted toward him and then stepped to one side. Jack was ready for him and hit him with a heavy tackle. The loss of balance was enough, Jack twisted behind the man, avoiding the swinging fists. His arm wound around his victim's neck and the base of his thumb dug into his carotid artery. It was a hold that would cause a loss of consciousness in not more than a few seconds. Jack felt the man sag and let his weight sink to the ground. He had a very short time until the man would recover, he had to move swiftly. How many of them were in the house? At least one he was sure. He moved to the door and pushed it open, if anyone inside heard it they would think it was their companion returning from his smoke, or so Jack hoped.

He was in a small hallway. This was nothing like the house he had imagined, no, not imagined, remembered vividly, just a short time ago. This was an American ranch house, low ceilinged, walled roomed, cozy. But inhabited by danger, that was a common factor. Jack was acutely aware of the nearness of an enemy. He knew also that Kate was very close by. He had to find her.

He heard movement from the end of the hallway. A man, a large man, appeared and stopped with a puzzled expression. After a second he had made up his mind and marched toward Jack. The first punch he threw was wild and Jack found it easy to avoid. The second caught Jack a glancing blow on the shoulder. A quick one-two left jab put the big man on the defensive, a right uppercut took him by surprise, and should have knocked him out. Instead he fell toward Jack and grabbed him in a grip that was unexpectedly strong. Jack felt the breath being squeezed from him, he struggled to free an arm. The elbow blow he managed was not as strong as he wished but it hurt the other man enough to make him loosen his grip. Jack quickly broke free and brought a knee up towards an unprotected crotch. The man groaned with pain and bent double. A neck chop and he crumpled to the floor.

Jack listened for signs of others, there was silence. He moved quickly through the house. On a table in the living room was a handgun. Jack was grateful that the big man had not been carrying it, he slipped it into his pocket. Where was Kate? He took the risk and called out her name. Silence. He shouted again and a faint sound replied. Her voice was coming from behind a closed door. There was a key in the lock. Jack turned it and pushed open the door. Before he rushed into the room he took the key and pocketed it, he did not want to risk being locked up when one of the two men came to.

Kate was sitting on the floor, her back against the wall, her hands tied behind her with a rope. Jack dashed to her. "Are you hurt?"

"This rope is killing me."

Jack fished the Swiss army knife from his pocket and began sawing at the rope. "We need to get out of here."

"Who are these people?"

"I'll tell you in a bit." He helped her to her feet as she rubbed her aching arms.

Kate's legs felt wobbly as they walked to the door and she almost stumbled. Jack held her round the waist. "Okay, I've got you."

"Sorry."

They walked out into the hallway. Miraculously there was still no sign of the two men Jack had immobilized. Then a sound stopped him in his tracks. Kate looked at him, puzzled. They could hear the unmistakable sound of a toilet flushing from the back of the house. So there was a third person, he had been otherwise occupied and was not aware of what was going on, yet.

They headed for the door. The big man was still lying on the floor but was stirring into consciousness. They passed him and stepped out into the night. Jack looked around for the smoker he had first encountered, he was nowhere to be seen. Helping her he guided Kate along the pathway toward his truck. They rounded the curve and the house was out of sight, the truck was clearly visible, a short walk now. Kate stumbled again and he held her tightly.

The crack reverberated through the still air and Jack felt the wind of the bullet as it whizzed dangerously close past his head. Instinctively he pushed Kate into the shelter of the trees. Twisting back he saw the shooter standing with his weapon cocked for action. Jack had the gun from his pocket and ducked down in a crouch. He took quick aim and, at the same time he squeezed the trigger, saw the gunman's arm jerk from the recoil of his weapon. Then the jerk stiffened his whole body as he collapsed to the ground. Jack felt the punch of the bullet in his shoulder and spun with the impact. Then he saw the house and heard the explosion. The sound seemed to come from inside his head. He pictured flames shooting from the windows, smoke pluming upwards. There were screams from those trapped in the inferno. His eyes were closed.

He opened them and saw the man lying still on the pathway, the house peaceful and whole. The sound of the roaring flames was replaced by the buzzing in his brain. He tried to shake the memory from his mind but that image burned like the shadow of a flashlight when the brightness has gone. Jack could feel his chest tighten and his breathing labor. He closed his eyes against the dizziness and fought to stay alert. The pulse pounded in his head and his vision began to dim. The last thing he saw was Kate rushing toward him, her face distorted in an expression of terror.

FORTY

Mark Butler fought back a feeling of panic. He had held a winning hand and the stakes in the Internet poker game were high, high enough that his winnings would reduce his burden of debt to an almost respectable level. He had experienced that euphoria of winning, of collecting what was due to him, what he deserved. The shock of losing had hit him like an ice cold shower. The disbelief had quickly evaporated and the stark reality of his situation loomed before him. He was now so deep he could hardly see the surface. As he drove to start his evening shift in the Emergency Room his mind tried to plan what he should do. His medical license was almost certain to be taken away from him, the hearing with the Medical Board was only a few weeks away and he was not at all optimistic of its outcome. He had nothing to lose by making medical mistakes. His malpractice insurance was covered by the group he worked for so he was financially safe against being sued. He had to be careful not to cross criminal lines but, apart from that, his options were open.

By the time he walked into the Emergency Room and took over from the evening shift he was feeling a little more optimistic. If only the right patient came in, and he could make the right mistake, a mistake that could cause pain and suffering, enough to persuade a jury, then he could call it the jackpot.

His first two hours were unproductive, routine stuff that offered no scope for improvisation. And then things changed.

Kate drove as quickly as she could. Her arms still felt stiff and painful, her legs were trembling. Jack sat beside her in the truck, he was breathing more easily now. She had checked the wound in his shoulder, she was not able to determine how bad it was but she could see it was bleeding heavily. She was worried about the breathing difficulty he seemed to have had. She had checked his rapid pulse and made sure his airway was clear. She used his shirt as a makeshift tourniquet. With considerable difficulty she had managed to get Jack into the truck. All the time she had been aware that there were two more men in the house and that they could appear at any moment.

She closed the passenger side door after strapping Jack in with his seatbelt. Dashing around the truck she climbed into the driver's seat and started the motor. The tires scattered driveway oyster shell as she headed out to the road. Glancing in the rear view mirror she thought she saw a figure running down the pathway but she was accelerating away so quickly she was not sure.

Kate hit a curve in the road and grunted as the truck's tires squealed in protest. She was barreling along the narrow country road, not sure if they were being followed and knowing that Jack needed urgent medical attention, for his bleeding shoulder wound and for the mysterious breathing difficulty he had experienced.

Headlights appeared around a bend in the road and dazzled her, she was aware of the speed she was traveling as meeting vehicles whizzed past her, disturbingly close on this narrow highway.

Jack groaned and muttered something she could not decipher, she had her concentration focused on the road and did not reply.

The lights of suburban Deep Wells appeared, the traffic increased and their journey was frustratingly delayed.

A red light stopped them. Kate could see the lights of the hospital in the distance, so near. She glanced over at Jack. His breathing seemed normal now but his eyes had a dull dazed expression. There was an alarmingly large pool of blood covering the seat. Kate stared at the red traffic light, it seemed as if it would never change to green. When it did she took off with a spinning of tires.

Kate swung into the entrance to the hospital and screeched to a halt outside the Emergency Room doors. She raced inside. In the waiting room people stared at her as if she was some sort of curiosity. The young woman at the reception desk looked up from what she was doing and recognized there was an emergency situation. Kate explained that Jack had been shot and was in the truck. She felt breathless from the journey and the anxiety she was experiencing. Why did it take so long for the receptionist to grasp the situation, why was everything happening in slow motion? She wanted to tell the medics with the gurney to hurry up, to get Jack into the building where he could be taken care of. She followed them to the truck and watched as they helped Jack out and onto the gurney. She walked behind them as they wheeled him through to the treatment area. Then there were several people crowding around, working as a team, checking vital signs, hooking up monitoring systems, putting in an IV. Kate felt excluded from the process, an onlooker with no active part to play. Then she looked up and her heart skipped a beat. This was not what she wanted to see.

FORTY-ONE

Liz was excited, she could hardly wait for the sun to set before she began her evening's tasks. She was not at all nervous about what she was going to do and the thought of being caught never occurred to her. Her previous successes and the luck she had with them convinced her of her own immunity. The careful planning and anticipation of results had not been part of this plot, in fact she was not quite sure of the consequences of what she was about to do.

First a casual stroll around the outside of the hospital building. She paused at a door that led into the Emergency Department. And then at another door, and four more. She was quick as she slipped the wedges under the doors and kicked them into place. No one would notice them in this light. Their discovery would only occur when those trapped inside tried to open the doors. And then it would be too late.

Her heart was thumping with anticipation as she walked to the main parking lot and her car. How her life had changed, from those days of wondering and worrying where her next meal would be coming from and how it would be paid for. How had he found her? And why was she so valuable? She realized that her position in the medical records department, although not an important one, gave her access to patients' details, diagnoses, treatment schedules, and physician contacts. She had managed to maneuver the electronic records to confuse the operating room staff and force the error that resulted in the surgeon removing a healthy eye. She had spotted the drug resistant infection and had acted on her own initiative to spread that infection to the nursery.

This time she had merely relied on instinct. He had shown his lack of enthusiasm but she was determined to go her own way. She would be lucky again.

Kate recognized him as soon as he walked through the door. She hunted her memory for his name. Mark something - Butler. She recalled their previous meeting when Jack had suffered his concussion and the comments Michael Mahoney had made about the Emergency Room physician, and now Jack was in the same doctor's incapable hands. Dr. Butler did not inspire confidence even if she had not had contact with him before. His body language spoke agitation; he walked with a jerky movement glancing around as if uncertain of his surroundings. He stared at Jack with an expression he might have while inspecting goods in a supermarket. He caught a brief eye contact with Kate but did not show that he recognized her. He stood beside the gurney and touched Jack's shoulder. He felt for pulses. He loosened the piece of Jack's shirt that Kate had tied to try to hold back the bleeding. The ooze of blood increased, puddling onto the gurney. Kate wanted to rush forward and do something.

"We need a surgical consult and to get him to the OR," muttered Butler.

Get a move on, thought Kate. She resisted the urge to move forward and help Jack.

A door opened, a young man in surgical scrubs came through it. He headed toward Kate.

"Could you move your truck, it's blocking the entrance."

Kate was not ready to leave Jack, although she was not active in what was going on. She hesitated.

"Please Ma'am."

She looked back at the gurney and Mark Butler. He had made the decision, she could do nothing to help, her truck was causing an obstruction. She tore herself from the room and hurried out through the waiting room. She climbed into the truck and drove to the main parking lot. It was full, she drove along avenues of parked vehicles looking for an empty space. She found one a considerable distance from the hospital entrance. As she began her walk back to the building she felt a sudden release from the tension that had held her captive for the last many hours. She let the memory of her capture and the realization that she would not survive the ordeal sneak into her consciousness, and the fact that Jack was in a serious condition sent her hurrying toward the lighted entrance to the Emergency Room. As she forced her legs to move faster she could feel them start to tremble. The adrenaline rush of what had kept her going was beginning to wear off. She felt alone and hopeless in this parking lot full of cars and empty of people. Her body seemed to be dissolving into a fatigued jelly. Like walking over wet sand she headed for the entrance. The door felt heavy and resisted her push. She found the room she had left just minutes ago. Nothing had changed, Jack was still lying on his gurney, Mark Butler was leaning over him. Doing what? Kate had an ominous feeling that something was going horribly wrong.

Mark Butler saw possibilities, like a mirage in the desert the image suddenly appeared. The patient was a man who had been shot and had lost a lot of blood. Ideas clicked in Butler's mind. He had been obsessed with the gamble that had not paid off, the denial was giving way to anger and he was prepared to face some more risk. A delay in stopping the bleeding and in transfusing the patient with life sustaining blood could cause complications – and pain and suffering. It was obvious that the patient needed urgent referral and surgical intervention so a slowness in this response might produce results.

Butler approached the gurney. There was a considerable amount of blood, the patient was semi conscious, the vital signs monitor showed that his blood pressure was alarmingly low. He could sense the atmosphere around him, he was being observed, the people in the room knew what was expected, he had to show good reason for his actions.

Liz was dressed in blue surgical scrubs and a long white coat. A paper cap covered her head and she wore a surgical mask over her face. The clipboard she carried gave her an authoritative image. She walked into the Emergency Department as if on official business. Something was going on in one of the treatment rooms that was attracting attention. Good, she thought, no one will notice me.

She pushed open the door to another treatment room. A young woman holding a whimpering baby looked up, the expression on her face changing from a look of relief that medical help had arrived to one of disappointment as she realized Liz was not the person she was expecting. Liz raised a hand in silent greeting and strode confidently to the head of the treatment table. On the wall was a collection of dials and controls. Liz selected a handle and turned. A slight hissing sound came from somewhere on the wall. Liz nodded, waved a goodbye to the young woman, and left the room.

She repeated the same routine nine times. The patients occupying the exam rooms did not question what she was doing. The next room was empty. Liz smiled, her luck was running with her. She took a small candle from her pocket and a book of matches. Carefully she struck a match and lit the candle, balancing it near the head of the examination table. Then she turned the control handle on the wall and hurriedly left the room.

She was not sure exactly what was going to happen but she wanted to be well away from the Emergency Department when it did.

Mark Butler had given orders to one of the nurses beside him and had then turned and walked way. The nurse looked puzzled and frowned as she caught the eye of one of her colleagues. Kate stepped forward, she felt as though she was in some sort of nightmare, hoping to wake up to reality but knowing that she was experiencing reality. She introduced herself and quickly instructed the nurses what to do. Her eyes were focused on Jack. His breathing was shallow, his eyes half shut. He was not fully conscious but Kate sensed that he was aware of her presence. She touched his hand and felt for his pulse. It was rapid and faint. She checked the IV and the EKG tracing on the monitor. She increased the rate of the IV, he needed to replace the fluid loss from the bleeding. She was aware that too much IV fluid could risk a worsening of his bleeding and was careful to avoid overdoing it. But, more than that, he needed blood. Or rather packed blood cells. It would take time to get some units typed and cross-matched, she hoped there was type O blood available.

She detected a quivering sensation from Jack's wrist. Then a twitching of his body. His breathing became snorting jerks of inhalation.

"Trendelenberg," she snapped, meaning she wanted the bed tilted so that Jack's head was lower than his feet increasing the blood flow to his brain.

"Can't tilt this gurney."

"Okay, pillows under his legs, keep his head down."

There was a scurry of activity. Kate kept an anxious eye on Jack, his usual healthy and animate face was pale and flaccid. She glanced toward the entrance to the ward. Where were they?

"What are you doing?" Mark Butler had appeared as if from nowhere.

"I'm trying to save this man from dying of blood loss." She resisted the urge to add, where were you?

"I'm in charge here, please leave."

Kate wanted to be able to grab him by the front of his shirt and toss him away just like the movies, but this was not the movies. Jack's life was at stake and she was alone here trying to save him. There was a strange look in the Emergency physician's eyes, not an expression that invited confidence. Kate was not ready for this, she was exhausted from the day's trauma and was terrified that she was going to lose Jack. For a moment Kate thought that Mark Butler was going to attack her, he was clearly agitated and seemed unsure of what he was going to do next.

The tense seconds were interrupted by the arrival of a young man in scrubs carrying a package. He was slightly out of breath and sweating. Kate watched as he handed the container of packed red cells to a nurse. A sense of guarded relief seeped into her as the nurse quickly and efficiently began to hook up the plastic bottle to the IV line. Thank goodness they had type O blood available, how many more bottles, she wondered.

She noticed a movement to her side. She turned and stared in disbelief as Butler reached out to grab the IV line. The nurse pushed him away and he staggered, momentarily off balance. Then, wildly, he recovered and lunged toward the bottle that was now delivering life saving fluids to Jack. Her instincts took over, an open-handed blow to Mark Butler's jaw stopped him, he looked at her with an expression of incredulous surprise and then there was an explosion of anger, a wild eye narrowing threat of extreme violence that terrified her. Figures appeared, uniformed security and people in scrub suits, chaos ruled. Kate felt as is her head was about to burst, she closed her eyes and tried to imagine herself away from this nightmare. When she opened them again she saw Mark Butler struggling unsuccessfully to free himself from the grip of a burly security officer. Someone nudged her and she was conscious of the gurney being wheeled away. She followed as Jack was taken from the ER to, she assumed, the operating room. As the elevator door was about to close behind them she heard a whooshing sound and felt a rush of air. The door slid silently shut but not before the echo of a distant scream of panic leaked its way into the elevator.

FORTY-TWO

Kate felt as though she had been tossed into a world of jumbled experiences and images. She was not quite sure what was real but she knew that she was surrounded by things that were not good. Her hours of capture and the threat of what might happen to her had frayed her nerves. The narrow escape and Jack's injury had worn them further. Now, as she rode the impossibly slow elevator, she was not certain of what the future held. Jack was hanging on by a tenuous thread, that reality was a constant presence. Hope kept her going.

Richard North was the surgeon she had asked the ER nurses to contact and he was waiting at the OR entrance. He wasted no time on pleasantries, bending to examine Jack and then instructing the operating room staff before disappearing into the scrub up area. Kate watched Jack being wheeled through the doors to the OR that slammed closed behind him. She was alone, waiting to find out his fate.

She paced, she sat, she cried, she tried to calm herself with deep breathing. Time wore heavily, she felt very alone. And then the noise of a door opening. The expression on Richard North's face sent her heart spiraling in a denial-provoking descent. Something really bad had happened.

"He's a tough one." Richard shrugged and a faint smile touched his mouth. "We stopped the bleeding, he's had more packed cells and his vitals are looking good. Surprisingly there's not too much damage done, he should make a good recovery."

Kate stepped forward and hugged her colleague. "Thank you Richard."

"How are you doing Kate? What happened?"

"It's a long story Richard." She fought back the tears that suddenly welled.

"Later."

"Yeah, later."

Jack was drowsy and dopey, but alive. She sat with him in recovery and then when he was transferred to his room on the ward. The night was a watch interrupted by episodes of fragmented sleep. Kate found that reality and her dreams became intertwined, she was back in her captive state and its threatened conclusion, then in the hurried dash to get help for Jack. And now in this hospital room, shaded lights, beeping monitor, IV drip silently feeding fluid.

Dawn arrived, unseen in this windowless confine, and the lights were turned up in respect for the new day. Michael Mahoney was an early visitor, a courtesy call for her as a member of staff. He greeted Jack with an enquiry as to how he was feeling.

"Not too bad, thanks." Jack was certainly more alert this morning and seemed free of pain.

"You're up early." Kate noticed a certain tenseness in the CEO's manner.

"The ER business is still being investigated."

"What happened with that doctor, it was all so quick?" Kate remembered the incident when Mark Butler had tried to grab the bag of blood cells that would save Jack's life. It was all a jumble now, the day had been a nightmare, the following night a stressed waiting. What had happened?

"I need to ask you what happened Kate." Michael Mahoney looked Kate directly in the eye. She felt a challenge, almost an accusation. She remembered taking over the management of Jack's care, the threat she had felt, the blow she had struck. She recounted the events she recalled while Mahoney listened and nodded occasionally.

"You did the right thing, Kate," said Mahoney. He glanced over toward Jack and smiled.

"And the doctor?"

"He is under suspension, we're not sure if he was involved with the fire."

"Fire?"

"Someone turned as many oxygen supply lines as possible and set up a naked flame in one of the exam rooms."

"Was anyone hurt?" Kate remembered the whooshing sound and the scream.

"No, fortunately there wasn't enough flammable fuel in the first room to allow the fire to spread."

"What is going on, Michael?"

He shrugged. "I don't know, but I'm going to get to the bottom of all this." He held out a hand and then gave her a brief hug. "The police want to talk to you and Jack, they should be here soon."

They arrived in less than an hour. Ed Powell was a serious middle-aged man, slightly overweight and graying at the temples. Pete Black was younger, tousled dark hair and a fidgety demeanor. They asked if Jack was fit to answer questions and found two chairs which they drew up beside his hospital bed. Ed Powell did most of the talking while his partner scribbled notes on a yellow legal pad. They followed the story of Jack's arranged meeting at the lake and asked searching questions on the background of his conflict with the board of his company and in particular Tom Windle.

"Thank you Mr. Stone." And the two officers turned to Kate. Again there were many questions. Kate found herself reliving the nightmare of her capture and shivered at the memory of it.

"Would you recognize these men?" asked the younger policeman.

Kate nodded. "They made no effort to hide their faces."

The officers glanced at each other. Kate knew what they were thinking, her captors had no intention of releasing her they planned to kill her whatever Jack had done.

"We've found the house that might be the one you described. There was nobody there but there were bloodstains on the roadway where the man Mr. Stone shot could have fallen."

There was a silence, the questions had all been asked.

"What happens now?" asked Kate.

"We find the men who did this and we bring them to justice."

The officers thanked them for their information and left. The room seemed very empty, Kate felt something was missing, a gap in the gaggle of events that had involved them.

"Are you really feeling okay?" She knew Jack had a way of playing down anything he might be suffering. It annoyed her although she realized it was his way of protecting her from concern.

"Really. The shoulder twinges a bit but I feel fine." This time she believed him. Then it came to her.

"I have to go to the house."

"Wait until later, I'll come with you, in fact I can drive you."

"No, they won't release you for hours yet, maybe not even today."

"This is not a prison, I can just leave."

She gave him a look that did not require words to express its meaning but she said "No" anyway.

"What's the hurry?"

"My phone, it's gone and I rely on it to keep in contact with my patients. There's a back up phone at home. And I need to clean up anyway."

A momentary expression crossed his face, and then a reticent smile. "Okay. Be careful."

Kate climbed up into the pickup truck and started the motor. The big engine throbbed into life and she guided the heavy machine out of the parking lot and onto the highway. She felt a little light-headed after the restless night and the trauma of the day before and drove carefully. The truck was not like her own light handling sedan and she had to concentrate on her driving. She left the outskirts of Deep Wells and was on the quiet country road. It was much calmer than the race of the previous evening and she began to relax. She remembered the look on Jack's face, the expression before the smile. "Be careful," he had said. What did that mean? The three men in the house, the way they had treated her. They intended to kill her. Did Jack know something that worried him? Was she driving to an empty house in the country that might be a threat?

She found that she had slowed down, the foot on the gas pedal seemed reluctant to press for further acceleration. A voice in her head told her that she was making a mistake, she should have stayed at the hospital.

The familiar road into Mill was not the welcome entrance to the quiet retreat she was used to experiencing. It was a trip into the unknown, the return to the place from which she had been snatched. The house was no longer the safe haven that offered her shelter from the busy schedule of the working day, a comfortable nest she shared with Jack, a lovers' rendezvous.

She turned into Middle Way Road and inched slowly along. The street was empty of traffic, she could see no sign of neighbors. No one would know if she arrived, or whether she departed, or how. She could turn around now. But she didn't, her practice relied on her availability and she needed a telephone for that. The telephone was in the house and that was all she was here for. Her mind was numbed as she drove into the driveway. She found the garage door opener on the rear view mirror and watched as the door rolled slowly open. She guided the truck into the dark space of the garage and turned off the motor. An ominous silence surrounded her. She remembered the violent assault of her kidnapping, the subsequent threats and humiliation. Should she risk facing the same thing again?

"Come on," she told herself, why would they still want her? Logic said that she should not feel threatened but instinct told her that there was danger in this house.

She climbed down from the cabin of the truck and walked to the door leading into the house. It felt like a walk to the gallows, the silence, apart from the clinking of the cooling engine of the truck and the distant background of birdsong. The house was quiet. Kate listened for signs of waiting assailants, half expecting sinister figures to emerge from doorways.

She knew where her back up phone was but she felt obliged to tour the whole house, the kitchen with its innocent view out to the decking and beyond, the living area, their bedroom. She pushed open the door to Jack's study. She could sense his presence here. The floor was empty now but she remembered the time she had first seen the drone and the skepticism she had felt. She had been wrong. Had she been wrong about other doubts she had had about him? She pictured him now in the hospital room, anxious to be here, home with her. Was he really feeling as well as he claimed, he tended to downplay his own problems, he made an effort to hide things that might cause her concern. It shouldn't have, but it did bother her. She liked to be in control, to know what needed to be cured. A niggling thought rose. She recalled their escape from the house yesterday. Jack had been coolly in control. And then he had been shot. What happened immediately after that scared her. She had let it fade to the back of her recall, there had been more immediate concerns to worry about. Now the picture of Jack and the expression on his face came back to her in vivid detail. She saw him jerk as the bullet hit him then a wild look as he stared at the house. He had closed his eyes as if fighting some inner demon and when they opened again there had been a look of terror. His breathing was desperately labored, she had rushed to his aid anticipating a need for immediate medical intervention. She remembered the instinctive reflex of her medical training, the personal aspect numbed by the urgency. But now, in retrospect, Kate was puzzled by the clinical presentation. There had been the gunshot wound and the blood loss, but there was something else. What?

She took a deep breath of the air in his room and went to the drawer and her spare phone. Her practice depended on her being available at all times, this was made possible by the smartphone that was always with her. She made contact with the office computer and checked any messages that may have come through. There was nothing that was urgent, she would take care of them later.

A hurried shower and change of clothes, Kate felt some of the stress inching its way out of her body.

She drove her own car out of the neighborhood and onto the highway. Jack should be ready for discharge soon, she hoped so. But she couldn't help worrying about what she had seen happen to him yesterday.

FORTY-THREE

Troy Lopez had just a few pieces of the puzzle to fit into place. Marvin Barnet had given him the original clues and he had followed his instincts from there. Barnet had almost talked himself into a confession in the murder of Angela. There was enough evidence to convict him anyway. A hint that some leniency might be earned by his co-operation had encouraged Barnet to offer more information than he might have. Troy had put together what he learned in talking to people in Kate Westbrook's office and had made a wild guess as to what might be going on. His interview with Michael Mahoney had revealed some enlightening facts, and an interesting common factor.

He had found himself outside an inconspicuous building whose sign announced that it housed the Regis Law Firm. Troy sensed a strong atmosphere of resentful suspicion when he introduced himself and presented his credentials as a police detective. Ernest Feather, a tall, sharp-featured young man had made it clear that he was not welcome.

"I'm sorry to have to bother you," he said, "but I am investigating a homicide and I have reason to believe you might be able to help."

There was a noticeable jolt in Feather's attitude and Troy saw the man's prominent Adam's apple jerk as he swallowed.

"Perhaps I could see one of the law partners?"

"Mr. King is really busy."

"I don't want to inconvenience him more than to ask him some questions here in his office. I won't take up much of his time."

Troy knew that these people were not involved in anything to do with Angela's murder, but Feather did not know what he was talking about. There was also the possibility that he had the authority to force Mr. King to attend an interrogation that would waste a great deal of his time.

Ernest Feather disappeared into the back of the building and returned a few minutes later.

"Mr. King will see you now."

The rest had been easy. Sam King was a puffy faced man in his late forties. His office was lined with overfilled bookshelves, his desk was piled with paper files. A gold Rolex was on his left wrist, a diamond clip held the silk tie to his custom made shirt. He listened with a poker face as Troy spoke.

"And if what you say is true, there is no crime involved, at least not on our behalf."

"Unless you were aware of what might have been going on."

"That, of course, is absurd, all we do is fight for our clients' rights."

Troy sensed that King was on the defensive, he was probably not liable but he had been dancing on the edge of an ethical dilemma and he knew it. Negotiating the next step was simple.

The man who looked like Buddy Holly was surprised at the response to his call. He had been concerned that his contacts were thinking of reneging on their agreements. There was no legal binding of course and he knew that he had very little power to threaten them with anything. But they owed him, owed him big, and he did not intend to let go. He was not expecting they would contact him, it was his move.

Ernest Feather answered the call. Buddy was careful not to sound too antagonistic, but also to project a tone of confidence and a sense of being in control. Feather's easy compliance with his request took him by surprise. They made their arrangements and Buddy ended the call. He felt a huge wave of relief, maybe this would be the end of what was becoming a risky and compromising situation. But, as he breathed a relaxation he experienced an uncomfortable uncertainty, something did not seem to fit. Tomorrow was a convenient time for the transaction, the location was satisfactory although it was usually he who chose where the handover would be.

What was happening in the hospital? He had not heard from Liz. The last time they had communicated he had tried to restrain her from what he considered an over-ambitious project. Had she acted on her ideas? The more he thought about it the more he felt inclined to terminate this part of his career. Yes, he would collect what was due to him tomorrow. But he would change the plans just a little bit.

The meeting was to take place at Starbucks in the Arboretum. Buddy was not happy with this for two reasons. He had not chosen the rendezvous location himself and they had used this meeting place quite recently. He believed in changing things, a fixed routine invited observers to take notice. He

chose the Target store at Four Points, the electronics
department.

He arrived early and strolled around the menswear section,
down to the display of bicycles and then a return to ostensibly
inspect the shelves of cell phones and tablets.

"Can I help you sir?" Buddy was taken by surprise. He
hadn't realized he was so nervous. The prize today was huge,
he knew that and was somewhat puzzled that it was coming so
easily to him. The young man who had offered assistance had
the familiar red Target badge, he was anxious to help.

"No. No thanks, I'm just looking."

Buddy felt uncomfortable at having made a contact here. He
was meant to be anonymous, unobserved. He turned away from
the helpful employee and pretended to study the latest Bose
sound system. He checked his watch, it was a minute after the
scheduled meeting, he was beginning to feel nervous, a little
out of control. An instinct told him to leave but the thought of
the money that was due to him and was almost in his grasp
kept him staring at headphones and speakers.

He recognized him, the man with a bright orange tee shirt
and a Texas Longhorns burnt orange baseball cap, a
combination of colors that was hard to ignore. He was carrying
an envelope, an envelope that would soon be in his hands.
Buddy felt a wave of anticipation as he approached his contact.
The handover of the envelope was a smooth exchange. Buddy
gripped it with an eager hand and turned to head casually
toward the exit of the store.

"Excuse me sir." Again he was taken by surprise but this time it was not a Target person who accosted him. Buddy saw the flash of a police badge and sensed the presence of other men around him. The urge to attack and run was quickly suppressed when he saw that he was surrounded. Thoughts of survival raced through his head. Don't resist, co-operate. The envelope, evidence, his money but enough to convict him. He dropped it and it slapped to the floor. Troy Lopez bent and picked it up. "You are under arrest," he said and read Buddy his rights.

FORTY-FOUR

Kate checked her telephone messages while Jack drowsed in his hospital bed. A patient who had called yesterday sounded as if he could have something seriously wrong. Kate felt a tight band of anxiety knot around her temples as she called the number back. She explained that she had a technical malfunction with her phone and apologized for the delay in response to the patient's call. She questioned the man about his symptoms and listened to his replies with increasing relief. He did not seem to be experiencing what she had thought and felt very much better today. She plugged her phone in to charge and leaned back in her chair. Time to wait.

She must have drifted off to sleep, she was suddenly aware of Richard North being in the room. She shook her head trying to clear her thoughts. Richard was examining Jack, he checked the medical chart and nodded with a satisfied expression.

"Time to go home," he said. "The discharge nurse will give you instructions on wound care, although you probably don't need any lessons." He smiled at the now alert Kate. "Hemoglobin is still on the low side, we'll need to keep a check on that."

Kate was about to mention the strange attack she had seen Jack go through after he had been shot but Richard had already left the room. He was a brilliant surgeon but could improve his bedside manner.

It was late afternoon when they climbed into Kate's car.

"You okay?" she said as she noticed Jack wincing.

"Yeah, it stings a bit when I move." He smiled. "I'm okay. Really."

Kate stared for a moment. Could she believe him? She started the motor and drove out of the parking lot.

"Jack," she said as they entered the highway. "You had some sort of attack when you were shot, do you remember that?"

Jack was silent. She glanced sideways at him, no denial, no reassurance that he was okay really.

"Jack?"

"I was hoping you wouldn't see something like that."

There was a hint in his tone that alarmed her, she had never experienced anything but confident reassurance in him. She veered off the road and into the parking lot of the H.E.B. grocery store. She stopped the car and turned to face him. "What do you mean?"

He half-closed his eyes and took a deep breath, preparing himself. "It was when I was in the Middle East. We had a mission, there were four of us." He paused as if finding the memory painful.

"This was when you were in the military?" He had never spoken in detail about his military career although she did gather that he was involved with special services.

"Yes. It was a dangerous situation, we were behind enemy lines, although that didn't mean a lot, they were all over the place. The house had to be checked, they were hiding everywhere. It was quiet in there, but that didn't make it safe. We checked each dark room." He stopped again and swallowed. "Then I came out, it was getting dark. There were sounds, I couldn't see where from. I knew I had to get back into the building, I was totally vulnerable out in the open."

"And, what happened?"

Jack looked as if he was about to burst into tears. His lips trembled, he ran a hand across the short hair on his scalp. Kate waited for his answer.

"I never made it. There was a rumble and then a bang. I could feel the heat, I felt the explosion. There was smoke and the smell of it still haunts me. I have dreams. Sorry. Yes, I have dreams."

"But you survived."

"One out of four, yes, I survived. They didn't."

She reached out and touched his hand. "I'm so sorry."

They stayed, silent, while shoppers came and went around them. Jack was clearly fighting the memory. "And since then, if something sparks it, I have a problem breathing and staying conscious."

"Post traumatic stress disorder."

Jack grunted a mirthless laugh. "To put a word on it." There was a look in his eyes she had not seen before, almost as if a window had opened, she could see beyond the confident self-control into the vulnerable mind behind his personality. And she felt a deep empathy with what she knew he had been trying to hide, the stubborn British pride, his insistence on protecting her from his own problems. She felt a tear well. "I love you. Let's talk about it."

"We will." And the window closed. There would be time later to broach the subject, they now had an opening, he no longer had a secret.

Kate put the car into drive and drove back onto the highway. Her mind was reeling with emotion, the trauma of the last few days, the unknown of the future. A thought hit her. "The three men who grabbed me, the police haven't got them yet?"

"Not as far as we know."

"Do you think we are in any danger, could they come to the house, is your business with them finished?"

"No, not to worry. They're not a problem." It was a familiar optimistic tone. Kate glanced sideways, expecting to see the accompanying smile.

But there was no smile on Jack's face.

FORTY-FIVE

Her phone sounded just before she was about to drive to the office. She did not recognize the number but answered it anyway.

"Detective Pete Black." The voice gave her no clue and the name was only something in her fuddled memory. Detective was the domino that started the release and it was only seconds before she realized who was calling. The rather hyperactive younger police officer who had questioned her and Jack in the hospital. What did he want with her now?

"We have two suspects in custody who we think may have been involved in your kidnapping."

"Well. That was quick."

"Yes. Thank you. I wonder if we could ask for your help."

"How can I help?"

"We would like you to identify them if they are responsible for the crime."

"It would be my pleasure." Kate pictured herself staring at a line of men, each staring back at her. Then, seeing one she recognized, she would point her finger. She hoped the two men were the ones, she would feel much safer if they were behind bars. But what of the third man?

"Could you take the time to call at the Department, it shouldn't take long."

Kate thought for a moment, she would be driving almost right past the building in Deep Wells on her way to the office.

"I could do that in about twenty minutes if that is okay."

Detective Black voiced his appreciation and promised he would be ready for her. Before leaving the house Kate left a message at the office telling them she might be late and could they shuffle patient appointments to take care of that. She trusted Sally Snooks and Nick to fill in the gaps.

She found a parking space and walked into the Police Department building. The outside appearance was unimpressive, a plain square building, red brick, ordinary looking windows, boring. Inside, the air conditioning was turned down low, there were uniformed officers at desks pecking away at computers, there were people of indeterminate status lounging around. Kate made her way to where Pete Black had directed her.

His office was small. There was a desk with a computer on it and untidy piles of paper surrounding it. Black rose from his desk chair to greet her. He explained that he would be showing her photographs and he wanted her to identify any person she recognized. Kate had expected a parade of real people and was relieved that she would not have to meet her former captors face to face.

After a few preliminaries Kate was seated at the desk, now with space cleared, and six or seven photographs were placed before her. She scanned them, faces of strangers, men who stared out at her with unwelcoming expressions.

She recoiled as she recognized the weasel face and its narrow eyes, the expression of lust and malice, the evil behind that pseudo smile. The memory of her ordeal in the captive house hit her and she felt a chill run through her. Her finger trembled as she pointed to the photo.

"That's one of them."

"You sure?"

"I'm certain."

Another set of photos and another jolt of recognition. She was surprised at how vividly she recalled those faces. Pete Black seemed pleased with what had transpired.

"Thank you for your help," he said and there was the hint of a satisfied smile on his face.

"There were three of them."

The smile faded. "Yes. We're still looking for the other man."

As Kate retraced her steps and left the building the image of the third man teased her memory. He had been a tall massively built man, silent and threatening. As she started her car and drove on to the office she wondered what had become of him.

Jack waited until he guessed Kate had finished at the police department before calling her. She was driving on her way to the office.

"How did it go?"

"They definitely have two of the guys."

"And the third?"

A slight pause. "They're still looking."

They chatted for a few minutes. Jack had an uncomfortable sensation that he had somehow failed her. He could not forget her questioning his posttraumatic episode. For all his intent on keeping this part of his life a hidden secret he had confessed to her. She now knew that he had his weakness. At the end of the call he let his mind dwell on the events for the last few days. He had thought he would lose her. His emotions had convinced him that his life was nothing without her. But what about Kate's feelings? Did she really want to spend the rest of her life with him? She had shown her doubts in the past, would this last brief episode in their lives persuade her that their relationship was not going to last?

The whirlwind adventure of her kidnapping was clearly the result of Tom Windle's machinations, or in Jack's view it was. Would the police agree, would there be evidence, would his problems be resolved?

In spite of, or perhaps because of, recent close escapes from nasty situations Jack felt a deep insecurity. He considered his own situation was nearing a conclusion, and he had a good hope that he would emerge as the winner. But there were so many other things that gnawed at his mind. Kate had gone through so much and was now heading for another day of solving her patients' medical problems. She was vulnerable to making mistakes, she needed all her facilities to cope with the workload she faced. He knew that the series of mishaps occurring with her patients had bothered her a lot. She had talked about them in an academic way but Jack had sensed she was more emotionally concerned than she wanted him to know. He felt a surge of something he could only define as love for her. He had always thought of it as a sense of possessiveness and protectiveness, and he knew he was guilty of over-exhibiting both, but now there was more. He did not want to lose her, he would not lose her. But, did he have a choice?

"Are you okay?" Maureen stared at her as if examining for damage.

"I'm okay." Kate was determined to put on a brave face.

"The TV news people called just now, they wanted to know if you'd be in the office this morning. What happened?"

Kate recounted the events of the weekend. As she did so she realized what trauma they had gone through. Was it all over? She shuddered as she thought about the big man who had not been caught yet.

"They want to come and interview you."

"Who?"

"The TV people."

Kate groaned. She pictured the day and the stream of patients and the effort to keep from running late. She did not have time for interviews. But it was not the television reporter who arrived first. Troy Lopez was apologetic when he saw how busy the clinic was.

"I won't take up much of your time but I think you should know what I have discovered."

Kate listened and could hardly believe what she heard.

"I spoke with Mr. Maloney yesterday and apparently there was an incident in the hospital emergency department that might be connected."

"You mean the arson attempt?"

"You know about it? Sorry, of course, you are Chief of Staff."

"No. I was personally involved with a patient there." Kate explained what had happened to her and Jack that weekend. Time was ticking by and the waiting room was filling up. She hoped Sally and Nick, and the robot, could keep up. She felt an unreality begin to overwhelm her, the situation had taken on a meaning that was more than unbelievable. "There was also a very weird episode with the ER doctor."

Kate described Mark Butler's strange behavior. As she did so she remembered Flora Robbins and the way he had mishandled her case. Was this part of the same story? Troy Lopez thought it might be. He would follow it up.

Kate rushed through the rest of the morning, apologizing to patients for keeping them waiting. A television reporter, who she vaguely recognized, and a cameraman arrived and she allowed a rapid and highly unsatisfactory interview. She kept thinking about what Troy Lopez had told her, but that was a different story and would no doubt air in its own time.

There was not time for lunch and she hit the afternoon running on adrenaline and caffeine. She cheated just a bit and grabbed a large cup of coffee instead of the usual cup of tea. There was one house call requested. The drone would take care of it.

She programmed the robot with the patient's details and watched as it rose into the air and buzzed away to its destination. Jack's machines had been so successful but she still had the fear there would be a failure and a patient would be harmed. Was she being old fashioned, did she still believe in traditional medicine? The fact that the practice was treating patients in the traditionally old fashioned way suggested that she did, the use of the robots allowed her to believe she had enough of modernistic attitude that she was able to incorporate the latest technology into her practice.

She waited for the drone to arrive at the patient's house. What if it couldn't find it? What if it failed to land? Too many what ifs. The computer screen showed the patient's face and Kate listened as the dialogue between machine and human proceeded. To her mind the exchange was flawless and she activated the control that would return the drone to the office. Why did she have such doubts? That was a question she could not answer.

Her mind was a whirl as she drove home. She felt as though she had been wound up tightly and then left to spin. She concentrated on keeping control of her driving, other traffic on the road seemed to be threatening, the natural instinct that enabled her to drive without thinking about it was wearing thin. What was happening to the familiar skin that protected her from the hazards of life, was she slowly going mad?

She reached the outskirts of Mill, and then the quiet street on which she lived. The garage door opened at the touch of her remote control. She stopped the car in the garage and killed the motor. She took a deep breath and closed her eyes. She could smell the dying engine, she could hear it cool. She was home. Her sigh of relief was interrupted by the image that came suddenly into her head. The big man, the man they hadn't yet caught. Where was he, was he still a danger?

Why did she feel a sense of apprehension as she climbed from her car, why was opening the door and walking into the house an act of bravado?

It was quiet, dusk was a while away but the sun was about to bid its farewell across the valley, she could see the shadows forming across the decking outside. She resisted calling out Jack's name but she wondered where he was. The silence weighed heavily, she walked with leaden footsteps through the den and out onto the wooden decking. A bird shrieked and fluttered away, she jumped at the sound. Then she saw him. He was sprawled on a lounger, legs awry. His head was at a strange angle, his eyes were closed.

Kate felt her heart stop in her chest, a sliver of emotions pierced her brain. Something had happened to Jack, was she in danger herself? Her reflex took her to his side. Her touch brought an immediate response, a wakening, a brief confusion, a recognition.

"I fell asleep."

"Is everything okay?" She had overreacted. He was staring at her.

"How about you?"

Kate felt as if she was about to burst into tears. Her throat was constricted, her voice was choked, she could feel a sob swell in her chest. She turned away and rushed from the room.

He was with her in the bedroom, his good arm holding her, whispering words of comfort. She wanted to resist, to be alone in this moment of weakness but her body began to melt. He cared, he was alive, what if what she had imagined had been true? She put her arms around his neck and clung to him. She could feel tears tracking down her cheeks but the violent sobs had faded, her self-control was returning.

When she met his gaze she could see the worried expression, the uncertainty in his eyes. "I'm sorry, I thought –"

He put a finger to her lips. "I know." Then his lips touched hers. The kiss was a reassurance, passion was below the surface, compassion flowed like a wave.

"Detective Lopez came to the office this morning."

"Anything new?"

"Oh yes."

They sat out on the decking. The sun was sinking sending long shadows toward the east. Kate wondered where she should begin, she was still feeling shaky inside but the tears had dried.

"Could I have a cup of tea?" She almost laughed as she heard herself ask for the British answer to most of life's problems. Jack went inside and put the kettle on. "Won't be long," he said as he came back. "What did you find out today?"

"Troy Lopez is certain that Marvin Barnet killed Angela, he more or less confessed to it. He also thinks he murdered David."

There was a silence.

"He thinks it would be difficult to prove but Barnet is a violent man – look what he did to Angela, and to you. He was clearly upset to find out that Angela and David were having an affair and Troy guessed that he had staged the killing to look like suicide."

"So our imagined solutions could have been near to the truth."

The sound of the kettle boiling came from the kitchen. Jack got up to make the tea and brought back two steaming cups.

Kate sipped hers gratefully. "There's more." Jack held his cup and nodded for her to continue. "Troy Lopez questioned the staff at the clinic and picked up clues. He had time, he said, so he followed up on a hunch he had. He was curious about the number of medical mistakes that had been made, it seemed to be more than a coincidence."

Jack raised his eyebrows.

"I know, the third most common cause of death."

Jack held his out his hands, "Just kidding."

"He also noticed that one law firm was handling most of the malpractice cases that were being filed."

"Regis?"

"Yes, Regis."

The sound of Kate's phone came from the house, breaking the silence around them like a rude intruder. She rose and went to answer it.

Jack's mind was digesting what Kate had told him. So Regis was somehow involved with this. What else had Kate heard?

The telephone call was presumably from a patient, he worried that the continued stress of being on call would harm her, could force her into making a mistake. Again he wondered about the Regis Law firm.

Kate came out carrying her phone. She placed it on the table and sat down. She had a smile on her face.

"That was Detective Black, he wants me to help identify another suspect."

"They caught the third man?"

"They think they have him. He was in a hospital in Austin being treated for a gunshot wound."

"That's a relief, let's hope they can sort out who was behind all this. But tell me about Regis."

"Well, Regis has been getting information on cases of possible medical malpractice and has filed dozens of suits. I'm not sure if what they were doing is illegal but they have been paying their informant."

"Why should they do that?"

"A malpractice case can bring in a lot of money. Even in small claims the insurance company might settle out of court to save legal costs. A few of those sorts of cases and that's easy money, and if they have access to more than a few that money can mount up."

"Makes you squirm doesn't it."

"Well here's something that will really make you squirm."

Jack was still trying to absorb what he had just heard, he waited for Kate to continue.

"The informant didn't just find instances of medical malpractice he actually manufactured them."

Jack was beginning to see where Kate was leading. "Angela?"

"Angela was one, there were others. He would find people who were financially challenged and who could be employed somewhere in the medical field. Angela was chronically short of money, there was a secretary from medical records who had access to patients' information, and that odd ER doctor, he was in massive gambling debt and was desperate."

"So he paid them to make medical mistakes and sold this information to Regis?"

"Regis denies knowing that the malpractice was deliberately planned but they should have been suspicious."

"And perhaps they were but who can prove that?"

They sat in silence and watched the sky glow and darken. Stars appeared, buzzing insects hummed around them. They both felt exhausted, they asked each other questions, they marveled at how they could have been involved in such events.

They went to bed early and lay awake in each other's arms while sleep drifted over them. Each had more questions, their future was still something of a mystery.

FORTY-SIX

The explosion was muffled and faint, it hardly bothered him.
It faded into a distant silence. The specialist Kate recommended
had helped him almost obliterate the effects of the shocks he
had experienced in those traumatic situations of his military
career.

He opened his eyes and blinked at the daylight shining
through the bedroom window. Kate was lying beside him, her
dark hair spread on the pillow, her eyes gently closed, her
breathing shallow and even. He gazed and wondered at his good
fortune. He slid from the bed and made his way to the kitchen,
the kettle, and the teapot.

The day was blessed with picture perfect central Texas
weather.

The sky was clear and an endless blue. The temperature was
warm, yet a gentle soughing breeze caressed the flesh. Bright
light filtered through the glossy dark leaves of the old oak trees,
and the small chapel stood there to greet them in this, their
field of dreams.

Kate wore a simple cream silk dress. Her hair swung down to her shoulders and her eyes sparkled with pure joy. Deep within her, behind the soft silkiness of her gown she felt a fluttering, as if the unborn baby was also experiencing the thrill of the day.

Jack turned to gaze at her as she was framed in the old wooden doorway of the little country church. His vision blurred as he drank in her beauty.

It had been a year since they thought they were losing each other, and now they were to be fused in a bond that seemed to grow stronger with each passing day.

Their vows were short and simple. Jack with an uncharacteristic quiver in his voice as he said, "I do"

Then he kissed his bride.

After the simple ceremony they mingled with the small cluster of friends who had come to witness this union.

Kate chatted with Michael Mahoney. She had not seen so much of him since her year as Chief of Staff had finished. The problems he had faced a year ago were resolving as far as the hospital was concerned, but Kate could sense that Michael was still agonizing over the suffering and loss that had so affected innocent patients.

Then he saw Sally Snooks standing arm in arm with Nick White.

Sally was reaching for her phone and began walking from the chapel with it to her ear. How wonderful it was to have her as a partner and a friend, not just as an employed locum. And Nick as her nurse. The practice was keeping busy but the workload was manageable as a shared burden, and also a joyous setting to spend the days.

Maureen ran over and hugged the newly weds, her smile encompassing her entire sweet face.

Jack turned toward Roger Fado, and they exchanged hearty handshakes. But Jack sensed that the lawyer looked serious.

"Looks like your friend Tom might be heading for jail," he said with a grim smile on his face.

Jack reminisced about his ex partner, then he recalled that Tom could have been responsible for Kate's death. Jack was relieved that he had won the battle, and that Tom had not; so now let the justice system take care of Tom.

They all clustered beneath the ancient old oak trees and raised a toast to   the couple's future. Jack's eyes met Kate's.

" And now it all begins," he thought.

Made in the USA
Lexington, KY
17 September 2017